P9-BYR-351

I'll Be There

HOLLY GOLDBERG SLOAN

DISCARDED

LITTLE, BROWN AND COMPANY
New York · Boston

This book is a work of fiction. Names, characters, places, and incidents are the product of the author's imagination or are used fictitiously. Any resemblance to actual events, locales, or persons, living or dead, is coincidental.

Copyright © 2011 by Holly Goldberg Sloan

I'll Be There

Words and Music by Berry Gordy, Hal Davis, Willie Hutch and Bob West
© 1970, 1975 (Renewed 1998, 2003) JOBETE MUSIC CO., INC.
All Rights Controlled and Administered by EMI APRIL MUSIC INC.
All rights reserved.   International copyright secured.   Used by permission.
Reprinted by permission of Hal Leonard Corporation

All rights reserved. In accordance with the U.S. Copyright Act of 1976, the scanning, uploading, and electronic sharing of any part of this book without the permission of the publisher is unlawful piracy and theft of the author's intellectual property. If you would like to use material from the book (other than for review purposes), prior written permission must be obtained by contacting the publisher at permissions@hbgusa.com. Thank you for your support of the author's rights.

Little, Brown and Company

Hachette Book Group
237 Park Avenue, New York, NY 10017
Visit our website at www.lb-teens.com

Little, Brown and Company is a division of Hachette Book Group, Inc.
The Little, Brown name and logo are trademarks of Hachette Book Group, Inc.

The publisher is not responsible for websites (or their content) that are not owned by the publisher.

First Paperback Edition: June 2012
First published in hardcover in May 2011 by Little, Brown and Company

Library of Congress Cataloging-in-Publication Data

Sloan, Holly Goldberg, 1958–
   I'll be there / by Holly Goldberg Sloan. — 1st ed.
   p. cm.
   Summary: Raised by an unstable father who keeps constantly on the move, Sam Border has long been the voice of his younger brother, Riddle, but everything changes when Sam meets Emily Bell and, welcomed by her family, the brothers are faced with normalcy for the first time.
   ISBN 978-0-316-12279-5 (hc) / 978-0-316-12276-4 (pb)
   [1. Brothers—Fiction.   2. Family problems—Fiction.   3. Fathers and sons—Fiction.   4. Selective mutism—Fiction.   5. Family life—Fiction.   6. Mental illness—Fiction.]   I. Title.   II. Title: I will be there.
   PZ7.S633136Ill 2011
   [Fic]—dc22

                                                                                    2010042994

10 9 8 7 6 5 4 3 2

RRD-C

Printed in the United States of America

For Gary Rosen...
who is always there.
And for Max, Calvin, Madeline, and Alex...
who are my inspiration.

1

The days of the week meant nothing to him.

Except Sunday.

Because on Sundays he listened to pipe organs and pianos.

If he was lucky, handheld bells, pounding drums, or electronic beat machines might vibrate while people sang and sometimes clapped and on occasion even stamped their dressed-up feet.

On Sundays, wherever he was, whenever he could, Sam Border woke early, pulled on his cleanest dirty shirt, and went looking for a church.

He didn't believe in religion.

Unless music could be considered a religion. Because he knew God, if there was one, was just not on his side.

Sam always came in after things had started. And he always left before the service was finished. He sat in the back because he was there only to visualize the patterns in the musical notes. And maybe grab a glazed donut or a sticky cookie on the way out.

If someone tried to speak to him, Sam nodded in greeting and, if he had to, threw in a "Peace be with you." But he had perfected the art of being invisible, and he was, even when he was younger and little, almost always left alone.

* * *

What he could remember, when he thought of the dozens and dozens of towns where he'd lived, were sounds.

Even Junction City, where he'd spent a whole winter and made a friend, was now gone, except for the ping of the rain hitting the metal roof on the apartment off the alley where the city parked all its noisy trucks.

That was three years ago. Fifteen towns ago. Another lifetime.

After Junction City they'd been outside of Reno for a while. And then in a trailer that rattled as if every screw and corresponding piece of corroded metal was ready to come undone.

The trailer was in Baja California, and it felt like living in a cardboard box, which was one of his many recurring nightmares. But he'd appreciated those five months south of the border.

Being an American automatically meant he was an outsider, so for the first time in what he could remember of his blur of a broken life, he'd felt like he could relax. He was different. It was expected.

But even fitting-in-because-you-don't-fit-in didn't last.

His father got them out of the country and back to the U.S. just as Sam was learning to speak Spanish and figuring out how to swim.

For weeks, while his brother and father slept, Sam had gone down right after sunrise to the crashing waves. Teaching yourself a skill, especially one that could kill you if things went wrong, wasn't easy.

At first, he only went in up to his knees. And then, gradually, he ventured into the swell, moving his arms in the cold surf like he'd seen people do from a distance.

He was pretty sure he looked like a real idiot.

But he was always able to get back to the gritty beach, even on the morning when the ocean suddenly shifted gears and began to pull him sideways down the shoreline. For what seemed like miles, he slapped his arms against the waves and thrashed his legs in a fury as he swallowed mouthfuls of icy salt water.

Because something inside him, even when he most wanted to give up, just wouldn't.

After that day, Sam figured he had once gone for a real swim. But he assumed that whatever he'd learned from the experience would disappear, like so much that had come and gone in a life dictated by his father. There were so many things that were a mystery. That's what happens when you've never gone to school past second grade.

But the good thing was that he didn't know what he didn't know, and that made it all easier.

* * *

Emily Bell was a collector.

And what she gathered and sorted and prized was carried with her wherever she went.

Because Emily's obsession was with other people's lives.

Her grandmother had once said that Emily would have been the greatest spy ever born. But only if spies didn't have to guard secrets as well as unearth them. Because Emily's own emotional wall of self-protection was see-through. She wasn't hiding anything about herself, so why should anyone else?

It was disarming.

Emily's interest in personal histories made her accessible to people's deepest emotions. It was as if she had some kind of magnet that pulled at someone's soul, often when he or she least expected it.

And that same magnet, which had to have been shaped like a horseshoe, allowed someone to look at her and feel the need to share a burden.

Hers was a gift that didn't have a name.

Even she didn't understand what it all meant.

Emily just knew that the grocery store clerk's cousin had slipped on a bath mat and fallen out a second-story open window only to be saved because the woman landed on a discarded mattress.

But what interested Emily the most about the incident was how the cousin had subsequently met a man in physical therapy who introduced her to his half brother who she ended up marrying and then running over with her car a year later after a heated argument. And that man, it was discovered, had been the one to dump the mattress in her yard.

He'd saved her so that she could later cripple him.

Emily found that not ironic but intriguing.

Because everything, she believed, was connected.

Now, at seventeen years old, Emily's question was how she fit into the big scheme of things. Where was her minor incident that would change the course of major life events? So far it had all gone according to plan. Good parents. Decent younger brother. World's greatest dog. Loyal best friend.

There had been no dramatic hairpin turns in her road. And not even any real bumps to speak of.

But she had lived in one town, and she had seen how small things changed big things. She saw every person as part of a ripple effect.

And, because of that, she believed in destiny.

At least that's what she would later tell herself.

*   *   *

Emily took a bite of whole wheat toast and stared out the window. She did not have a beautiful singing voice. She could carry a tune, but that was the extent of the situation.

So why was she going to sing a solo at church?

The answer was right across from her, drinking coffee.

Tim Bell was a college music professor. But on Sundays he was now also the choral director of their congregation. And, as Emily chewed, she decided that he really must not care about that new position if he was going to subject the people to her rendition of "I'll Be There."

Because it wasn't even a church song she had to sing.

It was a classic pop melody that the Jackson Five had made famous, and people had heard this song and seen this song performed and they all knew how it was supposed to sound.

Which made her singing it even worse.

Her father had a theory — because he had theories about everything — that love ballads could be used in places of worship and reinvented to have a spiritual dimension. Being an instructor, he knew that the key to emotional involvement with music was familiarity.

So the way Emily saw it, he was basically tricking people.

He was using songs that already made them feel good. The only problem in the scheme was her. It was just plain wrong to make her a guinea pig in the plan.

Emily had tried all week to appeal to her mother, who was always a voice of reason. But Debbie Bell was an emergency-room nurse and she said that she handled pain and he handled poetry, which meant she left music to her husband.

In desperation Emily had even worked on her little brother, Jared, who was only ten years old and, being seven years younger than her, would pretty much do anything she said. But even Jared didn't think her singing was a big deal.

Emily shut her eyes and she could hear her own voice,

sped up suddenly like a cartoon chipmunk, singing: *"I'll be there. Just call my name. I'll be there."*

It was a total nightmare.

She would just have to grit her teeth and get through it.

But was it possible to grit your teeth and still sing?

2

Sam's father, Clarence Border, heard voices.

But they were voices of people who were up at odd hours and who lived exclusively inside his head. They were voices of people whose jobs were primarily to warn of danger — sometimes real but mostly imagined.

When you first met Clarence Border, you understood you were talking to someone who was anxious. His thin body seemed to crackle with energy. His fingers fluttered at his sides when he spoke, moving like he was playing an invisible piano that must have been located on the tops of his bony thighs.

It wasn't that he twitched. He was more in control than that. It was that he was hardwired to run in the blink of an eye.

And to take you with him.

Clarence was a good-looking man. He had a full head of dark hair and a strong jaw. When he was dressed in his always clean black jeans, you couldn't see that on the inside of his left leg, curled around the calf, was a tattoo of a black snake. He'd given it to himself, and it looked like it.

Clarence stood over six feet tall, and you could tell in a single glance that he knew how to throw a punch — and that it wouldn't take much to get him to do it.

His voice was deep and steady, and you'd think that would be a good thing, but then his fingers would start moving and it was like he was getting a message from some far-off place, not from circuitry in his frontal lobe that just didn't seem to work right.

There are many ways Sam's father's life could have played out. He could have stayed in Alaska, living near the old cabin where he was born, hunting and fishing and on occasion taking something that wasn't his and selling it to get by. But he'd gotten caught trying to unload an outboard motor to an off-duty patrolman.

The arrest uncovered a string of other misdeeds, and Clarence found himself at the age of twenty-two in prison for three years. When he was released, he left the state, and the only thing he knew, truly deep in his heart, was that he'd never go back to living behind bars.

Which was not to say that he was going to live a life of virtue. Far from it. Clarence Border's vow wasn't one of decency. It was a vow of preservation and desperation. He'd do anything, to anyone, to keep one step ahead of the government.

For a time, life in Montana, which was where Sam was born, was without major incident. Clarence had met Shelly at the Buttrey Food & Drug store. She appeared in the aisle just as he was preparing to slip a box of cheese-flavored Goldfish crackers into the back of his bulky winter coat.

Shelly was ten years older than he was, and he could tell right away that she liked him. Since she was wearing a name tag, he just needed her phone number. She gave it to him without his even asking.

Six weeks later, Shelly was pregnant with Sam and she was living with Clarence above her parents' garage. He worked odd jobs under the watchful eye of her family, and while the whole arrangement didn't actually work, it wasn't yet a colossal failure.

Shelly's father, Donn, was an electrician. If he'd had more opportunity, he'd have been an engineer. He understood not just wiring and current and all things mechanical—he also understood operating systems.

The first time Donn met Clarence Border, he knew that his daughter had hooked up with a man who had a busted mainframe. He tried to warn her early in the game, but Shelly was pregnant before anything could be done.

Donn then took a different approach. He'd teach the shifty snake a profession. As the months wore on, a new plan took shape. If he couldn't make Clarence understand electricity, Donn could electrocute him and probably get away with it.

But the snake struck first.

The voices in his head couldn't be ignored, and the morning of the bite they told Clarence that he'd need to be righteous when someone had done him wrong.

Donn wouldn't let Clarence smoke cigarettes when they were in the truck, and when they got to the Weiss Sand and Gravel Company, there was a No Smoking sign in the work area.

Clarence seethed as he unloaded their tools. Someone would pay for the way he was feeling.

Shelly's father was up on the roof attaching a new transformer to the pole when Clarence unhooked the ground wire. The old man was cooked in a single jolt that flung his body halfway across the roof into the company's TV dish. Smoke came off his body.

All Clarence could do was stare at the No Smoking sign and feel a sense of satisfaction.

* * *

After that, Shelly and Clarence moved from the garage into the main house, and Shelly's mother, consumed with grief, stopped speaking to him. He'd look back on this period as a time of focus.

When Sam was almost four and a half, Shelly got pregnant again and then, a month early, tiny Riddle was born. From the start, Riddle cried all the time. His weak sobs drove Clarence out of the house and back into the garage apartment.

The kid had colic. And some other problems. His nose ran constantly, and he squinted as if the sun were in his eyes even on rainy days. Because of his red face, Shelly named him

Rudolph but he was known as Riddle from the second his father picked him up and he made his first squawk.

By the time Sam and Riddle were seven years old and two, the house had liens and the bill collectors didn't just make calls, they paid visits.

Shelly's mom couldn't take it anymore, and even though she'd grown attached to the two little boys, she moved down to Louisiana to be with her deaf sister. She said she'd send money when she left, but no one had believed her. Clarence hadn't worked in forever, and his wife finally went back to stocking the aisles at the Buttrey.

Shelly came home after an eight-hour shift on a cold, rainy day in March and the front door was wide open. The truck wasn't in the driveway, and the garden hose by the garage was missing. Clarence had taken the two kids, some power tools, one suitcase of clothes, and her Indian Head penny collection, which had belonged to her great-uncle Jimmy.

Sam was in second grade and the star of his class, reading books for fifth graders. Ten years later, he could still picture exactly what that classroom looked like.

He'd never seen another one since.

* * *

Since they'd left Montana, Sam's father always told the same story. His wife had died giving birth to the young one, and then he'd lost his business. Riddle always looked like he was either just getting over a cold or just coming down with one.

He'd squint out at the world, and people just naturally felt bad for the whole motherless family.

Clarence said he'd been in auto parts. Not many people asked him about auto parts, and that was a good thing because he knew next to nothing about them.

He'd explain that he couldn't pay his employees health-care insurance premiums, but he'd chosen his workers over profit. He kept it going for as long as he could, and then finally the government came and forced him into Chapter 11.

Riddle first heard the story when he was a toddler, and back then he thought it meant that his father had been trapped inside a book. But somehow the tyrant had gotten out, and that had to be why Clarence hated teachers and any kind of learning, really.

Sam and Riddle's father believed in life experience. That's what he told the two boys. That's why he'd never let them go to school once they took to the road.

But they really didn't go to school because Clarence didn't just hate all teachers, he loathed the whole system.

* * *

The two boys had slept late for years. Now that they were older, their father didn't bother to even try to feed them, and they always woke up hungry.

Sam and Riddle had been taught to stay out of sight during school hours because people wanted to know why two boys were wandering around doing nothing. Plus it was better to let fast-food places open and have trash build up before they headed into the world.

They made a habit of not hitting the streets until the sun was high in the sky and knew to say that they were home-schooled if anyone asked. But Sundays were different. Sundays, they could be seen at any time.

And Sundays there was music.

Sam pulled on his shoes and stared at his little brother, who was asleep on the stained mattress on the floor in the corner. Riddle's breathing, as always, was heavy, and his permanent congestion had the wheeze of some kind of new bronchial infection.

Sam thought about trying to prop his head up higher on the pillow because sometimes that helped, but instead he took a pen off the floor and wrote in large letters on a scrap of paper:

BE back sOON.

* * *

Sam had seen the First Unitarian Church when they originally came to town.

Was there a Second Unitarian and a Third? Was it some kind of contest?

Because now, standing in front of the brick building on Pearl Street, he could see that this house of worship was much more upscale than what he was used to. These First Unitari-

14

ans were the winners. The parking lot was mostly full and the cars were new and clean, and that wasn't right for him.

This church was in the best part of town, and nothing about it looked desperate. He didn't go into places like this.

The way he saw it, the less money people had, the more instruments they played and the more food they put out. And the easier they were for him to be around.

But Sam had been all over his own neighborhood and, without Riddle at his heels, he had walked faster and somehow had ventured farther than before.

Sam had heard the pipe organ playing from down the street. It was just too intriguing. And now he could see that the First Unitarian's large wooden doors at the front were propped open.

He could get in and get out.

And maybe catch a glimpse of what was making the amazing sound.

But it wasn't that easy.

The first problem was that no sooner had Sam entered than a man appeared from nowhere and closed the oversize doors. It sounded like the closing of an entrance to a vault.

Sam slid silently into the pew in the last row. The organ stopped playing almost immediately, and a minister appeared. He wore a robe but also a tie. He leaned into a microphone and offered up some words. Sam never heard anything these people said. Instead he studied the large space.

To Sam, a room that was clean and smelled vaguely like flowers and candles was exotic. And scary. He was now giving this place his full attention.

The walls were covered in wood that looked to him like pieces of soft leather. There was a large light fixture that hung from the ceiling up front, and it had rows of tiny candles, but they weren't really candles. They would look better, he thought, if they weren't fake. But then it would be impossible to light them without a huge ladder. And also they might drip down onto people, which would be painful.

The long wooden pews were not comfortable. But they never were. If you want people to pay attention, it was important to keep them from settling in. Hadn't his father taught him that?

The man in charge finally stopped speaking, and a choir stood up from a section off to the side. The singers were all ages and shapes, wearing white robes, and they looked to Sam like birds. He didn't know the names of many types of birds, but he'd seen his share, and he felt sure that some place must have big white birds with clean feathers and hairy heads.

Then the organ again began to play, and Sam watched as a girl in the group started to weave her way through the other singers. He could see that she was his age. And he could tell, as she edged toward a microphone, that she was very nervous.

*　*　*

Emily was feeling all sweaty but sort of cold at the same time. This was just ridiculous. Her father, who was standing off to the side waving his right hand in some way that was supposed

16

to be significant, was for sure not going to ever get any eye contact.

Once she got to the microphone, she seized on her strategy.

She was going to focus on the back.

The way back.

Because that's where the people sat who checked their e-mail and monitored sports scores. The back of the church was filled with bodies that were there but not there. The nonlisteners.

Those were her people.

Or her person.

Because when she raised her eyes from the floor, she could see that today there was only one body in the last row.

Emily lifted her chin and opened her mouth and now sang directly to him:

> *"You and I must make a pact*
> *We must bring salvation back*
> *Where there is love,*
> *I'll be there"*

She could hear herself. But not hear herself. And that was the only blessing of her day. Emily knew the song. She knew the words:

> *"I'll reach out my hand to you*
> *I'll have faith in all you do*
> *Just call my name and I'll be there*
> *I'll be there to comfort you*

17

Build my world of dreams around you
I'm so glad that I found you
I'll be there with a love that's strong
I'll be your strength, I'll keep holding on
Let me fill your heart with joy and laughter
Togetherness, well that's all I'm after
Whenever you need me, I'll be there."

She was singing this all to a guy who she'd never seen before.

She could see that he was tall and thin. He had dark brown hair, which was wild and messy. Like it wasn't cut right.

The person who she was singing to was tan, like he spent a lot of time outside, even though it was still late winter.

And she realized that he looked uncomfortable. Like he didn't belong back there. Just like she didn't belong on the platform up front.

And he was intently watching her.

Pretty much everyone was watching her.

But what suddenly mattered was only that he was watching her.

Because all that had mattered to her was watching him. And now she'd made that commitment and she couldn't stop.

She was definitely giving the words of the song new meaning. Isn't that what her father had wanted? A heartfelt reinterpretation?

Was she having an out-of-body experience?

Her mouth was moving and sounds were coming out, but that didn't make sense.

What made sense was in the back row.

* * *

She could not really sing.

That was just a fact.

But it was also a fact that she was riveting. She was raw and exposed and not really hitting the notes right. But she was singing to him.

Why him?

He wasn't imagining it.

The girl with the long brown hair had her small hands held tight at her sides and, maybe because of how bad she was, or because she was staring right at him and seemed to be singing right to him, he couldn't look away.

She was saying she'd be there.

But no one was ever there. That's the way it was. Who was she to tell him such a thing?

It was intimate and suddenly painful.

Not just for her.

But now for him.

Very painful.

3

For a long time Sam was certain his mother would rescue him and Riddle.

Once she realized that they were gone, she would have called the police or the fire department (didn't they take cats out of trees?) or Mrs. Holsing, his second-grade teacher. Or even the neighbors. The ones named Natwick at the end of the street in the blue house who always waved when he walked by. People would be looking. He was sure of it.

Which of course was the case in the beginning. But his mother wasn't the kind of woman to lead an effort. She lacked not just the determination but also the organizational qualities of leadership. And it wasn't her fault.

When Shelly was a baby, her mother had placed her on the kitchen counter when she came in from the market. She'd only turned her back for a moment and the small child had wiggled free of the plastic bucket that was one of the early versions of a car seat. The straps were so complicated. Who needed them?

Shelly's head hit the floor with a thud that sounded like a bat hitting a watermelon. She was unconscious for a full five minutes, only coming around as their station wagon pulled into the emergency-room parking lot.

The doctors kept baby Shelly overnight and said everything was probably fine. The family couldn't deny that she was a loving child, calm and easy to care for. But after that day, she no longer had the potential for her father's brainpower or her mother's musical ability. If her mind was some kind of computer, that fall to the kitchen floor wiped away whole sections of her hard drive.

Once Sam's father took off with her boys, Shelly started going to My Office. The gimmick of the place was the revolving front door. There wasn't another one in town, and this piece of salvaged metal and glass, from a former savings-and-loan building in Denver, made it appear that you were really going into a place of interest.

In reality, the inside was just the corner space of the neighborhood mini-mall, and the only other attempt at an office setting was that a wall of dinged file cabinets made up the bar.

Shelly went straight there from work, which got her through the hardest time of the day. Dinner hour was when she most missed her two boys, and if she wasn't drinking, she found herself cooking for people who no longer existed.

At My Office, Shelly always sat facing the door sipping Shirley Temples because they reminded her of the kids. But her Shirley Temples had two shots of vodka dumped in with the red syrup.

Clarence had been gone for only six weeks when she got hit. She was walking home after a half dozen sweet drinks when, according to the police report, she darted out into traffic. It was impossible to know if it was suicide, an awkward street crossing, or both. She was pronounced dead on the scene. But they took her to the hospital anyway.

The nurse who admitted her body was the same nurse who had been there the day, over forty years before, when she had come in as an infant. The nurse had been young then, fresh out of school. Now she was in her sixties and had arthritis in her knees.

But she remembered.

She wrote the words *Head Injury* on the form for the death certificate and at the last minute added in parentheses *preexisting condition*. She believed in full disclosure.

Six months later, the town's local chief of police retired. The new man in charge of the department was an outsider who was all about responding to the immediate needs of the community. With no one pressing for updates on the missing boys, the case moved lower in priority.

Shelly's mother passed away from a stroke the following year and, after that, even if they had been found, there was no one to return the boys to. The missing Border children were an open file that was in reality closed.

But of course Sam didn't know that.

He imagined his mother in the old house waiting. Even in his fantasies, Shelly was never in the world looking for him. She was always sitting by the phone, staring out the window, longing for him to come through the front door and into her arms.

With time the fantasy faded, as did his image of his mother, until when he thought of her, which was rare, she was always in deep shadows, her face unseen. As the years passed, the whole house had turned dark and lost its shape.

But now, glued to the wooden pew in the back row of the First Unitarian Church, he felt an old feeling flooding over him. Sam's mother was there, somewhere, reaching out to him. She was trying to show him a way home.

Because hadn't she played this song? Hadn't she sung "I'll Be There" to him? Is that why he knew this music so well?

And with the connection, the knot, which was permanently twisted in his stomach, released.

* * *

Emily knew her face was flushed.

Deep red. She told her friends that when that happened, it was chemical — related to having one of her parents descended from northern Europe — and that it had to do with blood pressure. Her best friend, Nora, read somewhere in a magazine that a red face meant a person was more likely to have some kind of throat cancer later in life.

But maybe she'd made that up.

It was confusing. But everything was now confusing.

This guy, this person, this stranger sitting in the back of the church, was causing her to feel weird. Was it him, or was

23

it all in her? Was she feeling something real or just projecting? But wasn't singing one of the things that most exposed your soul? And wasn't her soul exposed enough?

The choir joined in, harmonizing with the words "I'll be there."

And then suddenly it was over.

The organ hit the last note. But instead of stepping back and taking her place in the choir, she moved through the other singers to the steps and left the sanctuary.

She went down the dark hallway that was hidden by the altar, and she opened the single rear exit door and bolted out into the harsh light.

* * *

Sam watched her flee.

He understood completely.

Hadn't he spent his whole life running? The girl with the off-key voice and the glossy sheet of brown hair and the watery eyes was now gone.

The choir continued, seamlessly moving on to another song. But Sam was up on his feet as well. He didn't care that the big wooden doors made noise. He pushed down on the brass bar and was outside.

In moments he was around the back of the church and standing next to the girl who was in some kind of distress. He put one hand on her shoulder. Her eyes were all watery. He didn't want her to cry. If she cried, he might cry. Why would they go to that place?

But he'd learned how to make emotions go away. He was an expert at that. So why was he back here behind the church right now? He was supposed to be invisible. Right?

Right?

And then he found himself saying:

"You're going to be okay. Really . . . It's all right. . . ."

He was comforting her. The girl who couldn't sing and who had been so exposed. Her choir robe parted, and she shook it off and he could see she had on black pants that fit over her perfect little legs and a crisp white shirt that clung to her now small, sweaty body.

Sam suddenly wanted to scoop her up and maybe get on a motorcycle and drive away with her. Except he didn't know how to ride a motorcycle, but he'd seen that in a movie once on TV and the guy was wearing a military uniform and the girl knew him and she wanted to be scooped up.

And then, as she stared at him, it was all too much. She abruptly turned away.

And that's when her breakfast of toast, eggs, and bacon made its second appearance of the morning.

Because this girl didn't know him and, if she did, she would never want to have anything to do with him. This girl had taken one long, intense look at him and that, combined with her singing, had made her sick. He reached out and instinctively took hold of her long hair to keep it from the next retch.

25

He wished he had a rag or a towel or something she could use to wipe off her mouth. But he didn't and then the side door of the church suddenly opened and a woman was standing there. She said:

"Emily, are you all right?"

Sam dropped his hands and released her hair and stepped away and it was over.

Broken.

Done.

He turned on his heel and took off, moving fast but without running.

Away.

Away from her.

* * *

Emily looked from her mother, now heading toward her, over her left shoulder and then her right shoulder to the boy, and she realized that he was going, going, gone. That caused a second wave of anxiety. Where was he? But more to the point, *who* was he?

And then her mother was with her, and she picked up the choir robe off the ground and she used it to wipe her daughter's face, which was sweaty and hot.

You and I must make a pact
We must bring salvation back
Where there is love, I'll be there

But she didn't know his name. She didn't know anything.

Emily shut her eyes. In the orange and red sparkles, which were her eyelids, she saw the parking lot and the Unitarian Church. Maybe she had made it all up. She had a way of constructing stories out of nothing. She saw expressions on people's faces and imagined all kinds of incidents. That's just who she was. Curious? Born with too much imagination? A little off-center?

But then she opened her eyes, and in the distance, on the sidewalk going up the hill toward Cole Street, was a receding figure. He was real.

He had been there.

4

Sam went home to get Riddle. But his mind kept flashing pictures of her. The girl. With her gaze locked on him. The girl who couldn't sing.

Riddle would make the images stop, because he had a way of bringing everything into perspective. With his gray eyes and his wheezy breath, Riddle needed Sam. Even though the brothers were only five years apart in age, it seemed like even more — to them and to the outside world.

Where Sam was tall and lanky, Riddle was short and compact. Sam had dark hair. Riddle was pale and looked faded. Riddle understood only the detail of an object. Sam saw the big picture. And that was important, because he could figure out what they needed to do to get through the day.

Riddle couldn't. He spent his time drawing intricate pictures of the insides of things, strange mechanical sketches with his left hand twisted tightly around the pen. He didn't need blank paper to satisfy his compulsion, which was a good thing, because he rarely had any.

Riddle had an AT&T phone book from Memphis that had been with him for two years, and every single page had the details of something sketched across the original printing. There was the inside of a radio. The grid of the back of an old truck's radiator. A busted toaster with the bottom off. And all this was drawn on top of lists of people's phone numbers or advertisements for plumbing-supply places and Italian restaurants.

Riddle, for the most part, did not speak. He relied on Sam to get his ideas across, especially when it came to their father. Their father didn't like to listen to other people, so having a kid who was on mute most of the time suited him.

The two boys spoke with one voice—it just came out of the older kid. Clarence wasn't a deep thinker. There was a reason he called his second-born child Riddle.

*   *   *

Sam walked down the dirt driveway and passed by the old truck. His father was asleep in the front seat. The truck was packed, but that's how Clarence always kept it. He wanted to be able to leave on a moment's notice. And he never took the stuff they cared about with him.

When the voices inside Clarence's head told him to expect danger, he took a blanket and slept in the front seat. He was on high alert. He often stayed up all night, finally giving in to fatigue as the sun came up.

29

Sam looked in through the side window. He could tell by the angle of his father's head that he'd be immobile for hours. One less thing to worry about.

When he got inside the run-down house, Riddle was, of course, drawing. He squinted and a half smile lit up his face when he saw his big brother. Sam stayed in the door frame and said:

"Pizza ends or tossed tortilla chips?"

Riddle, as could have been predicted, just shrugged and wiped his runny nose. Sam answered for him:

"We'll hit the Dumpsters and then head over to the mini-mart."

He dug into his pocket and pulled out a handful of coins, mostly pennies. A lot of them were greenish-looking copper.

"I scooped up change from the fountain in front of the bank. So we've got some choices."

Riddle was really smiling now. He lifted a ratty-looking backpack off the floor, shoving his battered Memphis phone book inside with a pen, and the two boys started out the door.

*   *   *

No one knew who he was.

Mr. Bingham, who was the self-appointed permanent usher at First Unitarian, thought that he was Nick Penfold. When Emily explained that Nick was in Florida at his grandmother's funeral, Mr. Bingham only scratched his head.

Her investigation continued. No new families had joined the congregation. Mrs. Herlihy in the office confirmed that. He didn't go to Churchill High School, that much was certain. And there was only one other high school in town.

Emily had her friend Remi drive her over to César Chávez High that afternoon, because she heard they had a Sunday basketball game that attracted a large crowd. She hung around pretending to watch, but she literally was scanning the group, face by face. Nothing.

The next morning, she told her best friend, Nora:

"Okay, so you know how I puked at church yesterday?"

Nora nodded but continued checking something on her phone. She didn't look up as she said:

"After you sang."

"Right. But there's something I didn't tell you."

Emily shared everything. So this was surprising. Nora's eyes lifted to meet her best friend's.

"What?"

Emily took a deep breath.

"I know why I got sick...."

Nora's head tilted slightly to the side. Nora liked medical things.

"Because you were so nervous?"

Emily exhaled.

"It was because of a guy."

Nora looked confused. Emily never got to the giddy place about boys.

"What guy?"

Emily felt her face flush.

"I don't know who he was."

"Start over. I missed something."

"I sang to this guy. In the back. I was singing just to him. And he was really listening."

Nora peered at her friend. She now looked concerned.

"And that caused you to puke?"

"Let me finish."

"Sorry...."

Emily continued:

"We connected."

Nora waited. Emily seemed to be done. Nora said:

"Are you okay? A lot of people are getting the flu."

Emily obviously wasn't getting her point across.

"Nora, listen, I know it sounds weird...."

Nora's face scrunched up on the left side. Emily knew that meant something was bugging her.

"Did you talk to him?"

Emily felt herself get defensive.

"He came outside to help me. He pulled back my hair. He touched my shoulder. He told me it was going to be all right."

Now Nora seemed to be getting bored.

"And?"

Nora had been together with Rory Clerkin for almost four months. And before that she'd been with Terrance Fishburne. She had real boyfriends. When Emily hesitated with her answer, Nora continued:

"Guys really like you. And you're not interested. But some guy you don't know watches you puke, and you're into that? Bobby Ellis is hot. I don't know why you won't go out with him."

Now it was Emily's turn to scrunch up her face.

"What does Bobby Ellis have to do with this?"

Nora shot back:

"Everything. If you'd just hook up with someone, you wouldn't be so worked up when a random cool guy looked at you."

Emily seemed to hear only two words.

"Cool guy? I didn't say he was a 'cool guy.'"

Nora shrugged.

"Cate Rocce told me. She said there was a cool guy in church who left as soon as you sang."

Emily's eyes were wide.

Cate Rocce had seen him. Emily hadn't thought to ask Cate Rocce. Because she didn't like Cate Rocce. The girl just wasn't very nice. But Cate Rocce had called him cool. Maybe Cate Rocce knew who he was. Emily couldn't stop smiling.

But unfortunately, when she tracked down Cate Rocce in PE class an hour later, the girl knew nothing.

* * *

Sunday finally arrived.

Since her solo, she'd been allowed to quit the choir. Emily figured her father finally knew for certain that he hadn't passed along his musical talent to either of his kids, because her little brother was even worse at singing than she was. It happens.

Now, as she climbed into the car, she realized she'd been counting down the days. How ironic that church, which was the most boring part of her week, had become the focal point of all her efforts.

But he didn't show up.

For an hour and a half, she basically stared at the back doors and hated herself for doing it.

That afternoon she tried to push it all out of her mind. Was she mixing up the emotions of bombing in church with something else? What was happening to her? She was turning into one of those girls who made her crazy.

But if she felt this way about a stranger, she should be able to work up some emotion about someone she actually knew.

Right?

5

The next day before class, when she first saw Nora at her locker, she said:

"I thought about what you said...."

"About what?" Nora asked.

"About Bobby Ellis. He's kinda nice, I guess."

Nora smiled wide as she grabbed Emily by the arm.

"Really? I can't wait to tell Rory! So do you wanna do something—we could all go to a movie! Or maybe go get food and watch a movie at Rory's house—you know, if his mom's going to be out—or maybe—"

Emily interrupted her:

"Slow down. I only said he was okay...."

Nora's face fell.

"You said he was nice. He's one of Rory's good friends. He's perfect for you."

Emily tried hard to sound enthusiastic.

"I want to get to know him better. That's all I'm saying...."

Nora was back to her wide smile.

"Right. You set the pace. I'm going to tell Rory to have Bobby call you."

Emily felt a tidal wave of dread wash over her body as she nodded. Maybe in the next hour she could change her number or lose her phone.

The idea of talking at any length to Bobby Ellis was second in creepiness only to the notion of sitting next to him in a movie theater. What was wrong with her? Plenty of girls thought Bobby Ellis was totally great. She guessed they didn't notice how he laughed at just about anything anyone said. Or how he got too close when he was talking.

She'd read that good memories pushed out the bad ones. But what if it was the other way around? What if bad memories pushed out the good?

Bobby Ellis had always sort of bugged her. It was hard to think that was going to change.

* * *

Sam thought about going back to the First Unitarians. But it wasn't possible.

When you spend ten years being invisible, when you no longer know where you were born and are not even sure when you were born (it had to have been the summer, because there were memories of an ice-cream cake and running outside through a sprinkler), when your father changed your last name and you can't remember clearly what your mother even looked like, a room with that many strangers was as terrifying as a bed of sharp knives.

So was it just a coincidence that he took Riddle and went to Superior-Cuts for free haircuts? The sign in the window said they needed volunteers. Had they ever volunteered before for anything? They weren't supposed to talk to people. Wasn't that the rule?

Their father had cut their hair when they were little, whacking it off as if he were cutting cord. For the last few years, they'd been doing it themselves with a pair of scissors Clarence kept in the glove compartment of the truck. Who cared if there was any kind of style to the whole thing?

Sam didn't put together his thoughts of the girl singing with his desire to look different. He just saw himself in the reflections of store windows and realized that he and his little brother looked strange. And suddenly that seemed to matter.

Neither of them had ever been inside a hair salon before, at least not that they could remember. After Sam explained that they wanted to volunteer, the process began with a "before" picture taken with a digital camera.

Riddle made Crystal, the stylist-in-training, anxious. He didn't look her in the eye or acknowledge anything that she said. With his stubborn, bone-straight blond hair, he stared at his feet when she took a photo. His attention, as always, was on Sam, who stood, like the parent, only two feet away.

It wasn't going to be easy.

Riddle made it clear, in his own way, that he didn't want his hair washed. And then when Crystal used her foot to make the salon chair rise, he jumped out. He'd had enough of a problem with the plastic smock that snapped shut in the back, not the front.

Sam took Riddle to the corner of the salon, where they huddled together in front of the bathroom door. When they returned, Sam looked apologetic and explained that his brother didn't need any kind of styled cut; he just wanted to have his head shaved.

Instead of being upset, Crystal was thrilled. She buzzed his hair in what seemed like sixty seconds, and Riddle, now looking unrecognizable, took his Reno phone book and happily went to wait outside with his pen.

His "after" picture was taken against the exterior of the building. He was squinting up into the lens with a head of yellowish peach fuzz. Riddle spent the next hour drawing an intricate picture of the hydraulic lift at the base of each of the styling chairs.

Sam was up next.

With Riddle out of the way, she now took her time. She started by washing his hair, not once, not twice, but three separate times, working her fingers into his scalp as she leaned straight over his body. Her blouse somehow opened up an extra button, and Sam shut his eyes to keep from staring right at her pink push-up bra. Suddenly he felt like Riddle; he just wanted out of this place.

But Crystal didn't seem to notice.

After she'd done what seemed like an eternity of washing, she rubbed special conditioner deep into his scalp. Then with him back in the regular chair, she began to work on his haircut as if her life depended on the outcome. It took a while before Sam realized that the other two stylists in the salon were now watching.

Sam had a lot of hair. It was thick and dark and wavy. In the past he'd tried to cut it all the same length. Crystal had other ideas.

She layered the front and part of the back. She thinned and she clipped and she feathered. For forty-seven minutes she worked with total focus and commitment. When she was finished, it would not have been an exaggeration to say that the haircut was her greatest artistic achievement.

That's when the salon owner got involved. He covered Sam's face with wet towels and then warm shaving cream. The owner then pulled out the sharpest blade that Sam had ever seen, and the seventeen-year-old was now certain that he was going to die.

Feeling powerless to do anything, he closed his eyes, and then the salon owner took the steel straightedge and shaved off the fuzz that grew on Sam's chin and his cheeks and parts of his neck.

It struck Sam as interesting that when he thought the man was going to slit his throat, he felt a resigned sense of peace and didn't fight back.

The salon owner took the "after" picture himself, insisting that Sam stand by a mirror so that the front and the back of the cut could both be seen. Then the owner made Sam sign some kind of paperwork, which he called a release.

Sam had no idea what he was talking about, but if signing

a release meant he could leave, he had no problem scribbling his name on the form. He was starting to really get anxious. Everyone in the place seemed to now be involved.

While the owner completed the paperwork, Crystal took a plastic bag and filled it with what she called "product." She put in more than two dozen small containers of samples — shampoo and conditioners, hair gel, and even some kind of skin lotion. Sam was silent. He sometimes used a bar of soap on his hair. Mostly he just stood under the water and hoped the dirt would wash itself out.

Crystal pushed her card into Sam's palm with the bag of hair-care supplies, which now also included a package of disposable razors.

It wasn't until they got home that Sam saw that she'd written her cell phone number in purple ink on the back along with the words: *call me*. She'd signed her name underneath with a lopsided heart. Sam threw the card in the trash.

Their father, as could be expected, was not happy when he saw the boys. Riddle's shaved head didn't alarm him as much as Sam's new stylish one. The tall boy looked mainstream now. Better than mainstream, was the truth. And that unnerved a mind already unhinged.

Sam ignored his father's ranting and raving as best he could. But when it got to be too much, he grabbed his beat-up guitar and took Riddle and they disappeared into the woods. When they came back, it had been dark for hours and Clarence was gone.

It wasn't until the next day when he and Riddle went out

in the afternoon looking for lunch that it hit him: maybe their father was right.

Now they were no longer invisible.

* * *

As soon as the two boys left, the salon owner gave Crystal her own workstation. The girl had talent. No question.

The owner, Rayford, went to look at the release form. The older kid had signed his name: Sam Smith.

When Sam Smith had walked out, he looked as if he'd stepped right off the pages of a European fashion magazine. His worn jeans and his faded T-shirt that didn't quite fit right only made him somehow more appealing. The kid had an incredible look.

Rayford knew it when he saw it. He'd lived, after all, in Manhattan for three years. And if Sam Smith were in a big city, people would be trying to exploit him. But here, in the out-of-the-way college town with its two closed lumber mills and its double-digit unemployment rate, not likely.

So it was a no-brainer, putting together an ad with a "before" and "after" photo of Sam in the PennySaver flyer that was delivered to the mailboxes of the better houses north of Main Street on Fridays.

People were so predictable. Rayford would bet his left arm that no one for five hundred miles looked like Sam Smith, but he could guarantee that most of them hoped all that separated them from doing so was a good haircut.

* * *

Hours of being by themselves with a lunatic had made the boys strange. Sam knew that.

His brother's obsession with drawing wasn't something that people easily understood. No one had ever told Riddle that there was a right way or a wrong way to sketch something or that he might consider subjects other than the insides of mechanical objects. And while Sam didn't have Riddle's disconnect with the world, he was sure he did things that gave him away.

That was the problem with never going to school and never seeing how other people lived. You had no way of knowing how off you were in your presentation.

Maybe that's why most of the stuff Sam played on his guitar didn't sound like what he heard on the radio, even though early on he had figured out how to imitate songs once he'd listened to them a few times.

Sam could read well, and it was surprising how much stuff you could learn from magazines and newspapers. It was also surprising how many people threw interesting things away.

Every day in the trash cans and Dumpsters he found catalogs, letters, and manuals. Recycling meant that paper was usually separated, and it was there that he found an even better selection of reading material, which often included actual paperbacks and hardcover volumes of all kinds of things. People tossed textbooks, yearbooks, old almanacs, and even scrapbooks.

No matter what town they were in, he and Riddle went at

least twice a week to scavenge city dump sites. What was there wasn't, to the two of them, garbage. It was just stuff that people didn't want—and that you wouldn't get in trouble for taking.

Riddle would wander off, looking for mechanical things to draw. Sam stayed at the drop-off area. People would drive in with a pickup truck full of crap, exhausted from a long day of tearing something apart, or with the remains from trying to put something broken back together.

Sam would step forward and lend a hand, oftentimes doing most of the work. If they had books or anything interesting he wanted, no one cared if he set it aside. And at least half of the people reached into their wallets and gave him a few dollars for helping out.

Every now and then someone would put a five- or ten-dollar bill into his hand, especially if the person happened to see Riddle and figured out that they were some kind of damaged team. People were, for the most part, nice enough.

But after he got the haircut, they were suddenly nicer.

A lot nicer.

Housewives with station wagons filled with old lawn furniture and worn-out kitchen appliances smiled at him as they handed over money. Old guys with slumped shoulders and stained T-shirts slapped him on the back as he hauled old drywall out of their pickup trucks, joking that there was nothing like doing some after-school work to get ahead in life.

Suddenly it was as if he'd changed teams. He was on the other side of an equation. The world now seemed bigger.

He wondered if that's what happened when people could see you.

* * *

Riddle opened his phone book and looked at one of his drawings. A brown moth landed on the yellow paper. Riddle stared at it, his thoughts swirling:

Some things are born with wings. Like butterflies. Or birds. And they can fly.

Some things only have legs. Like spiders. But they have lots of legs so they can crawl and run and hide. When you have two legs, it is harder to hide.

Light is always moving. Even in tiny, tiny, tiny ways.

Light makes all shape.

I taste wild berries. Just by seeing them.

I listen. Always. If you are quiet, you hear more than things that make noise.

I see the insides. Turning pieces. Even if the pieces are broken. I put them back together.

I start downside up.

It hurts, but the inside is always worth seeing.

Then Riddle shut the phone book hard, crushing the moth.

He opened it slowly and stared at the flattened insect, now only a lifeless smudge against two pages. And his eyes filled with tears.

6

Bobby Ellis could drive with other kids in the car.

He was eighteen but in the same grade as Emily. His parents had told him that he'd had the mumps just before kindergarten and missed the first three weeks and so they had him wait a whole year later to enter school. They said he wasn't held back. He just had a false start.

The plan had been in place all week. Bobby would pick up Rory. Then Bobby and Rory would get Nora. Then Bobby, Rory, and Nora would get Emily. Emily had secretly hoped that her parents would say that driving with Bobby Ellis was a bad idea. But part of the new philosophy of giving her freedom since they'd made her sing solo meant they said yes to more things.

Tragic.

Emily took a shower after school and picked out what she thought was a nice sweater. It looked good, but it didn't suggest that she was trying too hard.

After Emily was dressed, she put on her favorite song and listened to it three times in a row. That was usually guaranteed to put her in a good mood. She was trying to psych herself into caring. But it was hopeless. With twenty minutes remaining before they were supposed to arrive, Emily went downstairs to have a yogurt.

Her parents had gone to a music recital at the college. Her little brother had a friend over, and they were playing some kind of annoying video game that involved a lot of screaming.

The mail was on the counter. It was always just a bunch of bills, so she ignored it except when a good catalog showed up. And this batch of stuff looked unremarkable.

Emily got a spoon and then went to the refrigerator and took out a peach yogurt. She looked at the clock. Eleven more minutes before they'd arrive. The book she was reading was upstairs. Jared and the annoying friend had the big TV monopolized.

So she picked up the stack of mail. On top was the Penny-Saver with ads for dog groomers and Realtors. She flipped it over and froze, saying out loud:

"OhmyGod..."

There he was.

In two pictures.

One looking just like she'd seen him, scruffy, vulnerable, like he had some kind of secret. And in the other photo he was all cleaned up. And he looked amazing. Under his pictures were the words: *Sam Smith: Before and After. Superior-Cuts! We Make Change Happen!*

"Sam Smith."

He had a name.

And then the doorbell rang.

* * *

Emily had the picture in her purse. It took all the willpower she had to keep from taking it out and looking at it as they drove away from the house.

She could tell that Bobby Ellis was watching not just the road but her. Rory and Nora were in the back. They sat so close that Nora may as well have been on his lap. Nora was giggling about something and generally acting in a way that Emily had never seen before.

Up front, the radio was on. Thank God. She thought it made talking to Bobby Ellis impossible.

Wrong.

She suddenly heard:

"So what do you have on tap for the weekend?"

Emily's mind was still reeling from the photograph and her discovery. She'd lost her ability to concentrate. Or at least her ability to concentrate on anything other than the Superior-Cuts advertisement and Sam Smith. She did her best to ignore Bobby's question and pretended to closely check something on her left index fingernail. And then she heard:

"You got anything exciting going on?"

Emily felt herself tense. Didn't he know that his eyes should be on the road? What if he wasn't paying attention, and they got in an accident? Then she'd never be able to find Sam Smith. A small voice came out of her body:

"I'm just hanging out."

Hopefully that would put an end to it. She turned back into her own world. Sam Smith. Before. After. Superior-Cuts.

"Sounds good. People don't appreciate how important it is to do nothing. My dad and I are going fishing up at Blue Lake tomorrow."

He was talking again. She continued looking straight out the window. She just couldn't do this right now. Would it be wrong to turn up the radio? She couldn't bring herself to do it.

The awkward silence was broken from the backseat when Nora chirped:

"Emily likes fishing."

Emily turned around to look at the traitor. She scrunched up her face.

"I do not."

Nora looked confused.

"Yeah you do. You go all the time with your grandma."

Emily exhaled through her nose. Why was Nora selling her as some kind of fisherman? She and Bobby Ellis did not have common interests. And why was the conversation spreading to include the backseat?

"I like canoes. That's different. And I like hanging out with my grandma. I don't like killing fish. *At all.*"

The last two words were delivered with such intensity

that now even Rory was paying attention. He sort of snorted and said:

"Whoa, girl."

In the front seat, Bobby leaned forward and turned up the volume on the radio. Conversation was now impossible. Emily was both grateful and humiliated.

* * *

Walking toward the multiplex, Nora and Rory held hands. Bobby and Emily trailed behind them, but Bobby kept his distance. After they got tickets, Nora told the boys that she and Emily needed to go to the bathroom. Once the girls disappeared behind the swinging door, Bobby looked at his friend.

"Dude, she hates me."

Rory sort of laughed.

"Yeah. Seems like it."

Bobby leaned against the wall.

"The weird part is, she's always been so easy to talk to. That's what I liked about her. She's always seemed so interested. She wasn't one of those mean girls."

Rory shrugged.

"I guess you don't bring out the best in her."

Bobby half smiled.

"Guess not."

Inside the bathroom, Nora turned on her friend.

"What is wrong with you?!"

Emily opened up her purse and pulled out the Penny-Saver flyer. She handed it to Nora.

"There. It's him. Mr. Last Row."

It was bright in the bathroom, and other people were going in and out of the stalls. A few of them didn't hide the fact that they glanced over at the flyer. Nora looked down at the paper, confused.

"He's a male model?"

Emily pulled the flyer back.

"If he was a model, what would he be doing at Superior-Cuts? He got a haircut. They do before-and-after pictures."

Nora brushed it aside.

"Well, he looks like a model."

The tone of Nora's voice made it clear that this was a very bad thing. And then she continued:

"Emily, you are here with *Bobby*, not with some guy you don't know who does advertising for Superior-Cuts —"

Emily interrupted:

"I don't think they pay you for —"

Nora continued:

"You've got to turn it around. Right here. Right now. You're embarrassing."

Emily stared at her friend. Nora looked like she was shaking. Emily glanced back down at the flyer. She suddenly felt foolish.

"I'm kinda in shock. I mean, I only saw the picture when you guys showed up. And I didn't know his name. And now —"

Her voice trailed off. Nora's voice was still hard.

"You still don't know anything. So get over it."

Emily folded up the flyer and put it back in her bag.

"I'm sorry."

Nora started for the door.

"Tell Bobby that, not me."

* * *

Emily apologized once they'd taken their seats. She smiled at Bobby three times during the previews and tried hard to just relax.

The movie was about a crazy killer who wore a clown/nun costume, and a few times she found herself involuntarily gasping at some act of unspeakable violence. Once she even turned her head suddenly to look away and somehow ended up deep in Bobby Ellis's armpit.

And he seemed to like that.

By the time it was over, Emily was too worn-out to be agitated. As they walked to the new SUV, Rory suggested they go get pancakes.

IHOP was all the way across town on River Road. It was close to the freeway and far from the university, in the neighborhood with the car mechanics and discount tile and carpet places. Whenever Emily thought of River Road, she could picture the sign that said Low-Cost Cremation, which hung on the cement building a block from the animal shelter where they got their dog.

She was dying to just go home, but she tried to be

enthusiastic and agreed that pancakes sounded really good. So what if IHOP was a fifteen-minute drive?

The group found a booth at the restaurant in the back next to the windows. Nora was being nice to her again, and Bobby Ellis was in the middle of telling a story about someone throwing firecrackers at crows.

Emily was happy that he seemed to be on the side of the crows, but she was only hearing half of what he said. She stared out the dark glass and silently wondered if the waitress could bring her crepes with the lingonberry butter and the check at the same time.

And then two figures passed by outside on the sidewalk.

One was short with a shaved head. He carried something the size of a phone book. The other was tall. Even looking out a tinted window, half a block away, in the dark, she knew. Emily slid right out of the booth and got to her feet.

"I'll be right back."

Nora started to scoot out to follow.

"I drank too much Diet Coke. I'll come with."

But Emily was already moving down the aisle. And she was heading in the direction away from the bathrooms. Nora called after her:

"Hey, Emily..."

But she didn't turn around.

Outside, it had just started to rain. Emily angled past a middle-aged couple trying to open a broken umbrella and found herself in the parking lot. She looked down the street. They were in the distance now.

He was getting away.

Inside the restaurant, it was silent at the table as a waitress delivered their order.

Bobby Ellis took a bite of his pancakes. Rory poured half the container of syrup over his waffles. Nora scooped off some of the whipped cream from her crepes. More silence.

Then Bobby Ellis turned his head, and out the window he saw Emily run by on the rainy sidewalk. He looked back across the table at his friends, saying:

"She hates me."

* * *

At the corner, the two brothers started across the street. A city bus was approaching. Were they going to get on it? She had to stop him. Running hard now, Emily shouted:

"Sam!"

He turned. And he saw her. And he stopped.

The rain was coming down for real now, and in a few seconds she found herself in the middle of the street, standing across from him. Emily opened her mouth, and all that came out was:

"I…"

That was it. Nothing else. Just *I*. His eyes were locked with hers. He finally said:

"You…"

Apparently, she thought, they could only speak to each other one syllable at a time.

The younger boy next to Sam tucked his phone book farther inside his shirt to keep it from getting wet. He was looking at the ground. Sam glanced at him, his eyes reassuring, and his hand went to the younger boy's side and he lightly touched his arm.

When he turned back to Emily, she opened her mouth again and said the most heartfelt thing she'd ever remembered saying to a boy:

"I...I...I've been looking for you."

He nodded and the expression on his face made it clear he completely understood.

7

Rory was now in the front seat. Bobby Ellis, of course, drove. Emily, soaking wet, sat silently in the back with Nora, who was completely ignoring her.

After what seemed like forever, they pulled up in front of Emily's house. The rain was still falling, but it was only a drizzle now, and the windshield wipers scraped at the glass. Emily managed to say:

"Thank you. I'm sorry that I didn't...that I was so..."

Bobby turned around and looked at her. He wasn't mad. If anything, he only seemed sort of intrigued.

"No big deal, Emily."

Emily felt relieved. At her side, Nora wasn't being as forgiving. She was now texting someone. In the front seat, Rory looked down at his phone. He'd just received a text.

Emily addressed the whole car:

"Good night."

She had the door open and was moving fast now. It

sounded like more than one of them mumbled back "good night." She couldn't really be sure.

Emily entered her house to find her mother standing on the hooked rug in the entryway doing her best to not look like she couldn't fall asleep until her kid was home. Her mom gave her a tired smile.

"How'd everything go?"

Emily meant it when she said:

"Tonight changed my life."

And then she headed up the stairs.

*   *   *

They had made a plan.

She was going to meet him the next night in front of the restaurant with the blue roof at seven o'clock. Sam could tell time. But it meant nothing to him. He didn't have a watch. He didn't have a cell phone or a computer or anything that even displayed time. The clock on the dashboard of the truck had been broken for years and Clarence liked it that way.

Time for Sam was about the position of the sun. It was about feeling hunger in his stomach. It was about the temperature just after dawn. Time wasn't measured in minutes or even hours. It had a rhythm that had to do with days and seasons, animals and insects, flowers and plants.

Time was measured by the number of pages of drawings

in Riddle's phone books. It was seen in Sam's pants that were short since he'd grown another three inches. Very little in his life had been predigested and explained.

Now, staring up at the ceiling at a brown water spot that looked like a cowboy boot, he was worried.

Sam pushed those thoughts away and went back to thinking about the girl. She'd just appeared on the street. She'd called out his name. She knew him. No one knew him.

She told him that her name was Emily.

Emily Bell.

He could see Emily now, soaking wet, standing on the sidewalk. Because of her, he now had to organize a plan.

He would do laundry tomorrow. He'd gather up stuff and take it down to the Clean Quarter. Riddle liked Laundromats. A room of working machines was his idea of heaven. Yes, they'd go to the Clean Quarter.

He hadn't been there in about a month. It was amazing how many days in a row you could wear something before it just grossed you out. Maybe he'd throw in the two gray towels in the bathroom and wash them, too.

He guessed they might not just meet in front of the restaurant with the blue roof, but maybe she'd want to go inside. And then they might get something to eat. He'd only been in a place that nice on a rare, rare occasion, and that was really only to use the bathroom.

So he'd need to have some money. He wasn't sure how much. He'd better go to the dump early and help people unload stuff. He couldn't risk not being able to pay for something.

All of a sudden, everything was getting so complicated.

*　　*　　*

Emily wondered if he drove.

Since he was on foot late at night, she decided he didn't yet have his license. She could walk to IHOP, but she'd have to leave about two hours early.

Emily suddenly wished that they'd picked someplace closer. But what she really wished was that they'd exchanged cell phone numbers and e-mail addresses and regular addresses.

Because at this point, she couldn't call him or even find him online to change the plan.

She could ride her bike out there, but then she'd be stuck with it. And she didn't have a way to tell him to ride there to meet her.

She hoped he liked mountain bikes. She loved going up into the hills and riding down on the different trails that ran along the stream. It was rocky and the paths were full of turns and you had to be in a crouch, half standing, gripping the handlebars like your life depended on it. Because it sort of did. At least the way she rode anyway.

She figured he wasn't someone who sat inside playing video games at all hours, because he looked weathered, and those kinds of kids looked pale and sort of fidgety.

He probably did lots of sports. Maybe he played soccer.

She was glad that she was still on the school soccer team, even if she really wasn't even a starter.

She could see him skiing. But she liked to snowboard better than ski now, so she hoped he felt the same way.

Her family only went up a half dozen times a year, but they'd gone since she was a little kid. So of course she knew her way around the different runs. But what she really liked best about snowboarding was riding the chairlift and looking down on the snowy trees and pretending she was a bird, flying over the mountainside.

But she'd keep that to herself.

Like a lot of what she felt, which could be alarming to those who didn't see a painting and want to climb inside the picture to get to know the people. She couldn't help being that way.

Her mind drifted to his family. Did they like the outdoors? Did they go camping or love something like sailing? Were they a family that had a strong connection to art or some activity like rock collecting, which was what the Schiffs, who lived on the corner, did every weekend? They were all about quartz.

Or maybe they were big travelers. She hoped that was their interest. She loved getting on planes and flying places. Maybe his family felt the same way, and maybe his parents, once they got to know her, would want her to go on one of their trips.

She worried now whether her mom and dad would let her go.

Would they get all crazy and say it wasn't right for her to

travel with his family? Would her mother insist on calling his mother and going over all the details? She could imagine the whole embarrassing scenario. If this all worked out, she decided she would try to keep the moms to an e-mail-only relationship.

Emily shut her eyes and slowly let out a long sigh.

All of a sudden, everything was getting so complicated.

* * *

Every now and then, it actually occurred to Clarence that it might take the same amount of effort to do things in a legitimate way as it was to do them *his* way. But he'd quickly push that thought aside. Because there was no denying the fact that being a thief was a lot of work.

But he was used to the struggle.

Clarence kept his vehicle registration current by peeling off a sticker from the back of someone else's license plate. He took things from people's mailboxes — payments, money orders, free samples, and a favorite: credit-card bills with preprinted checks to cash.

He'd called himself John Smith for years. There were so many Smiths that everyone got jumbled up in the records. John Smith. One bad Smith don't spoil the whole bunch, girl.

Some of his crimes were petty — he stole magazines from newsstands and crates of produce from the loading docks of markets. But he tackled larger offenses as well.

He went to construction sites after hours and hauled away tools and building materials. He broke into cars and grabbed purses and cell phones and gas cards. He went to bowling alleys and walked off with other people's shoes. He took soap and toilet paper from storage cupboards in public bathrooms. He snatched dogs out of fenced yards and returned them, claiming rewards. He jacked potted plants, firewood, and spare tires.

And then, when he could feel the net closing in on him, he'd move on. That's why the truck was always packed. Ready when you are.

The cops had questioned him too many times to even count. He'd been taken in and held overnight in all kinds of places. Hell, there were warrants out for him in half a dozen states. That's why he went to Mexico. He thought he could just escape the whole damn country, but they had their own sense of justice down there. If he'd hung out any longer, he'd be missing kneecaps—or a lot worse.

The boys gave him a story. People felt sorry for a single father. And he'd done right by them. He'd taught his kids to survive, and that was the most important thing you could give a child. He rarely had to hit them anymore.

Now that the oldest boy had gotten so big, he'd laid off that. But he couldn't get the kid to come with him when he was working it. The boy just refused. Even when he was little. Even if you smacked him.

The younger one was a piece of work. Who knew what he was thinking? Clarence had seen him out in a meadow when he was four years old eating grasshoppers, and that's when he knew for a fact that the kid was a dud. He didn't talk much, but he could draw. Crazy-looking stuff. Too bad there was no money in that.

Sometimes the voices told Clarence that Riddle was out to get him. So he let the older boy deal with the little kid. He'd learned the hard way. Trust no one. Especially your own blood.

Clarence couldn't imagine sticking around this place much longer. He'd scammed the rental house, and soon they'd be after him for not paying. He was only still there because college towns had careless kids with money and lots of things that were easy picking. But he'd already had some close calls. People were too interested in his business.

Any day now, he'd get the boys in the truck and be moving on.

8

Bobby Ellis woke up and realized he was thinking about Emily. How messed up was that?

He knew he should have been really mad, but he wasn't. The truth was that he hadn't ever even really noticed her until Riley Holland, the most popular guy in their class, had pointed out that Emily looked like the quirky girl in the commercial for mini tacos that ran during the Super Bowl.

Riley Holland had good taste. Bobby knew that. And so after Riley made the connection, Bobby started paying attention to Emily. From-a-distance kind of attention to someone.

Now he went over it all in his mind. He didn't do anything. She was weird from the moment she got into the car. And she'd been nice to him all week at school. He'd called her three different times, and they'd talked about homework and their friends and music and even dumb stuff like the weather. She'd listened and even added in some curious comments.

So who was that other person who got in the car last night? And why did this other person, this crazy girl, interest him more than the nice one?

How messed up was that?

* * *

Emily told her parents she was going to meet a boy named Sam who she'd met at church. This was true. She told her parents that they would meet at the IHOP on River Road. This was true. She asked her dad if he'd drive her there and she said she'd figure out a way to get home or else she'd call for a ride. This was also true.

She told them that she was meeting him at 6:30 PM. This was not true. She didn't want Sam seeing her being dropped off by her father, so she was willing to wait a half hour to avoid that. It's not that she was embarrassed by her dad, not more embarrassed than anyone is by their dad, but, still, she was seventeen.

Sam got there early, too, because he really did not understand the time thing. It had been hard leaving Riddle, but he got him a meatball sub at Subway and a Coke. And he'd surprised his brother with a broken clock radio with the old-style digital eyes, the kind that flopped over the numbers instead of projecting them.

Sam had taken the back off the radio so that Riddle could see the wires and the small circuit board right away. And then he told him to stay in the house and that he'd be gone for two full drawings.

Once at the restaurant, Sam took a seat under a tree in the grass that grew in a thin strip in the parking lot. He watched as the silver car pulled up to the curb. Inside he saw Emily say something to the man driving—her father?—and the man smiled at her as she got out.

Even though he was in shadow, and it was dusk and he was at a distance, Emily saw him. Why could she pick him out from so far away and be so certain?

She walked over, and he got to his feet and he smiled. She smiled back and managed to say:

"Hey..."

He said "Hey" back.

And then they graduated to two syllables and then three and then sentences. And then whole ideas and the real expression of thought.

In every possible way, it was different from the night before in the car with Bobby Ellis. Bobby could and did, in her opinion, talk about nothing, and she found it hard to listen. Sam barely spoke, but everything he said was interesting.

They didn't go into the pancake house but just started to walk. There was no destination. She had so many questions but tried hard not to interrogate him.

He'd made a vow to himself that he wouldn't tell her anything, if he could help it, about his life, but little things dribbled out.

He'd only recently moved to town. He had a brother. They called him Riddle. He was the boy she saw with him on the street at night.

Emily said she had a little brother, too. She told him that she went to Churchill High. She said she wished he went there. He said he wished he did, too. But he said he was homeschooled and added that his father didn't believe in organized things.

She didn't understand but took the silence that followed to mean that she shouldn't pursue it.

He tried to answer questions without revealing that he did not follow half of what she said. And she didn't understand the silences and mistook his utter confusion for deep introspection.

She decided that he was the best listener she'd ever met.

She was talking about something called calculus and he thought maybe that was a medicine. She had played in something called AYSO since she was only five. She laughed and said that even then she'd never been any kind of star.

A star at what, he wondered.

He told her that he'd lived for five months in Mexico and that they moved a lot. He talked about places he'd seen and sleeping outside and how he had once walked with his brother and father for thirty miles in a single day when their truck broke down in the desert.

She said she loved to travel and that she was embarrassed to admit she'd hoped that his family felt the same way.

And then they were outside her house.

It was eight miles away, and Emily just naturally had gone there. She tried to get Sam to come in, but he wouldn't. He said he had to go. He told her that he didn't have a cell phone, but she gave him her number and he said he'd call her.

She asked him to meet her the next day, and he said he didn't think he could. He looked anxious now, and even though he was still there, he was suddenly far away.

For Emily, he was more than she could have imagined. He wasn't like the other boys she'd done things with. He didn't try to tell outrageous jokes or bore her with stories where he was some kind of hero. He didn't boast about stealing his parents' vodka and drinking with friends or staying up all night to pull a prank. He didn't take out a cell phone and check for messages or have all kinds of attitude.

For Sam, she was like someone from another planet. Planet Contentment. She had energy and enthusiasm, and she had to have never seen what he'd seen, because she was so open and so trusting.

Sam had no idea what the next step should be.

He was filled with confusion and, now, standing on the edge of her herringbone-brick driveway, what he wanted, more than anything, was to get away. To escape. To make all of the emotion he was feeling simply stop.

He then reached down and took her hand and brushed it up against his lips, and he lightly kissed the inside of her palm. He then whispered:

"I will always remember walking with you tonight...."

He then let her hand go and turned away and she watched, immobilized, as he headed down the sidewalk, around the corner, and disappeared into the night air.

* * *

Sam didn't call.

Emily heard nothing from him.

Not the next day or the next day or the next.

Emily became one of those girls. She checked her phone constantly. Neurotically. Obsessively. She was angry at him, and she was angry at herself. She literally had trouble concentrating. How had this happened to her? Why had it happened to her? And how could she make it stop?

After the first two days, she started looking for him. She walked to the IHOP after school and sat inside, staring out the window. On her third day there, the floor manager offered her a job as a hostess. After that, she never went back.

Emily knew Sam's last name, but that got her nowhere. She didn't know where he lived. He'd said he didn't go to school. He'd said he moved a lot.

So had he left town? Even if he had to go, even if there had been some big emergency, why wouldn't he call to tell her? Why wouldn't he call to say good-bye? Why wouldn't he call to say *anything*?

The ripple effect of her disappointment hit everyone.

She and Nora got in a fight about nothing, and they were no longer speaking. Her father, clueless as to what was really going on, worried that her dark mood had something to do with making her sing.

But her mother knew anxiety when she saw it. And her cheerful daughter was now experiencing real angst.

And then Emily woke up from a dream believing Sam

had been hurt. Hit by a car. Run over in the dark walking home. That had happened to their neighbor Pep Kranitz on a trip to Nebraska and he'd almost died.

She called the two hospitals in town and asked for a patient named Sam Smith. He wasn't at Sacred Heart, which was where her mother worked. But he was listed at Kaiser. Room 242.

She knew it.

Emily put on a dress and bought daffodils. (Was it right to give flowers to a boy in the hospital? She wasn't sure. And she wasn't going to ask her mother.) When she got out of the hospital elevator, the man at the nurses' desk told her that room 242 was at the end of the hall. *Smith, Sam* was written in Magic Marker on a wipe board by the door.

Emily held her breath as a heavyset nurse emerged from the doorway lightly touching her arm as she whispered:

"He passed."

Emily stepped into the room to find a skeletal old man in the metal bed, hooked up to tubes and monitoring devices. His marble yellow eyes with cloudy blue centers were open, staring lifelessly up at the acoustical tile ceiling.

An elderly woman was folded over the bed gripping the sheet. And then she saw Emily and she pulled herself up and wrapped her arms around the young girl's neck as she heaved a sob. The daffodils fell from Emily's hands onto the bed, and she held on to the old woman and began to cry with her.

She would find out, later, that the Smiths had been together for fifty-nine years.

It was another first in Emily's life. A dead man. A dead man named Sam Smith.

* * *

Making a connection to a person can be the scariest thing that ever happens to you.

Sam knew that now.

He'd walked around coiled rattlesnakes. He'd jumped off a train trestle to avoid an oncoming train. He'd lain in bed shivering at night with infection and no penicillin. He'd been pulled out to sea by the current when he couldn't swim. He'd dodged the flying fist of his father. Many, many times.

But this scared him more.

This scared him so much that he couldn't face her again.

He'd come home that night, and things had not gone well. Clarence was hearing voices and when he discovered Riddle by himself, the voices got louder. Where the hell had Sam gone?

Once Clarence started kicking walls, Riddle took off out the back door. He ran into the nearby woods, and Sam spent an hour out there after midnight trying to find his little brother. When he did, Riddle was shaking from the cold, hiding like a small, injured animal, which, Sam thought, of course he was.

The next morning, when Sam was feeling as if he were going to jump out of his skin if he didn't go see her, he burned her telephone number. But that didn't stop him from thinking about her or where she lived.

It was a yellow house with dark blue trim. It was two stories, made from wood, and it looked like something that you'd see in a brochure for happy people. There were flowers in the front and a wide green lawn. Two cars without dents were parked in the long brick driveway. There was a basketball hoop attached to the big garage in the back. Wicker furniture was on the front porch, and it had cushions that were clean.

You could tell that people sat out there in the warm months of the summer and drank lemonade or something in glasses filled with chips of crushed ice, and they probably ate homemade candy.

After three nights, Sam went there. But only very, very late at night. He knew from experience that in towns of a certain size, only drunks, thieves, insomniacs, and people who heard voices were out on the streets once bars closed. Now he added to the list a new category: the heartsick.

Sam used alleys and side streets to get there, staying in the shadows. When he arrived, her house would be dark except for a small yellowish light that glowed downstairs behind a gauze curtain by the front window.

He'd look up at the house and imagine what he thought was her room and he'd picture her under blankets peacefully sound asleep and he knew he'd done the right thing. He'd kept his mess of a life away from her.

But the room he stared up at wasn't even her bedroom. It

was her brother's. And what he also didn't know was that most nights she, too, was awake. She wasn't asleep under a down comforter; she was awake thinking about him.

* * *

By the fourth day, Sam had played his guitar so much that the calluses on his fingers were cracking. He had to find something to do besides empty people's trash and work out new chord arrangements.

So he started to make something. At first he didn't even know it had anything to do with her.

He'd go down to the river with Riddle and they'd gather sticks from the shoreline. Riddle liked it there. He'd look for redeemable bottles and stare endlessly at the minnows that darted around the shallow, slimy rocks.

* * *

The tiny fish move like clouds of smoke.

But the smoke is underwater.

They stay together and turn like one thing. Because they are many things that understand the one thing:

And that is sticking together.

I do not see one of the little silver fish swimming alone. I look. But I do not ever see that.

* * *

72

Sam would bring bundles of river sticks back to the run-down house and he'd arrange them into shapes. There was a piece of scrap plywood in the heap of trash in the alley and it looked like a worn heart. Now it all made sense.

Sam took small nails from one of the rusty cans of nuts and bolts and metal crap that his father kept in the back of the packed truck. He hammered the nails into the plywood so that the sharp points poked through. Then he carefully layered the worn river sticks on top, attaching them to the points of the nails.

In the end, he'd made a heart from many, many pieces of worn wood, weathered by wind and rain, the bark long gone, with only the smooth parts touching, like limbs.

It was a heart exposed.

And then Sam couldn't stop himself. In the middle of the night, he left it on her back doorstep.

9

He was always the first one out of bed in the morning. He turned up the thermostat on the furnace, put on the coffee, and let out the dog.

And on this day, he also brought in a wooden heart, made from one hundred and seventy-eight small sticks, intertwined like brown and gray fingers.

Tim taught music composition and theory at the local college. But he'd minored in studio art when he got his degree from the University of California at Davis. He held the wooden heart in his hands.

It was amazing.

Tim carried it into the kitchen and put it down on the wooden table. Five minutes later he was still staring at the thing when Debbie Bell came in dressed for work in her blue nurse's uniform. She stopped when she saw her husband. From her angle across the room, she could see only what looked like a big pile of the outdoors. She thought there might be an animal involved. Her voice was tense:

"What is it?"

Tim motioned with his hand for her to come closer.

"It's awesome — that's what it is."

Debbie headed for the table, her eyes widening as she came near. She stood next to her husband in awe.

And that's where they both were when Emily entered the kitchen. Their heads swiveled in unison in her direction.

"What?"

Her father indicated the table.

"I think someone left something outside for you...."

They were blocking the view of the table.

"How do you know it's for me?"

Her father answered:

"It has your name on the back."

Her mother stepped away, and Emily could now see the wooden mass and she walked over. She looked down at the heart — at the hours and hours and hours of work that had gone into finding the pieces of wood and then placing them together in a sculpture that could easily be in a folk-art museum. And for the first time in days, she smiled. Wide. Full. Complete.

"Sam..."

Her parents exchanged a look. Was this the beginning of the end of their daughter's trouble? Or was this the end of the beginning, and now they were on to something more?

Emily picked up the wooden heart. It was heavy, and she could barely carry it. Her father stepped forward.

"Do you need some help with that?"

She was standing there, but her happiness could be felt like light bouncing off the walls.

"No. I got it."

And as she headed upstairs to her room, she could hear her father, in a hushed tone, whisper to his wife:

"She's fallen for some kind of artist...."

*　　*　　*

So Sam wasn't gone.

Once in her room, she'd carefully turned the wooden heart to look at the underside. Carved on a stick in the back, in the tiniest of letters, was the word E M I L Y and then 4 U.

And on the very last stick was the word S A M.

Emily went to school that morning and apologized to Nora, explaining that she hadn't been a good friend, saying that she was sorry. Nora missed her and was happy to have her back.

Emily made an effort to participate in class, and she even smiled at Bobby Ellis, who now seemed sort of obsessed with her. She gave Pierre Ruff her math homework after lunch, because she could do it again in five minutes and apparently for him it was a struggle.

When school was done for the day, she didn't go right home but stayed and turned in a late assignment in history. She threw out a stack of old papers that were crunched up in her locker and ran all twelve laps that the soccer coach suggested they do as off-season training.

She was back to being herself, but with a difference: she had a secret.

He would return. She knew it.

And this time, she'd be waiting.

*   *   *

Emily set the alarm clock on her phone for two in the morning. She guessed that would be the earliest that he'd come. And then she put on her favorite jeans and a long-sleeve T-shirt and she climbed into bed.

Three hours later, when the alarm sounded, she woke with a start. She silently got out of bed, pulled on a sweater and her fleece-lined boots, and slipped into the hallway.

As she moved past Jared's room, she could see Felix, the family's nine-year-old dog, sound asleep on Jared's bed. The dog's legs were moving in his sleep and his tail was twitching.

Once downstairs, Emily took a heavy, red wool blanket from the top shelf of the coat closet and slipped out the front door. She then wrapped herself up and waited on the porch recliner.

She was surprised that she wasn't sleepy. Instead she felt just the opposite. She felt so alive. The night was cold, but spring was battling out there somewhere and winter was in full retreat. When she exhaled out her mouth, she could see her breath as a small explosion of white air.

At first it felt like the whole world was either dead or asleep. Silence. And then she realized this wasn't actually true. A bird was making a noise in the next-door neighbor's tree. Was it an owl?

And some kind of animal was chewing on something — or was it digging? — back by the garage. From far away she could now hear a train. And from another direction, a dog began to bark.

She sat in stillness, not once checking the time, realizing that she'd lived here for ten of her seventeen years, but she'd never experienced the house, the yard, or even the street at this hour.

That's what Sam was doing, she thought, giving her a new vision of her own world.

And then at some point, deep in her time-suspended experience of the dark serenity, she realized that the owl had stopped his rhythmic hooting. And the rodent was no longer digging.

And that's when she saw him, in the shadows on the opposite side of the street, heading toward the house. She didn't move. Her eyes followed his progress. He did not know she was there.

It was cold outside, but he had on just a plaid shirt, and he wasn't even wearing a jacket. Didn't he feel the chill in the moist night air? She could see that his hair was messy and his shoulders were hunched forward. But if anything, he only looked better than she remembered.

Sam passed by the edge of a pool of light that shone down from the high-pressure sodium-vapor streetlamp. His hands were in his pockets; his gaze was downward; he had no idea that she was there waiting. But when he stepped on the edge of her brick driveway, she got to her feet and he saw her. He abruptly stopped.

But she was moving now.

She went down the three stairs on the porch, across the small brick walkway, onto the lawn, and in seconds she was right in front of him. She looked up into his face and didn't say a word as she removed the red wool blanket and slung it around him, wrapping them both now as she pulled him near to her.

Their bodies were touching, the blanket like a red wool cocoon around them. She shut her eyes, pulled him closer, and he gave in.

He had no choice.

* * *

When Emily woke up, she knew it wasn't a dream, because her face was red, like she'd been skiing while it was snowing and she hadn't worn a scarf.

She was exhausted when she went downstairs for breakfast, but she had a lightness of being that lifted the spirits of her parents, who of course knew nothing about her experience in the driveway. Emily chewed on a spoonful of oatmeal and then said to her mother:

"My friend Sam is going to come over after school. We'll probably go for a walk or something."

Debbie Bell tried not to look surprised but nodded.

"He can stay for dinner if you'd like."

Emily only smiled, her eyes giving away her inner happiness as she said:

"Thanks, but not today."

Jared, who at ten years old always seemed a few steps behind, piped up:

"Is that the boy who disappeared on her?"

Everyone shot him a look. Who knew he'd been following the drama?

Tim Bell was surprised that the discussion unnerved him. Who was this guy? He'd caused some grief in his house so far, that much Tim knew. He wondered what lay in store for Emily in the future.

It sounded so old-fashioned to think, but Tim Bell hoped the kid came from a good family.

10

Ever since the night they'd gone to the movies, Bobby Ellis changed the route he used to drive home. The logical way was to go down Fairmont and cross Skyview, but now he turned earlier, on Agate Street, so that he could go past her house.

It felt like something a teenage girl would do.

Or a stalker.

He'd never actually seen Emily out front, or even inside through the window, thank God. But he kept at it, sometimes three or four times a day, as he came and went from his own house out into the world.

Keeping an eye on her was probably biological. Bobby's father was a lawyer, and his mother was a private detective. They shared offices and referred business to each other.

Bobby came from a family who believed that what you see is not what you get. They were a family that knew dirty laundry and, as an occupational hazard, believed in conspiracy. They were always looking for clues and always finding them. Which might explain why Bobby liked Emily so much more after their single, undeniably horrible, date.

Before that night, Emily was a cute girl who attracted a wide group of friends. But she didn't have any intrigue. She wasn't the most beautiful girl in their class. And she wasn't the most powerful or the most sought after. And Bobby Ellis liked competition.

But then he'd watched her chase after a really good-looking guy in the rain. He'd asked around, and no one knew the guy.

That right there raised suspicion and intrigue.

Bobby Ellis knew the difference between the ordinary and the out of the ordinary. Emily Bell was different. And now he wanted her to notice him. He wanted her attention. That wasn't normally a hard thing for him to accomplish.

Girls, in general, thought he was good-looking.

The problem was on his end.

He thought most of the girls at Churchill were boring. A more accurate statement would have been that the ones who weren't boring weren't as cute as the one who were boring. Or at least most of the things the cute ones were interested in bored him. That's how it seemed.

But Emily didn't fit that mold.

He knew that now.

Because besides detouring to drive past her house every day, he was also, as his mother would say, doing the legwork.

He'd checked out her grades, which wasn't hard because

he worked in the office two days a week during his free period, and he had copied all the passwords to the computer database one day when he found them in a file on the vice principal's desk.

With access to the system, he could see that Emily Bell was as good of a student as he was. Like him, she appeared to do it without really trying that hard.

He already knew, of course, that she played soccer. He didn't know until he started his digging online that she'd taken sculpture classes on Saturdays for three years at the Art Center and she'd won some contest for designing a piece that was on display in the college museum. Or that she'd broken her collarbone in a bike accident (he'd also accessed her medical file, which was part of her release to play a school sport). If knowledge was power, he had to be getting some kind of edge.

But he couldn't figure out his plan of attack.

Should he wait in the weeds? Or should he be more aggressive? And who exactly was this good-looking guy she liked so much? And how come no one knew him?

Bobby was turning all of this over in his mind when he came home on Thursday. His mother was in the kitchen. She'd put a stack of stuff from work on the dining room table. Bobby picked it up. Among her things was a printout of the local area's crime report. Both his parents got this as e-mail every Thursday, and his mother always brought hers home to study. She sometimes got clients that way.

Bobby was looking at the report.

"Anything going on in town?"

His mother answered:

"Theft was up. It's been a few months now. Somebody out there's got sticky fingers."

The police department's weekly update also came with a map that had little yellow dots of the addresses where incidents had been reported. Bobby liked maps and statistics. He studied the printout.

The map showed that most of the dots were in one neighborhood. South. Near River Road. He didn't get out there much. It was the low-rent part of town, because if the river flooded, so did the neighborhood. Even though that really didn't happen much anymore. But people still at least thought that it could.

The last time he was on River Road was the night he went to IHOP. It made sense that the thieves lived over there. He was sitting in IHOP when someone stole the heart of the girl he liked. That much he knew for certain.

*　*　*

The next day after school, Jessica Pope asked Bobby to go get a coffee with her. He thought about it, and even though she looked cute in her low-cut pink shirt, he took a pass. Jessica Pope wasn't Emily Bell.

Bobby told Jessica that he had to do some work for his mother. People always bought that excuse. They assumed he was up to something interesting and important. So after telling Jessica a lie, the idea was planted in his brain.

Bobby had kept his mother's crime-incident map. He wasn't sure why. But it was in his backpack. He dug it out, got into his SUV, and drove across town to check out some of the places where there had been problems.

The yellow dots.

Bobby was in the southbound lane of River Road, in the middle of the afternoon on a cloudy day, when he suddenly saw the guy Emily had run after that night. He was with the same little kid, and Bobby knew for sure it was them, because they were dressed in the same clothes. And the little kid was even carrying something against his chest, just like before.

On instinct Bobby went to the next traffic light, turned the car around, and headed back to follow them.

And that's how he found out that the two boys lived in a crappy house at the end of a line of run-down places out on Needle Lane.

*　*　*

Sam was relieved.

He'd been fighting thinking about Emily, and he'd lost. And now that he'd admitted defeat, it felt like winning. He never felt like he won at anything, so that further complicated things.

That week, at the end of every day after leaving Riddle at a picnic table at a park downtown with a candy bar and something new to draw, Sam went to her house. He didn't go inside but always just took a walk. Emily seemed to understand, without his even explaining much, that his life had complexities.

Emily had never met anyone like him. He was so different. He didn't seem to know about television shows or famous people. She couldn't tell most of the time if he was kidding around with her or if he really had never heard of most of the things kids her age talked about.

At the end of the week, she said that her parents wanted to meet him. She presented it as a good thing. He had seen them in the house, mostly shadows passing through a room. She said he should come over the next night and stay for dinner. He finally agreed.

But what was he going to do with Riddle when he went to her house? Leaving for a few hours in the afternoon was one thing, but staying for longer gave him much more reason to be anxious. Especially at night.

There was a large cardboard box leaning against the back shed, and Sam knew his father had to have taken it from someone. When he got his hands on big stuff, Clarence got himself in trouble. It was one thing to take someone's hedge clippers; it was another to lift their flat-screen TV.

And this time, if Clarence announced that they were leaving, Sam knew it wasn't going to be so easy to get into the truck and just drive away.

But Sam wouldn't let himself think about that right now. He was going to think about what to do with Riddle. He decided, in the end, on taking him to the movies, paying for his ticket, and telling him to sit through the show twice.

Movies were a big deal to them. They could count on two hands how many times they'd been in a real theater. Sam only hoped Riddle didn't go after the loose popcorn that accumulated on the carpet. Once before, they'd gone into a Cineplex and come out with a plastic sack of half-eaten concession items and, to Riddle, it was as if they'd won a lottery.

So Sam gave him money for his own food, slipping a can of soda into his pocket. He watched his little brother as the usher at the door tore his ticket in half. He'd picked a movie that featured robots, and Riddle was wide-eyed with excitement.

Sam's plan was to meet him at the bench in the park down the street after two shows, which would end up being over four hours later.

Since the buzz cut, he looked even younger and more vulnerable. But Sam decided that the haircut was good. Because Riddle's gray eyes and silence had a way of frightening people.

*   *   *

Emily was waiting, like always, on the porch when he arrived. Instead of going in the house right away, they sat together on the wooden glider. He had told her, that first night walking home, that he always felt more comfortable outdoors than inside.

In the kitchen, Debbie had *Weekend Edition* on the radio, and she listened while she supervised Jared, who had his spelling homework in front of him. Her son wiggled on the kitchen stool, his face sour.

"Why can't I go out there?"

Debbie continued to cut up tomatoes for the salad.

"Because your sister needs her privacy."

Jared closed the book.

"But I want to meet him."

Debbie felt the same way but only said:

"You will meet him."

"When?"

Before Debbie could answer, the two teenagers suddenly appeared in the kitchen doorway.

She was struck by how sweet they looked together. And how different the boy was from the fleeting look she'd seen of him in the church parking lot weeks ago.

This boy, or young man, really, was incredibly handsome. He had blue eyes, chiseled features, and, while thin, he had a strong physique. But he had none of the cockiness or body language to go with his exterior.

Debbie could see right away that he was different. He was…odd. That was the only way to put it. Not shifty but definitely ill at ease. Something was missing. Confidence? He didn't look nervous so much as out of place.

Debbie continued staring. Judging him. It was so unlike her. Emily, expecting her mother to say something, finally spoke:

"Mom? Mom, this is Sam…."

Debbie sounded flustered.

"Sam, we're so happy to have you here. I'm Debbie Bell...."

Jared, always a talker, was also now mute, staring in silence at the tall guy next to his sister. Debbie continued:

"And this is Jared — Emily's little brother."

Sam looked at Jared and gave him a half smile. Of course it did not strike Sam as strange to have a younger brother who was silent. Besides, Sam himself had yet to say anything since he'd crossed the threshold and entered the house.

The foursome stood awkwardly in the kitchen and then the cellar door suddenly opened and Tim Bell appeared. He must have heard all their footsteps overhead. His music studio was down below, and he spent most weekends working on compositions or doing choral arrangements.

He, too, when he saw Sam, had the three-second-pause-to-stare reaction.

Emily's eyes widened. What was wrong with these people?

"Dad...?"

Tim Bell then abruptly stepped forward, his hand outstretched.

"Nice to meet you, son."

Sam put his hand out, and they awkwardly shook hands. It didn't look like something Sam had done often, if ever. And Tim Bell had a solid grip. Sam instinctively tightened his hand in response. More clumsy silence. More hand shaking.

Then Jared, who was staring intently up at Sam, said:

"You're like the Dark Knight."

Ordinarily that kind of comment would have made everyone laugh, but no one did.

Jared seemed to have hit on something. It wasn't just that Sam looked like he could have been in the pages of a fashion magazine, it was that there was something about him that said he was living a double life or that he was in conflict, even pain.

And while the salad was not in the bowl, the rolls were only half-baked in the oven, and the chicken dijon hadn't been cut up, Debbie tried to defuse the situation by saying: "Well, everything's ready. Let's eat!"

* * *

He barely touched his meal.

That was concerning to Debbie and Tim Bell. What kind of six-foot-two, seventeen-year-old boy doesn't devour food? Especially when you can see in his eyes that he's hungry?

He was certainly polite but obviously on edge. In the course of the excruciatingly long twenty-one-minute sit-down dinner, he barely spoke, even when they asked him direct questions.

They started out with what should have been easy sledding for a teenage boy: what were his favorite sports teams? He claimed to not follow any team sports. Even Jared found this confusing.

Further questions revealed that he was homeschooled, but he wouldn't elaborate on anything he was studying, even when asked twice.

When questioned about his family, he said that he had a

little brother and that he didn't have a mother. They said they were so sorry, and he looked so sorry, too.

They said that they'd like to meet his brother and his father, and he had no response, other than to look, if possible, even more uncomfortable. He was distant, not unfriendly, but not able to engage.

He spoke English, but he didn't speak their language. And even Jared, who usually tried to dominate conversation, was silenced.

Outside it began to drizzle. And that's when he abruptly stood up and said he had to go. He had to pick up his little brother, who was at the movies, and he didn't want him waiting in the rain. They offered to drive him down to the theater, and he politely but firmly refused.

That's when Emily's mother, concerned about safety, said:

"Do you drive, Sam?"

He nodded and said:

"Yes. I've driven for a long time."

That seemed perplexing to the parents. They thought he was seventeen. Tim Bell followed up with:

"A long time?"

Sam nodded again.

"Since I was around twelve. But just my father's truck. No other car."

Debbie Bell's voice was tight now.

"Your father let you drive when you were twelve?"

Sam's voice was even as he replied:

"Yes, but I don't take the truck out alone. I just drive when my dad asks me to."

* * *

Emily thought it all went pretty well. Considering. Obviously the driving thing was strange, but she knew that Sam had lived in Mexico, and he'd spent time on farms and in remote places. Didn't farm kids all drive tractors when they were little or something?

Emily took an umbrella with her and walked Sam to the end of the street. She told him again that she wished he'd get a cell phone. He said he didn't think it was likely. She asked him to meet her tomorrow. He said that he didn't think he could do that.

She thought that he might say something about her parents, or her little brother, or her house, or the dog, or the food. But he didn't.

Instead, in a matter-of-fact way, he looked at her and said simply:

"I've never known anyone like you."

And then he walked away.

* * *

Emily stepped through the back door moments later, feeling so alive. He was a mystery. But he was her mystery, and every moment she was getting new clues and seeing new layers of someone who was, at this point, her biggest challenge.

But then the look on her parents' faces changed everything. They had questions.

"Exactly where does Sam live?"

"What does Sam's father do for a job?"

"How long has he been living in town?"

"Have you met Sam's brother? What is he like?"

"Why wouldn't Sam talk about being homeschooled?"

"Why didn't he eat his food?"

"What did Sam mean when he said that he'd been driving since he was twelve?"

She'd never seen them like this. Emily's face flushed deep red, and she raised her voice when she tried to answer.

After a few minutes, Jared came into the room and her father immediately ordered him upstairs. When he said he wanted to stay, they all shouted at him to leave. Now everyone was talking too loud.

Once Jared was gone, Emily demanded to know what, exactly, they were accusing Sam of. They couldn't articulate it.

Her mother managed to say:

"We've been around a lot longer than you have. We can see when someone isn't..."

She couldn't finish the sentence.

Emily fired back:

"Isn't *what*?!"

Her father completed the sentence:

"Isn't responsible."

Emily did a double take.

"Responsible?"

Her father held his ground.

"Yes, responsible."

Emily stared at her parents.

"How could you possibly know from one dinner that he's not responsible? What are you really getting at?!"

Her mother answered:

"The only thing we know about him is that he's very good-looking."

The way Debbie Bell stared down at the rug made it obvious that this was another strike against him.

Suddenly a thought hit Emily. A thought that was crushing. Her voice cracked when she finally spoke.

"What you're really saying...is that something must be wrong with him, for looking the way he does but liking me. Because it would make sense to you if he liked Bo Chubbuck, who all the guys think is so hot — right? Or Emma Allgyer, who even the teachers flirt with!"

Her father shot back.

"No, of course not!"

But then her mother looked away as if she had something else suddenly on her mind. And it wasn't convincing.

11

Sam got to the park, wet from the hour-long walk in the rain, and Riddle wasn't there. He waited for fifteen minutes and then anxiously headed down the street to the movie theater, thinking he'd meet up with Riddle on the way.

But he didn't.

By the time he got to the Cineplex, even though it was Saturday night, the place was pretty much deserted out front. The rain and the robots must have been a bad combination. Again, no Riddle to be found.

Sam's heart rate accelerated, and a voice inside was now saying that this whole night was a mistake. He shouldn't have had dinner at Emily's. Her parents were trying hard to be nice, but it was obvious to him that they were suspicious of everything about him.

And what was worse was that they were right to be.

The simple fact was that he shouldn't have left his little brother alone. What if Riddle had decided to walk home? He could imagine all of the distractions in the dark in the rain that may have led him astray. Now Riddle was lost, or worse.

So Sam started to run. It was three and a half miles back to the moldy old house off River Road on Needle Lane, and Sam was there in twenty-four minutes. He burst through the door, calling out for his little brother, but, again, nothing.

And it was impossible to tell if he'd been there and left or just not come home. Their father was nowhere to be seen. That was the only good news of the night so far.

Then Sam suddenly had another thought. He should have gone inside the theater to make sure Riddle wasn't still in there.

So Sam turned around and took off again, running back through the rain. He was soaking wet, freezing cold, and exhausted after the second three-and-a-half-mile run.

He had ten dollars left in his pocket, and he used it to buy a ticket. As he passed the refreshment stand he realized for the first time all day that he was really hungry. He had no appetite sitting with Emily's family. Now he'd give anything for a piece of that chicken with the weird mustard sauce.

Maybe he could try to get his money back after he'd checked the theater. He could explain there was an emergency. If this wasn't an emergency, he wasn't sure what was. Since he was incapable of lying, he'd do that. That was the ultimate irony of his life. His father couldn't tell the truth, and he couldn't lie.

Sam pushed through the double doors, and it was so dark that he had to stand in the back while his eyes adjusted. After a few moments, he took in the sparse audience.

No Riddle.

Sam was just getting ready to leave when he realized that the front row, which he thought was empty, actually had a single occupant. He saw the lump when the screen went blinding white during a shot of a robot in a snowstorm.

Someone was low in a seat off to the side.

Sam went down and found his brother sound asleep in what had to have been his third screening of the robot film. He was using his phone book as a pillow and his coat as a blanket. His 3-D glasses were on the floor, and popcorn pieces and a small pile of empty candy boxes and wrappers were scattered on the adjacent chairs.

Riddle slept like a small child, dead to the world. Sam woke him up and got him into the lobby, but Riddle fell back asleep leaning against a video game console. Sometimes too much visual stimulation gave him some kind of overload, and it was like he unplugged from life.

Sam left him there and went to plead for a ticket refund. In the end, the manager gave back five of his ten dollars. Sam then bought a hot dog and ate it in three bites. He woke Riddle up for a third time, but he just refused to budge.

So finally Sam got his brother to climb up onto his back, and as the rain continued to fall from the black sky, he carried him home.

And despite the fact that Riddle was small for his age, he was heavy.

* * *

97

Clarence never had a plan.

He believed this to be a great strength. And while he didn't have any kind of idea for his future, he did have exit strategies, but that was different. That was an understanding of the art of flight.

Clarence kept extra sets of license plates (which he stole from cars on the streets at night and replaced with ones he jacked from cars recently towed to junkyards). It was surprising how few people noticed that their plates had magically changed when they weren't looking and would drive with plates belonging to someone else's registered auto.

It was only when they were pulled over, sometimes years after the exchange had been made, when their registrations didn't match the car they were driving, that things would so quickly sour.

At all times packed in the truck Clarence had: two sets of license plates stashed along with two full gas cans, a shotgun, two boxes of ammo, a fishing pole, six magazines with naked girls, and a gallon of vodka.

He kept a large box of saltine crackers back there as well, but they seemed to burn some kind of hole in his brain in the middle of the night, and he usually ate them faster than he could remember to replace them.

But his biggest problem in life, as he now saw it, was technology.

Everyone was getting connected. He never understood computers, but people now carried the damn things in their hands, and that was just no good.

They could now call to report him lurking around in the alleys behind their unlocked garages. And what was worse, they could raise these handheld instruments of torture and snap his picture.

And then they could send these not-even-blurry shots to the bad guys. Because, for Clarence, the good guys were of course the bad guys. And he was the only good guy.

Now, just because you're paranoid doesn't mean someone isn't out to get you. And in the case of Clarence, there were many people who wanted more than a word with him.

One of these people was a man named Hiro Yamada. Hiro ran a business called Medford Coin in Medford, Oregon.

Ten years earlier, Clarence Border, then in his first year on the road with the kids and calling himself John Smith, sold Hiro an Indian Head penny collection.

Clarence had taken the pennies from Shelly's underwear drawer when he left. Shelly's great-uncle Jimmy had given it to her for her twenty-first birthday. Uncle Jimmy got it, before he died, from Grandma Arlene. She felt sorry for him after he lost his left ear in a painting accident when he fell off a wobbly scaffold.

So Grandma Arlene was the one who loved pennies. No one else in the chain knew a thing about them. And she was no expert.

Grandma Arlene found the 1877 Indian Head cent in the bottom of a sewing box at a moving sale in 1946.

She bought the sewing box and didn't find the penny until she got home. A classic case of finders keepers, losers weepers.

Only, these people didn't know they had the penny, so they didn't know they'd lost it, meaning there were no weepers. But there was a happy keeper.

Because this one penny was a very valuable penny.

Clarence, or in this case John Smith, didn't know that the 1877 penny was worth a bundle when he took the coins, placed in a blue cardboard coin holder that was really doing nothing to protect them, into Medford Coin.

Clarence almost made a fatal mistake.

The pennies were old and tarnished, and he'd decided to stop in a hardware store and have Sam polish them before trying to unload them. Had they removed the natural tarnish from the coins, he would have stripped the collectibles of most of their value.

But being lazy paid off.

Clarence went into the store and they had security cameras in the aisles, so he couldn't swipe the polish. And there was a line at the cashier and he didn't feel like waiting.

Later, at Medford Coin, Hiro silently examined the pennies as John Smith yelled at his two little kids to go back and wait in the truck. It seemed obvious to Hiro that the younger of the two had a horrible cold and shouldn't be in a truck to begin with. He should have been home in a warm bed. Or, from the look of the kid, maybe a crib. He was a tiny thing.

This was all ten years ago, and the boys hadn't yet figured out how to comfort themselves or at least figured out not to turn to their father if they needed help.

Hiro didn't like John Smith, and he thought that it was

obvious that John Smith didn't collect these pennies, because John Smith didn't know anything about these pennies. So despite the story that they belonged to his wife, who passed away and left him with the pennies and two little boys, Hiro assumed that they were stolen.

And that meant that if Hiro bought them, he would try to return them to their rightful owner. Because Hiro and John Smith were not men made of the same cloth.

The trick was to offer John Smith enough money that he'd take it but not enough that he'd realize the value of what he had on his hands.

John Smith walked out the door that afternoon with five hundred dollars in cash, a bottle of St. Joseph baby aspirin (which Hiro made him take), and Hiro's two-week-old sunglasses. Outside, when he knew Hiro couldn't see him, Clarence smiled wide. He'd driven a hard bargain. And taking the man's sunglasses was epic. He felt good inside.

Hiro knew that an 1877 penny, in poor condition, was worth four thousand dollars. But this penny wasn't in poor condition. It was in *superb* condition.

And while it had not been certified by the American Numismatic Association, and while there were a large number of counterfeit 1877 S coins out there, Hiro knew in his gut that this one was real.

And that meant it was worth around thirty thousand dollars.

Hiro put the penny in a protective Plexiglas case. It would take some time, but he knew that eventually he'd figure out where the rare coin, designed by James Barton Longacre, came from, and who was its rightful owner.

And he'd give it back.

There might even be a reward involved. But his real reward was knowing that some kind of larger order had been restored.

Because order, for most collectors, was what it was all about.

12

It was as if a layer of frost had formed inside the Bell house. It covered all the furniture, coating the walls and the floors. But it was thickest in the kitchen at the table, where the family ate most of their meals, now in icy silence.

Only Jared seemed unaffected by the chill, happy to play one of his video games in his lap and use his feet to wrestle with the dog under the table.

Sam came over to see Emily on Tuesday after school, and on their walk down to the river she gave him two things: a watch that had belonged to her grandfather Harry and a cell phone.

He refused them both. She explained that her grandpa gave the watch to her and that it was too big and she could never wear it. And then she looked as if she were going to cry. If he wore it, she would be happy. Someone would be using the watch. It was made for that, not to sit in a drawer.

And then there was the cell phone. She had to be able to talk to him, especially now that in her own house she had taken a self-imposed vow of silence. This way she could call him. They could make plans.

Sam finally agreed. But both things were on loan. He'd give them back later. But then she put the watch on his wrist and told him she never wanted it back. Ever.

He took it off and refused to wear it. She slipped it in the pocket of his old jacket when he wasn't looking, and he didn't find the watch until he got home. He put it on his wrist and was surprised that it made him feel so good and so bad all at once. What could he possibly give her in return?

When her parents couldn't reach her the next day, she told them she'd left her phone in her locker at school. She used Sophie Woolverton's cell to call home after soccer practice when she couldn't get a ride.

On Friday, when her mother couldn't reach her, Emily said she lost her charger and her battery had died. The girl who had no experience in deceit found herself learning a new game. She now found all kinds of excuses and fabrications.

Her parents took the fact that she didn't answer her cell phone as one more sign of her defiance. They had no idea it really meant that she now spoke to Sam several times during the day and always, every night, before she went to bed. She'd had a phone in her room for four years, but she didn't use it much. Now she was on it all the time.

To him, her phone was a form of magic.

It took three days before Sam did more than just receive calls, but then he finally dialed out, to her, of course. He was surprised at how quickly he came to find comfort from having it hidden in his worn pocket. It was his secret, and it gave him a feeling of power. It made him feel as if he were, for the first time, not completely on the outside of everything.

At night, when she called, he escaped into the back alley, sitting on a trash can in the cold, damp air. Since he went outside to play his guitar most nights, his father didn't question why he got up and slipped out in the dark.

Talking in whispers, she went over her day and he went through his, careful to omit what were usually the dramatic parts — Riddle's three-hour, nonstop nosebleed, his father's entrance at 4:00 AM with armloads of someone else's dry cleaning. He didn't talk about his two hours at the dump unloading a truck of old acoustical ceiling tile, containing (unknown to him) asbestos.

He told her about walking to the lake and catching a fish that Riddle insisted they put back (but which he would have otherwise fried up and eaten).

He told her about playing his guitar and writing new songs.

He talked about reading a book (taken from a pile in a brown paper bag left on the curb a mile from his house) about a group of people who traveled around the country on a bus.

She told him little stories about people, friends, even strangers who she'd come in contact with that day. She whispered confidences, and secrets, never knowing that while he told her small things, bits of the puzzle, he was keeping her away from his real story.

*　*　*

It wasn't soccer season, so the varsity team wasn't allowed to actually practice. Instead they met three times a week and ran around the track doing endurance and sprint work. They weren't supposed to even touch the soccer ball.

But of course they did. After an hour of hideous running, they did thirty minutes of informal scrimmage. Emily wasn't a standout, but she had enough speed and footwork to keep her side of the field from collapsing.

On Tuesday, Sam had said he would try to meet her when practice was over, but he showed up fifteen minutes early. He stood at a distance, leaning into the shoulder-high chain-link fence.

Haley Kolb, playing forward, saw him first. Jane Mann was passing to her, and then Haley's eyes fell on Sam and she completely whiffed the ball. When you propel your whole body forward to kick, you're supposed to hit something.

But Haley regained her balance and stumbled backward, thinking to herself that she was so uncool. She'd had a boyfriend for seven months now. She didn't even really look at cute boys anymore.

But this was an exception.

This guy was some kind of vision. He wasn't like anything in their whole town, that's for sure. Maybe he was part of some undercover reality TV show, and he was put there, staring at them, to judge their reactions. Great. Now she'd look like a total dork on national television.

Haley jogged over to Emily. They both were covered in sweat. Haley said breathlessly:

"Don't look right away, but leaning against the fence behind you is maybe the cutest guy to ever set foot in the state."

Emily's head instantly swiveled. Haley tried not to shriek, but it came out that way.

"I told you *not* to look!"

Emily smiled, and then as Haley watched, she ran across the field straight at the Vision in a Plaid Shirt.

With Haley immobilized, the other players stopped running.

Twenty-one girls now watched, dazed, as the boy/man/god put his arm on Emily's shoulder, drew her near, and with the old chain-link fence between their two bodies, gave her the sweetest kiss any of them had ever seen.

The next day, despite the fact that Emily was a junior, and despite the fact that she was one of the weaker players, the team voted her captain for the following season.

* * *

The other soccer players weren't the only ones who couldn't take their eyes off Emily and Sam that afternoon.

There was another person watching as the two seventeen-year-olds pressed against the zinc-coated mesh wire. Another person stood, dumbstruck, at a distance, dazed from the sight.

Bobby Ellis.

Did Emily know that this guy lived in a junky house, a

shack really, on Needle Lane? Shouldn't Bobby warn her that the neighborhood out there was shady?

Did she have any idea who this guy even was?

Bobby made a decision that he had to find a way to tell her without looking like he cared.

*　*　*

Debbie and Tim, in the car coming back from one of the college classical music concerts that Tim supervised, had to acknowledge that the *Sam Situation* was beginning to wear them both down.

Debbie let out a sigh that sounded like real defeat.

"We can't forbid her from seeing him. She's seventeen."

Tim nodded his head.

"And besides, that would just bring them closer together."

Debbie mulled over the options.

"So we need a new strategy."

Tim took his eyes off the wheel to look at his wife.

"Meaning?"

Debbie was thinking out loud now.

"We should include him completely in our lives."

Tim turned his full attention back to the road.

"Reverse psychology?"

"No. It's human nature. If something's really wrong with him, which we *know* is the case, we'll be able to identify it. We can't fight without weapons. We need more knowledge. We need to be able to point out his specific problems."

Now it was Tim who was nodding. He could do this. He had to do something. His daughter, with her new failure to communicate, was making his home life miserable. Who knew she was the emotional center of the place?

When they got back to the house, Debbie and Tim told Emily that they'd been unfair. They said they were happy she was seeing someone that she cared so much about. They wanted him to now be part of the family.

Emily didn't believe them, but she kept that to herself. They lived in a house that functioned harmoniously. Her father, after all, taught music. None of them could stand real discord.

So when Sam came over the following afternoon to see her, Tim Bell, with the new spirit of getting to know the kid in order to gain the upper hand to rid him from their lives, offered to take the tall teenager down to the cellar and show him his office.

*   *   *

Sam didn't want to go with the guy, but he didn't have much choice, as he suddenly found himself sandwiched between both of Emily's parents, who ushered him straight down the steep stairs to the cellar. He'd spent half his life in underground places. And he knew they could be a trap.

But Tim Bell's basement wasn't a torture chamber, it was a recording studio. A dozen different instruments were scattered around the room, which held an enormous collection of

CDs. Computer equipment and books took up the rest of the space.

Tim's own family wasn't very interested in his lair.

But Sam was.

He'd never seen anything like this place. Tim Bell, adopting the professorial mode he used in the classroom, began talking about doing music notation online, composing on the computer, and using the electronic keyboard. Sam listened, understanding about every third word, but his eyes were glued on the lone guitar resting on a stand in the corner of the windowless space.

Emily impatiently remained on the last stair. She hadn't officially even set foot into the room. She finally interrupted her father's mini-lecture to say:

"Thanks for showing us, Dad...."

She then gave Sam the international look for *Let's get out of here*. Only, he must not have known the look, because he turned to Emily's father and asked:

"Would it be okay if I checked out your guitar?"

Tim Bell gave up on the software lecture. His eyebrows lifted in what could only be called suspicion.

"Do you play?"

Sam nodded, managing to say:

"I just sort of taught myself...."

Tim Bell went across the room and retrieved his prize possession: his Martin Marquis Madagascar. It was made of rosewood, it cost more than anything else in their home, and it was Tim Bell's pride and joy.

Debbie Bell suddenly looked nervous.

So did Emily.

But what could Sam do with the guitar? Drop it? He wasn't clumsy; in fact he had a real grace to the way he moved. At least Emily thought so.

She glanced over at her father, who now looked anxious as he took the guitar by the neck and handed it, reluctantly, to Sam.

Sam had never held anything this valuable before. He seemed to get that much of the equation. He reached out to hand it back to Tim Bell, and Emily exhaled. She didn't realize that she'd been holding her breath.

Sam mumbled:

"It's amazing. Really. Thank you."

Tim Bell solemnly nodded. And then, softening, he surprised himself by saying:

"Go on. Try a chord or two."

Sam was now caught.

Should he give it back? Or should he check it out? What would please this intense man wearing round wire glasses and corduroy pants — trying or not trying?

It was impossible to know.

So Sam did what he was actually dying to do. He took a seat on the arm of the small sofa behind him, positioned the guitar in his lap, and he started to play.

13

Sam's musical education, if it could be called that, began at five years old, when his grandmother had taught him basic chords on a four-string guitar.

Once Clarence had plucked him and his brother from the plastic wading pool in the backyard and tossed them in the truck never to return, it would be a year before he'd hold another musical instrument. But when he did, he knew it was his salvation.

An old man who lived below them in an apartment house in Spokane played slide guitar. He was blind and made his mark on the world with his instrument. From the second Sam heard him, he was hooked on old acoustic blues.

When Clarence pulled the truck out of Spokane four months later, eight-year-old Sam had a beat-up guitar in his possession, a gift from the blind blues man.

It was the only thing he'd kept with him all these years, and he played it every day. For hours and hours. So while other kids were occupied with Little League or Nintendo, Sam Border, now known as Sam Smith, became proficient enough to play any song he heard on the radio and any song he heard in his head.

He didn't break a sweat playing school-yard kick ball, but he broke a sweat slamming the strings.

And now, in the basement of the Bell house, he shut his eyes and he let himself go.

* * *

When Sam stopped playing, a full nine minutes later, Debbie Bell was leaning against the far wall, immobilized.

Emily was now sitting in a chair next to her father, who was trying as hard as he could to hide the fact that the tears in his eyes were in danger of spilling down his cheeks.

For eighteen years, Tim Bell had taught advanced music classes at Baine College. He was now, at the age of forty-four, the head of the music department.

And he'd never had a student as talented as the kid sitting on his sofa.

* * *

Tim Bell drove him home.

Or to what he thought was his home.

Sam didn't lie, but he asked to be dropped at the curb four blocks from where he actually lived.

Tim Bell tried to give Sam his mountain bike, which was in the garage and something he never used, but Sam explained he'd never learned to ride a bike. Jared thought that was a bigger deal than the way Sam played guitar.

Now Sam sat with Emily in the backseat with Jared up front while Tim showed him the bus route and how to catch the number four bus over on Hilyard and how it would end up only two blocks from where the Bells lived.

Neither of Emily's parents wanted him walking an hour each way just to see their daughter. Not anymore.

Debbie Bell kept an extra cell phone in the glove box of her car, always charged, for emergencies. She worked, after all, in a hospital, and she knew firsthand the crazy things that happened to people. She went out and retrieved the extra phone and before Tim took Sam home, Debbie gave it to him.

She didn't like the idea of him not being reachable. Emily tried not to laugh, and Debbie mistook this for simple enthusiasm.

In the driveway, when Sam took Emily's hand, he slipped her old phone back to her. And the world no longer felt against them.

*   *   *

Everything changed after Sam played her father's guitar.

Her mom and dad went from the Haters to the Supporters. That night, after they dropped him off, Emily stood

114

in the hallway behind the closed kitchen door and listened to her parents talk. Her dad's voice was fast-paced and excited.

"He's a complete natural. An original. An innovator. He's got finger speed like a young Jimi Hendrix. He's got blues technique like Ry Cooder. He's some kind of prodigy!"

Emily could picture her mother's head bobbing up and down, because she was enthusiastically agreeing.

"He's a real musician...."

Her father jumped back in:

"No, he's more than that. I don't know how Emily found this kid. I don't know where he came from. But he's going places!"

Her mother's voice now sounded as if she were trying to calm him down.

"Well, right now he's just a kid. He's—"

But her father interrupted.

"I want him at the music department at Baine! He's homeschooled, so he'd just need to take the GED. He'll have no trouble passing and then—"

Now it was her mother who was interrupting.

"Tim, you're getting ahead of yourself. You have to find out if Sam's even interested. And homeschooled kids usually have parents with strong opinions about their education. You'll need to speak to his father. You'll—"

But Tim Bell would hear none of it. He had a vision for Sam Smith's musical future.

Emily walked away from the door.

Her father had big plans for her boyfriend. Maybe being a Supporter was going to cause more problems than being a Hater.

*　　*　　*

Riddle, more than anyone, understood change. And so he knew that Sam was changing before he did.

Riddle was outside staring at a line of ants moving into a small hole in the claylike, rust-colored earth. Behind him, sitting in the weeds, Sam was talking on a cell phone. But Riddle couldn't hear him. And he didn't want to hear him.

He comes and he goes now. But when he's here, he's far away. So even when he comes back to me, he's part gone.

I follow where I can follow where he will let me follow.

Like the ants follow in the line.

Because Sam is the only one who matters.

And if I lose my Sam, there will be nothing for me.

Riddle lowered his head and his left ear pressed hard into the clay earth. It felt wet and cold. But from this angle, he could really watch the ants move.

They were on his level now. And this close, they seemed blind, feeling their way forward with probing antennae, using smell and feel and taste.

Riddle remembered that Sam had said that ants march to find food. He remembered that they steal from other ants and capture ant slaves. He squinted past the now-large ants to his now-small brother in the distant background.

Had someone captured my Sam?
Was he now a slave?

* * *

The Bells wanted to meet his father.

Not possible.

There was nothing in the world that could make that happen. They could ask and ask and ask, but no. Never. Ever.

His father ruined everything.

Always.

Forever.

Was her father now going to ruin everything?

Tim and Debbie Bell shifted to wanting to meet his brother. They asked and asked and asked. And finally he said he'd consider it. And then eventually, worn down from their persistence, he agreed.

Maybe meeting Riddle would explain things. They'd know then that his life wasn't all about him.

And maybe they'd understand and stop asking the questions. It was hard enough when she asked the questions.

If it weren't for Emily, he'd throw the cell phone and the gold watch onto their front lawn and never look back.

* * *

What was better, eating together at a restaurant or staying at home?

Where would they feel more comfortable?

Emily settled on her house. It would be harder to keep her father under control, harder to keep him from dragging Sam down to the basement to get into music, but this was supposed to be about meeting Sam's little brother, and her father would just have to focus on that.

The night after Sam had played her father's prize guitar, everything switched. Her dad now acted like the kid with the crush, and she was the parent. Emily had to tell him to back off, to go slow. She had to tell her dad that he was overwhelming the situation.

They'd picked a Sunday. It would be an early dinner. Even though it was just spring, they'd set the picnic table. Sam told her that eating outside would probably be easier for Riddle.

Sam would not discuss his father, and Emily had come to accept that for now. They were at odds. It happened. Maybe because his mother had died. Maybe Sam felt his father didn't do a good job of taking care of his wife in the end. Emily's mom had told her about seeing all kinds of things like that in her years at the hospital.

But Sam was different about his brother.

He talked about him, in small ways, all the time. And he worried about him. Once Emily understood that this was part of what made Sam anxious, she felt even closer to him.

She could see that he was always holding the thought of someone else inside. He was always balancing people, and she was now one of those people. He was sharing as much as he

118

could. And sharing his little brother with her was a very big thing for him.

And that's how Emily knew Sam really cared about her.

* * *

They showed up early.

Sam and Riddle had gone to the Laundromat that day so that they would have clean clothes.

At noon, Sam left a ten-dollar bill on the cracked tile kitchen counter, knowing that their father, a born thief, would pocket the money and disappear. That allowed them to get dressed and leave in the afternoon without questions.

They took the bus across town, and Riddle, holding his phone book, stared out the window, for the most part, unblinking. Sam had explained that they were going to see Sam's new friend. Riddle had met her before. Remember? Outside at night in the rain?

Riddle remembered. Because he remembered everything. But he kept that, like almost everything, to himself.

They would eat dinner with the new friend and then take the bus home.

Riddle's favorite part was that the brakes on the bus made a loud squeak followed by a wheeze when it came to a stop. Every time this happened, Riddle smiled. Squeak. Wheeze. Smile. He saw it as some kind of joke.

Sam watched. In his own unpredictable way, his little brother was very predictable.

* * *

The dog saved the day.

Riddle related to animals much easier than to people, and Felix, the Bell's nine-year-old lumpy lab mix, got him through the meal.

Emily came out to greet them in the front yard, and she brought Felix with her. Riddle immediately crouched down low, making himself small to meet the dog. He seemed oblivious to Emily.

Riddle's head moved up and down in the same rhythm as the dog. Emily at first thought it was some strange coincidence until she realized that Riddle was imitating Felix, anticipating his moves.

Sam let him do that for what felt to Emily like a very long time before he said, in a low, soft tone:

"Riddle, this is Emily. You met before, and I've told you about her. We're going to have dinner here in this house with Emily. I want you to say hello."

Riddle, still moving like the lab mix, glanced up, briefly caught her eye, and then looked away.

Done.

Once inside the house, Riddle stayed close to Sam, appearing neither happy nor unhappy as he focused on the dog.

Tim and Debbie Bell introduced themselves and welcomed him to their home. Jared waited across the room at a distance, sizing up the situation. Riddle scared him.

After an awkward amount of time, filled in by Emily and Sam, they all moved outside to the picnic table. Debbie went back into the kitchen with Tim to bring out the food.

Inside the house, Debbie turned to her husband, speaking in a whisper even though everyone else was in the yard.

"He's got developmental issues. Autism? Maybe Asperger's."

Tim looked out the window. He could see them at the table. Sam, Emily, and Jared were talking. Riddle, sitting right next to Sam, was feeding Felix potato chips under the table. Tim shrugged.

"We just met him. It might be a little early to label the kid."

Debbie was all about quick diagnosis. And quick response. She continued:

"And he's got some kind of respiratory ailment. Asthma. Maybe asthma and allergies. I wonder what meds he takes. I hope he has a decent inhaler."

Debbie lifted the bubbling lasagna out of the oven and placed the hot dish on a tray. She was still whispering.

"You saw that he's carrying that old phone book. It's some kind of security for him."

Tim hadn't seen. But then again, he didn't notice half the things she did, even after she pointed them out. He now looked out the window and still was not able to locate a phone book. Did she mean something that was in his pocket or something larger?

Moments later, they were back out in the yard, dishing out the lasagna, salad, and garlic bread.

Sam and Riddle were not familiar with things that didn't come from a fast-food place or that wasn't cooked on a hot plate. They had eaten mostly what you find at the counter of a gas station for years.

But since lasagna seemed like a version of the fattest spaghetti with meat sauce ever made, they ate it.

Or in Riddle's case, Riddle and Felix ate it.

No one said anything about the fact that half of what was on Riddle's plate ended up in Felix's stomach. Jared made two attempts to point out the situation, and both times his parents shot him down.

Emily had told her mom and dad not to ask Riddle any questions. But of course they did. And Sam answered them.

But Riddle didn't seem to mind being interrogated. He ate food, he fed the dog, and he drank two tall glasses of very cold milk. It was very cold, because he put two cubes of ice in the glass.

After only seventeen minutes, Debbie Bell brought out a dump cake. She only made one on special occasions, which was strange, because it was less work than making any other kind of cake. Emily turned to Sam and Riddle and said:

"This is Mom's famous dump cake."

Sam's and Riddle's eyes met. Did these people go to the dump? Not possible. And it was also not likely that they had any idea that Sam and Riddle knew more about rubbish piles than a lot of people who even worked in garbage collection.

Debbie took the cake server and started to cut slices.

"We didn't make that name up...."

Emily continued:

"You take a box of yellow cake mix and then you dump in a can of cherries and a can of crushed pineapple."

Debbie added:

"You then mix in a bag of shredded coconut and stir in two sticks of melted butter."

Emily was smiling now. No one else was.

"It looks crazy, but you put that all in a pan and bake it."

Debbie offered everyone a slice of dump cake, starting with Riddle.

"Here you go...."

Despite the name, it was obvious, from the first bite, that Riddle loved the dessert. He had a sweet tooth, and his whole life he fought off hunger pains by eating candy.

Once his plate was bare, he held it back out toward Debbie. He wasn't smiling, but his eyes were. And Emily could see that. And that made her feel, for the first time all night, at ease.

Riddle didn't give any of his first cake piece to the dog, which was half the reason he took a second slice. He didn't feel right about not sharing with Felix (who, two hours later, barfed in a basket of unsorted socks in the Bells' laundry room).

After dinner, Jared went into the house and brought out a new Verizon phone book. He gave it to Riddle, who clearly was pleased. Riddle even looked at Jared and then said, as a matter-of-fact statement:

"I needed another book."

Riddle then opened up his existing phone book and showed Jared what several thousand hours of intricate, mechanical drawing looked like. Jared moved closer, no longer as afraid, and now in awe.

Tim Bell, liberated from the invisible harness thrown on by his wife and daughter prior to the meal, went into the house and returned with his prize guitar and a bass. He passed the Martin Marquis Madagascar to Sam, and he took the bass. It was getting cold outside, but they played anyway.

Riddle started to work on an aeronautical drawing of the inside of a cruise missile from the memory of a photograph he'd seen in a magazine. Jared was wide-eyed because of course they didn't have a cruise missile anywhere in their backyard.

Debbie took a seat across from Riddle to watch him work.

The dog went deep into the darkness to eat some green grass in hopes of doing something about his incredible stomachache.

And Emily stared at the group and decided that they were the human equivalent of a dump cake.

14

Eleven days later, Bobby Ellis continued his work on his first real detective case. He had run a property check on the crap house on Needle Lane and found that it was not just in foreclosure, it was also pending litigation in a title dispute.

And if that weren't enough, when he called the bank to discuss renting the property, he was told that the place had a mold problem and was not considered habitable.

How weird was that?

So why were people living there?

Bobby usually lifted weights after school, but on Thursday he decided to do more recon. And this time he hit the jackpot.

He turned off River Road onto Needle and saw the two boys again heading down the sidewalk. Bobby pulled over to the curb and watched.

* * *

Riddle carried a phone book, but it was his new one. He also carried something that he was quickly becoming even more attached to: an environmentally friendly, hydrofluoroalkane inhaler filled with Proventil.

Debbie Bell had insisted the night she met Riddle that she drive the boys home. Riddle was disappointed that he couldn't ride the squeaky bus but of course didn't say anything. They all piled into the Subaru, and soon it was clear that Debbie Bell had her own ideas about the trip home.

She drove straight to the hospital. Emily, once she realized what was going on, was as alarmed as the two boys.

So it was with some real effort that Debbie managed to get the three of them out of the car and inside the building.

After flashing her employee badge and explaining that she was giving a quick tour of where she worked to the three kids, Debbie entered the emergency room through the back entrance.

Dr. Howard was on duty. Goldie Howard was one of Debbie Bell's favorites. She was a kind doctor and into medicine for all the right reasons. Emily's mom, in complete violation of all rules and regulations, had the doctor spend fifteen minutes examining Riddle. A friend-to-friend thing. A worker-to-worker thing. An I'm-asking-for-a-big-favor thing.

No forms, no parental consent, no paperwork, just a doctor examining a kid who (unknown to them) had not seen a doctor since his immunization shots just after his second birthday.

Riddle, who was silent throughout the entire ordeal, ignored all of Dr. Howard's questions, which Sam answered.

Her diagnosis was the same as Debbie's: asthma. Possibly complicated by some form of acute allergy. She wanted Riddle to go see a pulmonary specialist named Dr. William Wang who was on Eleventh Street.

Dr. Howard wrote it all out on a referral form and then put two Proventil inhalers from the medical dispensary closet into Debbie's hands, signing the memo that they were taken out by Deborah Bell for Riddle Smith. Emily, who was friends with Dr. Howard's son, thanked her. Sam, at her side, did the same.

At the Bells' house, Riddle had been given a piece of the cake (wrapped in tinfoil and then placed on a paper plate as a take-home treat). He'd refused to leave it in the car and had it with him throughout the entire exam.

They had all said their good-byes (except for Riddle, who said nothing) and started down the back hallway when Riddle abruptly stopped. He turned around and went back to Dr. Howard and wordlessly handed her the piece of wrapped cake.

Done.

*　*　*

Now, in day eleven of the Proventil therapy, Riddle was feeling as if he could breathe. The thick spit that was always in his mouth, and forever stuck like a liquid hair ball somewhere in the back of his throat and halfway down his chest, had thinned.

It was crazy how strange he now felt.

It was like someone had been sitting on his chest for ten

years and then had decided to climb off. Riddle was so used to the tightness, the pressure, the literal squeeze it took to get a gulp of air, that he almost felt dizzy from the relief of being able to have oxygen flow.

Sam watched his brother and wondered if it were possible that Riddle had never spoken very much because it was literally a strain.

Because now he was really talking.

He could say what was on his mind, not just express himself in times of need or panic. Much of it involved repeating thoughts, sometimes obsessively. But he didn't seem like a fish out of water, gulping wide-mouthed in the air. He just seemed like he had opinions and ideas and now he wanted to share them. Sometimes over and over again.

That morning, they'd slept late. After they got up, eaten half a box of stale cereal (with no milk), and each drank a Pepsi, they'd gone to the dump.

Sam spent an hour helping an angry guy unload a U-Haul truck filled with stuff from an eviction. The guy gave Sam three bucks. It was better than nothing, but it wouldn't get them much of a meal.

When Sam and Riddle headed down Needle Lane they didn't know that Bobby Ellis was watching. The dead-end street had flooded frequently in the days before the Army Corps of Engineers put in the reservoir, and even though years had passed, the street held the memory. The soil was soft, rich from years of river runoff and thick with weeds and long-term neglect.

The houses on Needle were mostly built in the forties.

Some were vacant; none were well-kept. One of the neighbors had been busted for selling drugs back in September. Someone had spray painted graffiti of a happy face on the side of the drug-bust house.

Sam and Riddle walked past, and Riddle held up his inhaler, saying:

"What do I do when it runs out?"

Sam considered.

"You have a second one."

That didn't satisfy Riddle.

"What do I do when the second one runs out?"

Sam answered:

"We'll get you a new one."

Riddle was troubled.

"From the sweet-cake lady?"

Sam nodded.

"Emily's mom. Her name is Debbie. Debbie Bell. You know that."

Riddle's anxiety was not lessened.

"And what about when he makes us leave? What about when we can't find Debbie Bell, the sweet-cake lady?"

Now it was Sam's turn to be quiet. He had no idea what they'd do when Clarence announced, as of course he would, probably any day now, that they were on the run.

Sam looked over at his little brother. And this time he couldn't answer.

*　*　*

Bobby watched as the two boys slipped inside the house at the end of the road. Only moments later, a truck appeared on the street. Bobby sank a few inches lower in his seat and grabbed a handful of papers from his backpack. He pretended to be looking them over as the black truck passed by and pulled into the driveway of the last house.

The truck looked like it had been driven hard. Bobby watched as a man emerged. He was in his early forties; tall and thin, all angles.

Bobby quickly dug his phone out of his backpack and, as the man headed toward the back of the house, Bobby took a picture.

His phone was still raised when the man suddenly turned around. Bobby clicked again. The man now stared at him, defiant. Bobby dropped the phone and started his SUV. The man then turned back toward the house, and Bobby put his foot on the gas, pulling away from the curb at a speed that he hoped didn't look panicky.

With one hand on the steering wheel, the other hand wrote on the weekly crime report map: *License number: 7MMS 924.* He next jotted down the make, color, and model of the truck.

And then, because he was taught to do so, he quickly noted that there were two dents on the back of the vehicle and a cracked side-view mirror on the passenger's side.

It wasn't until he was three blocks away, waiting at a stoplight, that he looked at the photos he'd taken.

The man was small in the shot, and in shadow, but even from a distance it was clear that he was intimidating.

* * *

Sam was interested in the idea of school. For himself. And for his brother.

But he was interested in all kinds of things that seemed completely out of his reach. He'd thought about walking on the moon, but that didn't mean he'd taken any steps to make it happen.

Now someone else was taking the steps for him.

Tim Bell was obsessed with Sam.

Debbie Bell was obsessed with Riddle.

Jared Bell was in awe of Sam and sort of frightened by Riddle's obsessive drawing.

Felix the dog liked Sam and was in love with Riddle. But his obsession was the English setter named Cricket who lived three houses over.

And Emily Bell was finding herself more and more unable to control the situation. She was frightened by the obsessive nature of her own family. What was going on with these people?

After school on Tuesday, Emily came home to an empty house. Jared had basketball practice. Her parents were at work. She'd sent Sam a text message and hadn't yet heard back.

She let in the dog from the backyard and went into the kitchen to make herself a piece of toast. Debbie Bell's laptop was in the kitchen, and Emily opened it up. She wanted to go online without going to her room.

The screen brightened with the page that Debbie Bell had

131

been looking at when she'd closed the computer. Emily found herself staring at:

In order to enroll in PUBLIC SCHOOL you will need:

Proofs of Age, Identity, Residency, Immunizations

One or two of the below list:

- Birth certificate
- Passport/visa
- Hospital certificate
- Physician's certificate
- Family Bible
- Church certificate
- Parent's affidavit: legal notarized identification

Proof of Identity of Person Enrolling Student and Relationship to Student

Person enrolling student must present legal identification and proof of established relationship to student. Anyone other than parent or legal guardian must complete OCRM Form 335-73s along with:

- Photo ID
- Driver's license
- Passport

- Permanent resident alien card
- Naturalization papers
- Birth certificate
- Court order
- Separation or divorce decree

Acceptable Proofs of Residency

- Homeowners: If homeowner, a copy of your current property tax bill.
- Renters: If renter, a copy of your current (less than 1-year-old) lease. If lease is more than 1 year old, a copy of your lease and a current utility bill.
- Homeless Residents: If homeless, forms can be found in city hall to begin process. Note: Will require court date/hearing.

Physical Examinations and Immunizations

A physical examination is required for students entering public schools for the first time or transferring from a private school. The examination must be done before enrollment.

Acceptable Proofs of Full Immunization Compliance

Emily closed the laptop. She picked up her cell phone and sent a text to Sam. It read:

I need to talk to you.

15

Sam's mistake was to take a shower.

But he was dusty and sweaty from unloading trash at the city dump, and while that never bothered him much in the past, now it did.

Clarence came in the back door and he could hear the water running. The pressure in the shower was horrible, a dribble really, so it took some time in there to get any real dirt off.

Clarence saw a stack of clean clothes on top of a box in the hallway. The kid was going to the Laundromat an awful lot lately. That wasn't like him. And he was showering some-times twice a day. Maybe he was going to finally start taking after the old man.

That was one of the things about Clarence. He was always incredibly clean.

It was a tactic.

If you look good, most people assume you are good. It was

the book-and-the-cover lesson. People knew it, but they couldn't stop themselves from going along and judging just the same.

So while Clarence didn't feed his kids, had never let them go to school, and had ripped them from their mother's mortgaged-for-more-than-it-was-worth home while he had robbed his way crisscrossing states for ten years — he made sure to shave every morning and keep himself neat and tidy.

He didn't give a rat's ass how the boys looked nowadays, although lately they seemed to care. When they were young, and totally under his control, he ran things differently.

Clarence could hear Riddle in the other room.

He was humming something. The kid was making sounds lately. Not the usual wheezing and gasping but real noises. Like this humming.

Clarence didn't remember that before. Maybe his snotty-nose days were finally over. He knew the kid would outgrow it. Hadn't he said that for years? Hadn't he?

Everyone always thought the answer was medicine. That's what the world was about now. Got a problem? Find a way to let a drug company make money off of it. Hadn't they told him when he was in prison that they thought he should take something? What was it again? A blue pill? He couldn't remember. But he knew better than any of those half-wits in white coats what was right for his body.

Just let nature take its course. Water seeks its own level. Even dirty water.

What the hell was the little kid doing now in the other

room? Was he singing? Had the humming turned into actual words?

If he could just get Riddle to focus.

Or rather, to focus on the things he wanted him to focus on. Throwing away the phone book didn't help. He'd tried two years ago, and the kid cried for what seemed like six months. He wouldn't make that mistake again. Listening to the kid gulp for air while snotty tears soaked the front of his shirt was a nightmare.

As soon as he snooped on the older boy in the bathroom, he'd see what was going on with Riddle. The lock was broken, so that wasn't a problem. Clarence slowly opened the bathroom door. Sam was behind the mildewed gray plastic shower curtain and didn't see or hear him. Good.

Clarence silently congratulated himself on his skills. He still had what it took. He scanned the room. Sam's clothing was folded up on top of the closed toilet seat. That struck Clarence as strange. It should have been in a heap on the floor.

The kid had to be hiding something.

Moving nothing but his arm, Clarence picked up the pile and in a one-handed grip removed the clothing and was out the door.

He knew right away that there was something in the pants because they were heavier than they should have been. Clarence slipped his hand in the front pocket and pulled out the cell phone.

What the hell was the kid doing with a cell phone?

Had he stolen it? Was he finally beginning to pull his own weight?

Clarence looked closer. It wasn't a very expensive phone. And they were hard to unload anyway. He'd have to explain to the kid that if you were going to go to the trouble of breaking into a parked car, or walking off with someone's gym bag, you had to have some pay dirt at the other end.

Clarence started to put the phone down and then noticed that there was a message. He pressed the button and looked as the text appeared. It read:

I need to talk to you.

Clarence wondered if Sam had taken some girl's purse. That was the kind of thing that would be on a girl's phone. "I need." Girl talk.

Clarence looked at the previous message:

Do you and Riddle want to come to dinner?

He froze. His eyes now landed on the name at the top of the message. Emily.

Do you and Riddle want to come to dinner?

What the hell?

Clarence looked down at his hand. Adrenaline surged

through his system like a shot of tequila invading an empty stomach.

Think fast.

The voices now spoke to him.

Put it back.

Clarence slipped the phone into the pants pocket, grabbed the doorknob, silently turned, and in four seconds had the pile of clothing back on the toilet seat. He then expertly shut the door at the exact moment that the water was turned off.

Perfect.

He had just missed the scheming traitor.

Clarence, red-faced with fury, walked straight out the back of the falling-apart house and headed to his truck. He unlocked the door, climbed inside, and lit a cigarette. He needed to put this all together.

Those two good-for-nothing excuses for humanity were keeping things from him. They were liars.

He hated liars.

He should have realized lying would be because of a girl.

The two boys disappeared now for long stretches of time. And it wasn't to go out and jack something, which he would have approved of. It was to meet someone.

He should have seen the signs. When did the changes begin?

It all started with the haircuts. The clean clothes followed soon after.

So Sam had met a girl. And the girl had to have money, because she'd given him a phone.

The more he thought about it, the more he seethed.

He should take the shotgun out of the back of the truck and go in there right now and scare the crap out of both of them. He reached back and grabbed the gun. He held it in his hands and felt his heart rate surge. He'd let them know who was running things around here.

But no.

Think it through. Think it through. Think it through.

He lowered the gun to the seat. The voices were in a chorus now.

They could leave right now. He could pack up, get them in the truck, and be in another state so fast, they wouldn't know what hit them.

But no.

There had to be an opportunity here. A teaching moment. Isn't that what he'd heard a lady with an accent like she was in a circus call it? He had to teach them who was in charge.

Right now they suspected nothing.

The snake would strike first.

*   *   *

After Bobby snapped the photo, he drove to his parents' building.

Upstairs, Merle Kleingrove was at the front desk. She did the accounting and answered the phones and in general kept track of everything for both of his parents. Merle had known Bobby since he was a baby and fussed over him, like everyone did.

Merle looked at the handsome young man as he walked through the door. Expensive running shoes. Imported shirt from the online place his father liked. Jeans that were made out of lighter, softer, fine-weave denim.

He was spoiled.

Merle paid the bills, so she knew that. There was not a thing the kid wanted that he didn't get. But she had to admit that his mother and father were the ones piling the stuff on.

Bobby didn't ask for things. It wasn't his fault that he was an only child with parents who made good money. They'd rather buy him a new car than run out and get one for themselves.

But still. Merle gave him a big smile and told the handsome young man that there was half a box of donuts in the kitchen. His mother was out but should be back soon.

Bobby, always polite, thanked her, but went in the other direction.

*　　*　　*

They had connections.

That was one of the most important things a detective could have. And since his mother gave great bottles of twenty-year-old, single-malt scotch to all her friends at the police station every Christmas, they were hooked up.

It wasn't the first time Bobby had run a check on a license plate. And it wasn't the first time he'd done a property search. But it was the first time he'd been this excited about doing it.

Bobby dropped into the desk chair in front of his mom's computer and sent an e-mail. It took only three minutes before he had a reply.

The license plate he'd asked about was registered to a two-year-old Honda sedan owned by Evan Scheuer of Central County.

Bobby then searched his mother's telephone database for Evan Scheuer and found him living two hundred miles away in Backton. Bobby knew that the truck was certainly not a two-year-old Honda, but he still picked up the phone and called Evan Scheuer.

The phone rang twice, and then a man answered.

"Hello...?"

Bobby lowered his already deep voice and then, adopting the confidence and slightly bullying authority he'd witnessed both his parents exert every day of his life, he asked:

"Hello, my name is Andrew Miller, and I'm calling from the Department of Motor Vehicles about license plate seven-M-M-S nine-two-four, which was registered under your name to a Honda sedan."

The voice on the other end was neither friendly nor hostile.

"That car was totaled over a year ago in an accident on Route Ninety-nine."

Bobby nodded. Of course it was.

He could have just hung up, but he pressed on because, well, he could, and because he was now enjoying being Andrew Miller from the DMV.

"Yes, Mr. Scheuer, we're aware of that. I'm calling because the license plate from that vehicle appears to currently be in someone else's possession, and we are in the process of taking legal action. We may need an affidavit."

Evan Scheuer was now paying attention. The word *affidavit* did that.

"Okay, of course, no problem."

Bobby was having so much fun he forgot to lower his voice as he closed with:

"Thank you for your time, sir. We'll be in touch as the situation unfolds."

He sounded like a different person. But it didn't matter. He was still in charge. He hung up the phone and leaned back in the desk chair.

So Emily Bell liked a guy who lived in a crap house off River Road on Needle Lane. The guy had a father (didn't the creepy guy in the truck look like a lesser version of the kid she liked?) who drove a black truck with license plates that constituted at least a fifth-degree felony for stolen property.

Nice.

Bobby got to his feet and went to have one of the chocolate iced donuts with multicolored sprinkles that Merle had said were in the kitchen.

He felt that he'd earned it.

16

Sam and Riddle went out the back door of the house on Needle Lane. It was now dark. They passed by the front of the truck, and the driver's side door suddenly swung open, hitting Sam hard in the knees.

He stepped back, wincing in pain. Riddle, behind him, jumped like a frightened cat into the dark shadows.

Clarence appeared, now standing behind the open truck door, staring at the two boys. His voice was tight but controlled.

"Where are you two going?"

Sam looked at his father, the truck door separating them. He could see that Clarence had his shotgun in his hands.

"To get some food."

Clarence didn't move a muscle. He and the door were now effectively a barrier to keep anyone from going anywhere.

"Yeah? Where?"

Sam kept his gaze evenly on his father. To the world, he couldn't lie, but to his father, he had trouble telling the truth.

"We'll start at the 7-Eleven."

Clarence stared hard at the kids. Riddle was looking off into the distance, his head tilted at an odd angle.

But Sam kept his eyes connected with his father's.

It was a standoff.

Finally Clarence gave way, pulling the door in. Sam awkwardly went through the small gap that now presented itself between the truck and the peeling, painted side of the old house. Riddle was right on his heels.

Sam eyed the shotgun held in his father's twitching hands, but he didn't break his stride.

Moments later, the two boys were on the sidewalk, heading away from the house.

Clarence waited until they were at the end of the street before he set the shotgun down on the seat and started after them.

* * *

Moving in the shadows of yards, off the sidewalk, Clarence followed the boys down to River Road. They crossed over to the other side of the four lanes and then walked two blocks to a bus stop enclosure.

So they were taking a bus.

They were leaving the neighborhood.

That made it all the more interesting.

Clarence turned around and jogged back to the house.

Move quickly, but do not rush.

He was in the truck and back on River Road in less than five minutes.

Fortune was smiling on him, as he knew it would. He could see that the two boys were still in the distance waiting.

Clarence turned the opposite direction, went to the first light, and swung around, pulling to the curb away from the glow of the liquor store sign.

When the city bus chugged by, eight minutes later, he let three cars go ahead of him. And then he followed.

*　　*　　*

Clarence sat behind the wheel of the parked truck staring at the house. First a dog had run out. He couldn't stand dogs. Feed a vet, not a pet. And then a pretty girl seconds later was on the porch. Was this Emily? The boys had disappeared inside after the pretty girl had taken Sam's hand. It was all so disgusting.

Clarence reached under the seat and removed an old brown plastic bottle of someone else's prescription cough medicine. He took a swig of the purple concoction as if it were whiskey. Codeine was a friend. And the world had so many enemies.

His eyes took in the property. These people had big money, that was for sure. But how had Sam met them? And how the hell had he been able to get Riddle through the front door?

It was because Sam was good-looking. That was a fact. And obviously it opened doors. Doors in nice neighborhoods. Doors that wouldn't want to have anything to do with John Smith or Clarence Border.

Clarence ground his teeth. Hard. He looked down and saw the shotgun angled between the seat and the floor. He should go in there and let them know who was running this show. They were his boys. He'd raised them as a single parent. He'd sacrificed everything for them.

But the voices said:

Not yet.

Not now.

Knowledge is power. Better to know more before he pulled a trigger.

*   *   *

Sam and Emily sat outside behind the house at the picnic table. Riddle and Felix were inside.

Emily hadn't said anything to her mother about what she saw online about school. She wanted to talk to Sam first. But before she could even get to it, he blurted out:

"My father found the cell phone."

Emily waited for more. Was this a good thing or a bad thing? The look on his face said bad. He finally continued:

"He doesn't know that I saw him go through my things while I was in the shower. But he had to have found it. And now he'll cause trouble."

Emily's brow furrowed.

"What kind of trouble?"

His father was unpredictable. Sam had no way of knowing. But he guessed.

"He'll want to leave town. He'll pack us up and move."

Emily's eyes widened. What was he talking about...?

"You'd move because he found a cell phone? That doesn't make any sense...."

Sam hesitated. Emily stared at him. He wasn't going to continue. So she did.

"That's crazy!"

Of course it was crazy. Completely crazy. Her family had shown him for the first time just how crazy. Because, until meeting them, Sam didn't know there was anything in the world *other* than crazy.

Emily continued, trying to understand:

"Is it some kind of religious thing? Is he one of those people who doesn't use electricity or believe in technology?"

But Sam remained silent. This had nothing to do with God or technology. It had nothing to do with any kind of philosophy or way of organized thinking. It certainly didn't have to do with anything anyone believed.

How could he explain that his father was one of those people who didn't believe in anything but himself?

What did you call those kinds of people?

* * *

Inside, Riddle sat on a stool and carefully sliced the ends off of green beans while Debbie stirred three tablespoons of mustard into a bowl of potatoes.

This was their routine now. He did the prep. She did the

assembly. Debbie joked to her husband that Riddle was everything in the kitchen that she'd ever wanted. He loved to wash and cut vegetables. He liked to stir sauce and to clean pots and pans. Mostly he just liked being in the warm house when food was cooking and Debbie, in a low patter, spoke to him.

"I'm giving the potatoes a mustard bath. With the olive oil. And then we bake them in a really hot oven, and the mustard, which is coating the potatoes, turns crispy...."

She'd learned her technique in the ER.

Simply listening to someone speak, if the sound was in the right tone, could calm a person. It was part distraction, part plain audio comfort, and Debbie knew what she was doing.

So with Felix always at Riddle's feet to retrieve scraps of fallen food (deliberate and unintentional), and with Debbie moving around the kitchen, the two did a kind of dance.

Debbie was pulling him, almost literally, out of his old world and into a new one. She'd come to the conclusion that his deficiencies were, for the most part, with language.

But she felt that his chronic asthma and his multiple allergies had set him back much further than he would have been without these problems.

She had no way of knowing that he'd been locked inside a very small world that consisted of his brother and his interest in all things mechanical.

And now he was out.

What Debbie Bell really wanted was to get both of the kids in school. She'd made appointments with the pulmonary specialist, who couldn't see him for nearly two more weeks, but he was on the books.

And she'd arranged to take him to a child-development specialist.

Emily didn't know. And neither did her husband. Or Sam.

Taking him to see a friend in the ER was one thing. But how would she deal with the paperwork in a regular doctor's office? Who would she say that she was in this boy's life? A trusted friend? An aunt? A godmother? The mother of the boy's brother's girlfriend?

And who would pay for the appointments?

She'd cross that bridge when she came to it. That's what ER training teaches you. Deal with the here and the now.

So first she had to gain his trust. That's what the time they spent in the kitchen was about.

And it was working.

* * *

He was late.

Thursdays he had office hours instead of classes. They were set up to provide time to hear his students discuss musical issues but ended up being when college students came to discuss their grades. They all wanted an A. Even the kids who had no business being in a music class wanted the top grade.

Tim realized he was scowling.

Someone once told him that the most unhappy white-collar job in the world was to be a junior-high school music teacher. The instructors loved music, and they had to spend eight hours a day listening to kids butcher it.

At least he was a college professor. At least his students weren't being forced to play plastic recorders.

But so many of them still were joyless in their pursuit of the one thing, outside his family, that Tim Bell loved best. So many felt as if they were simply ordering off a menu that someone had put before them years ago, with the parental equivalent of a gun to their heads.

And then there was Sam.

He understood music; he loved music, in the most pure way that Tim Bell had ever witnessed.

Sam wasn't just a natural; he was something else. He had made his own musical language.

The boy had a gift, and it had been allowed to mature wild and free and apparently in some kind of vacuum of aloneness that made him completely, entirely unique. He did not have ideas about possible acclaim or reward. And as far as Tim could tell, he didn't even understand what a grade was.

Maybe there was something to this homeschooling thing.

What if there was some incredible secret to this way of teaching? If only Tim could speak to the boy's father. What if he were some kind of educational genius? Sam had his music, and Riddle had his drawing. How had they been nurtured?

Here was a kid who couldn't read music, who had no training whatsoever in the guitar, and he was doing things musically with the instrument that were completely innovative.

Tim turned up the volume on the CD playing in his car. Ali Farka Touré. Low-pitched vocals with minimal accompaniment. Tim rounded the corner and drove right past the black truck parked just down the street from his house, not even noticing as he flew by. He pulled into the driveway, cut the engine, and, grabbing his shoulder bag, headed to the front door.

Home.

Tim Bell realized that he was now smiling. That's what happened when he thought about the kid's potential.

Limitless.

That's the kind of future Sam Smith had.

*   *   *

Clarence got out of the truck and walked down the sidewalk toward the Bell house. When he reached the Subaru parked in the brick driveway behind Debbie Bell's car, he pulled a slim jim from the front of his pants.

The thin strip of spring steel had a notched hook on the end. Clarence expertly slid the tool between the car's window and the rubber seal, catching the rod that connected to the lock mechanism.

A subtle motion of his wrist, and the car door was open.

Inside the house, Felix had left the kitchen and was now at the living room window. He saw a figure in the driveway and lifted his head, sounding his bark for alarm/intruder.

At the TV set, Jared shouted for the dog to be quiet.

Clarence ignored the now-silenced dog and slipped into the Subaru. First thing first: vehicle registration. Clarence found it in the glove box.

Timothy Duncan Bell

Clarence shoved the piece of paper into his jacket pocket, his eyes darting around the interior of the car. Breath mints. Quarters and dimes for parking. Programs for musical events at the college. ChapStick. Half-empty water bottle. Windbreaker in the backseat. Sunscreen. Guitar pick. A handful of CDs.

Clarence scooped it all up, stuffing the things into a plastic bag. He then removed an eight-inch knife from a holder that was wrapped around his calf.

He turned to the passenger's seat and sliced the leather as if he were cutting the belly of dead animal. Clarence then slid out of the vehicle and moved to the back of the car, where he thrust the knife into the sidewall of the left rear tire.

Satisfied with his work, he pulled out the blade and headed back to his truck.

He was smiling now.

He'd introduced himself to Tim Bell. Too bad he didn't have time to meet the rest of his family.

17

Emily had no appetite.

She pushed the food around on her plate, trying to figure out what to do.

She watched the table. Whenever Debbie talked, Riddle looked at her with real interest. This all would have made Emily happy if she weren't so worried now about Sam's father. Who was this crazy guy who didn't believe in something as small as a cell phone? And why was she just now hearing about what a nut he must be?

Should she tell her parents what Sam had said? Should she just bring it up right here at dinner? Was that the right thing to do in front of Riddle and Jared? And when would her father, going on now about a musician named Ali Farka Touré, finish his dinner?

Emily calmed herself by making the decision to speak to her mom right after they were done eating. Whether Sam wanted her to or not.

But that didn't happen.

Emily's father went out to his car to bring in a CD he wanted to give to Sam. When he came back in, he was shaken. Someone had vandalized his car. The back tire was flat, the front seat was slashed, and all the things in his Subaru were missing.

Everyone rushed out to the driveway to see. There was lots of talking going on, but both Sam and Riddle were silent.

Tim Bell said he distinctly remembered locking the car, which showed no signs of break-in. No one was on the street, and no cars were parked nearby. Whoever had done this had come and gone.

They all shuffled back inside the house, and Tim Bell got on the phone to file a police report.

That's when Sam said that he and Riddle had to go.

* * *

Riddle was standing near the wall by Debbie, who was waiting near the phone as Tim sat on hold with the police department. Jared, now carrying one of his plastic saber swords, stared out the front window, looking for suspicious vehicles. Emily was trying to talk to Sam when he turned to his brother.

"We've got to go. Come on, Riddle."

But Riddle didn't move. He shifted his weight, making it look as if he were even closer to Debbie. Sam's voice got hard.

"Riddle, you heard what I said. We're leaving now."

Again, no acknowledgment. Sam crossed over and grabbed his brother by the sleeve of his gray sweatshirt.

"Let's go."

Riddle looked at Debbie and said in a whisper:

"We're sorry...."

And then he turned and followed his brother out the door.

Debbie didn't move. Empathy. Riddle had it. She knew that he did, but still the words directed just to her were like hearing a newborn's first cry. The relief was overwhelming.

* * *

They took the bus across town. Debbie Bell wanted to drive them home, but Sam wouldn't let her, and Tim's car with the flat tire was blocking the driveway anyway.

Emily stood on the lawn, watching them recede into the distance, and a lump formed in her throat. What was really going on? She then waited outside for twenty minutes with Jared and her father, because the police were on their way. Maybe she was mixing up everyone's emotions. Maybe Sam and Riddle weren't acting so strange. Maybe they were just upset like everyone else at the act of vandalism.

When she finally went inside, an hour later, she found the cell phone her mother had given Sam. It had been placed on the table by the front door. She checked her own phone and found a text message. It was the last thing he'd sent from the phone. It said simply:

i will never forget you.

And she knew that the look she'd seen in Sam's eyes when he'd left meant he wasn't coming back.

* * *

Sitting in the bus, driving back across town, Sam was certain. It had to have been Clarence. He had to have followed them.

And Riddle must have known that, too. Because when Sam looked over at his brother, who'd moved for the first time to sit by himself in the last seat in the back of the bus, he was leaning, glassy-eyed, against the window. And even the squeal of the brakes did nothing to break his dull stare.

The bus dropped them off two blocks from the house, and it was the longest two blocks they'd walked in their lives. They both knew what was on the other end.

Clarence was in the dark driveway, throwing the last ratty sleeping bag and pillow into the nest of crap in the back of the truck. The light inside the vehicle had been disabled long ago so that no one could see Clarence make off with stuff.

Hearing their footsteps, Clarence turned and aimed a high-powered flashlight that he'd lifted from a city utility truck right in their faces.

He could see them but, now blinded, they couldn't see him. But they heard him:

"Get in. I packed your stuff. We're out of here."

It had happened before. Many, many, many times. But never like this.

There were choices. They knew that they could have run. And they knew that they could have refused to go. But it felt, to both boys, as if those choices did not exist.

Because, if you cared about something, it would be taken away. If you stood up for yourself, you would be beaten down. If you spoke out, you would be silenced. They had only learned how to be there for each other. Other people could never be part of the equation.

Clarence had set up the rules of the game that way long ago.

Sam opened the truck door for his brother, but Riddle didn't get in. He headed for the house. Clarence called out to him:

"There's nothing in there. I took it all. Now get in the truck."

But Riddle kept walking. Clarence spat on the ground, turning on Sam.

"Get your brother into the truck. *Now!*"

The front door opened and closed, and Riddle disappeared inside. Sam didn't move. Clarence swung the flashlight from the door back to Sam's face as he said:

"I know where Tim Bell lives. And pretty Emily. Next time I'll slice more than a tire. Now go get the boy!"

Sam tried not to wince. He tried to bury his rage in the flat ocean that he would literally picture inside his mind. If he showed any emotion, Clarence won.

If it didn't matter that they were leaving, if he couldn't hurt him or his brother, Clarence wasn't as powerful as they were.

Only this time, it was impossible.

This time, he wanted to grab his father by the throat and squeeze until he could squeeze no more.

Instead Sam turned and walked toward the house.

Inside, the only light that was on was in the hallway. But it didn't take light to see that the place was a wreck. It had always been a mess, with mismatched, broken furniture and aggressive neglect.

But now it had the element of Clarence gone mad.

Chairs were tipped over, and the floor was littered with possessions.

Sam could hear Riddle move down the hallway to the back door. Sam stepped over a broken plate and followed.

Outside, in the small square of the backyard, Riddle did two things.

He went to the old metal trash cans at the rear of the property and removed a bag of cat food and a plastic dish from a hiding place. He then filled the dish and placed it on the ground by the fence.

Riddle then moved to the old oak tree that was growing up against the broken metal shed. Putting one foot on the shed, Riddle reached up to a tree branch and removed the second inhaler that the doctor had given him. It was wrapped in a clear plastic bag. He shoved it into his pocket.

Riddle then headed across the yard, down the narrow

driveway, and to the truck, where he silently got in the back-seat and closed the door.

Clarence was now waiting just for Sam. He shouted at the house:

"Sam! Let's go!"

But Sam was still in the backyard. His eyes were adjusting to the darkness as he saw two small cats, siblings, scrawny and wild, come out from behind the shed. They cautiously made their way to the bowl of dry food.

Riddle's secrets.

While Sam had left the house to see Emily, Riddle had found something to keep him company. Sam continued to stare as the cats ate, and it was only when he finally turned that he saw his guitar.

It was on the other side of the tree and it had been smashed to splinters.

18

After finding the cell phone, Emily convinced her mother to drive her to the bus stop. But of course they were long gone. She then talked her mother into driving out to River Road. But of course that was equally worthless.

They'd always dropped Sam and Riddle on the same corner and, now, looking down the dark side streets, she realized they could live in dozens of places. She had no idea.

When they finally got back home, Jared was still awake. He was now obsessed with bad guys and had unconsciously put on his old Spider-Man pajamas, which he never wore anymore, but which somehow still had the power to make him feel protected.

Tim Bell had kept himself busy changing the flat tire with the spare. He'd used duct tape on the upholstery so that the seat didn't look like such a victim. But he, too, was agitated.

It was late, but Debbie pulled out the custard she and

Riddle had made for dessert. She dished it into red-glass goblets, but no one had an appetite.

Debbie and Tim assured Emily that leaving the cell phone didn't mean much and that Sam would call or come back tomorrow to explain. No one said anything about a connection between the vandalized car and Sam and Riddle. But no one had to say anything. It was on all their minds.

When the family finally went up to bed, Felix was made to stay downstairs in his old wicker basket, which was placed by the front door.

And even Felix had a fitful night's sleep.

*　　*　　*

The kids weren't going to talk, and he didn't want to listen even if they did, so Clarence reached into the plastic bag of crap he'd scooped up from Tim Bell's car and popped in one of the CDs. It was some kind of crazy tribal music. So that's what fancy people listen to? Clarence hit Eject and tossed the CD out the window onto the highway.

Clarence drove all night, and they were in a different state five hours later. He was heading east. He'd decided that Utah would be their first real stop.

Riddle fell asleep not long after they got into the truck, but Sam, wide-eyed, sat in the passenger's seat staring straight ahead.

His mind was flooded.

He'd seen pictures of New Orleans after Hurricane Katrina,

and that's how he felt. His life was now underwater and, even if the tide somehow receded, everything that he had was now damaged beyond repair.

Looking over at his father, he considered grabbing the steering wheel and turning hard, sending the truck right off the road.

Clarence, who never wore a seat belt, would hopefully, upon impact with whatever they first hit, be catapulted straight through the windshield.

Sam blinked his eyes and could see the accident. Shattered glass, twisted pieces of metal, even an explosion when the full gas cans Clarence insisted on keeping inside the truck blew up.

But then, somewhere in the equation, Sam saw Riddle. He, too, didn't have on a seat belt. And he, too, would catapult forward.

Sam knew that, if it weren't for his little brother, he'd have been even more damaged, even more messed up, than he already was. Riddle had given his life purpose. And Sam would always, no matter what happened, not just protect his little brother but try to think of him first.

And so Sam kept his hands to himself, off the steering wheel and off his father's neck.

*　　*　　*

Emily refused to go to school the next day. Debbie took one look at the circles under her daughter's puffy eyes and let her stay home. Emily spent the day in her room, waiting for the phone or the doorbell to ring, even though she was certain neither would.

The next day, she was forced to go back to Churchill High. Debbie Bell knew about trauma, and contrary to what people thought, routine was a friend, not an enemy. People didn't need to be comforted as much as shown a line to stand in, a door that they had to walk through, and a task they needed to complete.

Emily believed that Sam and Riddle were in some kind of terrible trouble. But her parents weren't prepared to accept that.

They did deeply regret that they never had an address or a home phone number from the two boys. They did regret that they hadn't insisted Sam introduce them to his father.

* * *

Bobby Ellis could tell that something was wrong with Emily, but that didn't mean he was perceptive, because he wasn't. It meant that anyone could see that she was absent, upset, somewhere else.

He'd tried to find a chance to talk to her, but she wasn't in any of her usual spots, and she was keeping her distance from her friends. Bobby knew that Emily had D track free, and that's when she went to the library and did her math homework.

So on Friday, after days of trying to find a way to just casually get her attention, he took the initiative and cut class.

He could go into the office computer later and delete the absence.

He found her in the back sitting on the floor, leaning against a bookshelf. And she looked very sad. That much he could figure out. Nora had told Rory, and Rory had told Bobby, that there was a problem with the guy Emily liked.

So Bobby made a calculation. This might be the time to tell her about the crappy house where her supposed boyfriend lived. This might be the time to show her the photo of the creepy guy who was probably the boyfriend's father. And this might just be the time to bring up the stolen license plates.

Bobby edged closer. Even though it was a library, people didn't do more than slightly lower their voices when they spoke. He cleared his throat and felt it tighten as he managed to get out:

"Hey, Emily. . . ."

When she looked up, her face seemed to be saying, *Go away. Leave me alone.*

At least that's what he thought it was saying. But whatever it was that her silent face was expressing completely unnerved him. So while he had a whole plan, a whole way in which he was going to reveal his information, instead he blurted out:

"I saw that guy you liked over on River Road a few days ago, and I followed him home and took a picture of a guy who I think was his dad—and I have to say, Emily, it was all pretty damn weird."

He was not prepared for the fact that she would get tears

in her eyes. He had no way of knowing that she would be grateful and vulnerable and completely indebted. And so he was shocked when she jumped up and wrapped her arms around him and held him close once he showed her the photos on his phone.

And it was totally awesome.

*　*　*

Bobby hoped that people were watching as they headed across the high school parking lot to his SUV. He always parked next to the exit. His parents did that, so he did it, too. Detectives need to make quick getaways, even if it sometimes took a while to walk to your car.

Emily climbed eagerly into Bobby's shiny SUV, and he was still in amazement that some kind of switch had been flipped. He'd gone from deeply bugging her to being the Man. And being the Man was just so much better in so many ways that he couldn't believe it.

*　*　*

Emily held his phone while they drove, staring at the picture of Clarence, analyzing every detail of the shot. The intense man did look like Sam. She could see the resemblance. And maybe a little bit of Riddle but not much. The man in this picture was lean and sharp on the edges. And he looked angry.

After memorizing the photo, she forwarded it on to her own e-mail. She would need to show the picture to her parents and to anyone else who could help her.

It was so unlikely that Bobby Ellis would be the person to bring her the only real news about Sam that she'd had since they left. Maybe she'd misjudged Bobby. He seemed so caring now as he drove. And so focused.

Emily looked up from the phone. He was a deliberate person. She could see that. He even changed lanes with a kind of authority that kids her age didn't have. She didn't know what his attitude meant, or where it came from, but for the moment, she was simply grateful.

She realized that the silence in the car was suddenly awkward, maybe even unkind. And so she cleared her throat and asked:

"Now tell me why you were out there again?"

*   *   *

Fortunately, Bobby thought, he could answer that:

"Like I said, my mom gets the police report every week. And there's been an increase in crime in the last three months. A lot of the incidents — the burglaries — a lot of them were theft, you know, crimes of opportunity. Like say you leave your garage open with your expensive golf clubs right out in the open...."

Emily didn't have expensive golf clubs, but she nodded anyway.

"Well, a lot of these incidents were in the River Road area. Now here's something people don't really know, but criminals usually do most of their offenses close to where they live. They don't drive in their cars across town ... I mean, of course sometimes they do, but that's more for really targeted activity."

He could see that Emily's brow furrowed. And he wondered if he sounded like a real tool. It felt like he was sounding like a real tool. And now her brow was furrowing. Why was that? She seemed to have some kind of lie detector planted in her forehead. He continued spewing what was sounding to him like nonsense:

"So if you look at areas where there's a lot of this small-time crime, then the thieves probably live around there."

Bobby took a breath. Should he have made that plural? He felt like he was coming off the rails.

"My mom had asked me to drive to River Road and look for anything unusual...."

Lie.

He was heading into the big-lie stuff now. He had to get this out without revealing that he was obsessed with her. Then Emily said:

"But your mom doesn't work for the police."

Bobby shook his head.

"No. Private detective. But she has businesses on retainer, and when crime goes up, it's her job to spot trends and, you know, look for reasons. That's when she brings me in to help."

Was she buying it? Maybe. He exhaled; he'd been holding

his breath. That was not good. People who are at ease just let air flow in and out. In and out. He tried doing that a few times and then got back on track:

"So my mom had given me the crime map."

Lie.

"And she wanted me to recon the area."

Lie.

"And then I saw your friend...."

Emily was really paying attention now.

"And this was on Thursday?"

"Right."

"And so you followed him and his little brother?"

Bobby nodded and realized that he was now speeding. He put his foot on the brake. When he lied, it seemed to cause him to drive faster. Interesting. It was like he was literally fleeing himself.

"I recognized them. From the night at IHOP."

Not a lie.

But the next part was.

"They turned off River Road, and I was turning that way, too. I pulled over to check the map, and when I looked up, they were at the end of the street. I went down to do a U-turn there. That's when I saw the guy and took the photo."

Emily was nodding again. But then she asked:

"And why did you take his picture?"

Bobby could feel sweat run from his right armpit down his right side. Like a drop of water would. And now his left armpit was also dripping. But he kept his voice steady.

"The man appeared to me, from my past experience doing visual interrogation...."

He stopped for a moment. Visual interrogation? Where was this stuff coming from? He plowed ahead.

"He appeared to be suspicious. And, well..."

Okay, here was his bombshell. Here was the part that could tip the scales into stalker land. He just went for it.

"I ran the license plate on the truck in their driveway with the DMV that afternoon, and it didn't match the vehicle. It was stolen."

19

Riddle rolled up his sweater into a ball to use as a pillow. It smelled like her. It smelled like her kitchen.

He'd worn it the last night he saw her, when he measured the vanilla to put in the custard and he was sort of clumsy because that's just the way he was and some of what was in the spoon dribbled on the sweater. But she said it was okay because spilling was part of cooking just like tasting was part of cooking and touching food was part of cooking.

But he'd never cooked anything before he went into her kitchen.

I miss cooking now.

Before, I didn't miss cooking, because I didn't know cooking.

And I miss her. Sweet-cake lady.

Her name is Debbie Bell.

And I miss Felix the dog. And I miss the way he smells, which is like wet sweaters. But clean wet sweaters. Not the kind in the back of the truck.

And I miss riding the bus to their house. And I miss their family, even if sometimes they all talk too loud and sometimes too fast and sometimes at the same time.

I'm missing...

It all now.

Will someone find me? I will be good, if they can find me. I will try to stop missing.

I will try to stop missing everything I have always missed.

I will be good.

If you can find me...

You.

Find.

Me.

I am asking now.

I'm asking you in my inside voice.

And that's the voice no one ever hears.

✳   ✳   ✳

They spent a week in different places every night, and now they were in Cedar City. It was a town of twenty-seven thousand and that meant it was the kind of place that they'd be in and out of in a real hurry.

Cedar City was built around mining in a different century. Today it had a small branch of a state college, an annual Shakespeare festival, and a group of trusting people who left stuff out at night on their lawns.

The trouble was that stealing things was easy, but

unloading them was impossible. So Clarence could have had a warehouse of mountain bikes the first day that he arrived, but what good would it have done? After a few hours of trying to sell them, he'd have had the cops on his tail.

A place like Cedar City meant you had to have focus. There was a run-down motel when you first drove into town from the west, and Clarence took a room at their weekly rate. Two beds. The boys could sleep together, or one of them could sleep on the mildewed couch. He didn't care. He was sick of sleeping in the truck.

But now there were new rules.

The boys couldn't leave the room in the daytime. He didn't want them out wandering around meeting people. And of course there would be no phone calls.

Places like the Liberty Motel didn't have phones in the rooms anymore, so it wasn't like Clarence had to make that off-limits.

The world had gone cellular, and all that was left in room 7 was the old phone jack on the far wall. Someone had spilled some kind of red sauce on the carpet and while it had mostly been cleaned up, dried red spots speckled the phone jack and flecked the gray wall.

Sam found himself staring at the phone jack, imagining that he was some kind of bug that could climb inside the hole and disappear forever into another world and another life.

Since they weren't allowed to go out when it was light, the two boys spent most of the day asleep. It took a few nights to adjust to staying up late and being let out at dusk. Once on the street they'd go to the closest burger place and scrounge around for cold French fries and bun bits in the trash.

Clarence spent his time looking for small things worth money to finger. He'd unload them at their next stop, which would be a bigger town. He lifted a few wallets from a golf-course changing room. He helped an old lady put her groceries in her car and then followed her home from the market.

He took all of her jewelry when she left later in the day to play bridge. A simple broken glass pane on the back door, and he was in and out of her place in ten minutes. He took a Coke from her refrigerator and was considerate enough to put the can in her recycling container before he left.

Discovering the traitors had centered him.

He'd been neglecting his duties. He was a thinker. That was for sure. And lately he'd done a lot of thinking about his boys.

And the snake smiled.

* * *

Emily sat in Bobby Ellis's car, staring at the ramshackle house. It didn't look like any place she would have imagined Sam and Riddle living.

The houses and apartments out off River Road were all run-down and in general disrepair, so not connecting the two brothers to a specific one had been a way of protecting her from their reality.

But now it was staring her in the face.

Was he in there now? Were he and Riddle behind the faded old sheet that fluttered from the half-open, dirty window?

And what was worse — that he was there and hadn't contacted her in all this time? Or that he was gone? Bobby Ellis interrupted her thoughts.

"Do you want to go knock on the door or something?"

Emily nodded. Bobby looked at her. She seemed confused, but at least she wasn't hating on him, that much he could tell.

"Do you want me to go with you?"

Emily shook her head no and then opened the door and got out.

She walked to the front door and knocked. No answer. She knocked again. No answer. Then her hand went to the knob and she slowly turned it to the right. It wasn't locked.

Emily respected rules and privacy. She wasn't someone who was pushy and she didn't consider herself aggressive. But she didn't even hesitate. She simply pressed the door forward and walked in.

*　*　*

Bobby was watching from the SUV. Now what was she doing? Was she going in?

Bad idea.

He was up and out of the car.

Inside was a mess. Someone had moved out fast and had

made a point of trashing the place in the process. Emily stepped backward at the sight, bumping right into Bobby Ellis.

"Oh, sorry."

Bobby looked over her head into the room.

"We shouldn't be in here...."

But Emily was already moving forward on the ancient wall-to-wall carpeting, which was flattened into a dirty rust-colored sheet of former synthetic fibers. She called out:

"Hello...Is anybody here?"

Silence. And then a sound came from the back of the house. Someone was there. Bobby put his hand out to stop her, but Emily kept going and he had no choice but to follow.

"Sam? Riddle...?"

She called out, but no one answered. She continued down the cramped little hallway.

Bobby Ellis was more than six feet tall and played football, but he wasn't any kind of hero. And right now the last thing he wanted to do was violate Session law HB 0300, which, if he remembered the code as his father had taught him when they went to the firing range together, stated: *It is unlawful to enter and remain upon private property without permission of the property owner.*

So what were they now doing?

Bobby followed Emily down a narrow hallway. The sound in the back room was louder now. Bobby wanted to run. He wanted to scream and run. He had watched way, way, way too many horror movies, because he wanted to scream and run and hide.

But of course that wouldn't look good.

So he stayed right behind her.

*   *   *

She was angry now.

And it was the worst kind of anger, because it was at herself. Just the mention of the word *father* had changed Sam.

How could she have thought she knew him so well when she had not known him at all?

When she'd seen that look in his eyes, a look that had to be pain, how could she not have pressed him harder to explain his past? And to explain his present.

She moved toward the sound, calling out more urgently now:

"Sam?"

They passed a dirty bathroom and a small bedroom, where a mattress was on the floor. At the end of the hall was another bedroom. And that's where the sound was coming from. It was some kind of thumping. Emily kept going toward the closed door.

Behind her, she could now hear Bobby Ellis breathing. She was both glad he was there and resentful that he was seeing all of this. She wanted him to leave and she wanted him to be there all at the same time.

When she reached the closed door, she took the handle firmly and turned. She thought she could hear Bobby Ellis swallow. She opened the door, and the sound stopped. That's when she saw the two kittens.

There was an open window on the far wall, and they were leaping up, trying to return to the windowsill to get out. And from the look of things, they'd been at it for a while.

The room had stacks of paperback books in piles everywhere. Some looked like they'd been pulled straight from the trash; others looked as if they'd been in someone's house for decades. When the kittens jumped toward the window, they landed, most often, on the books, sending the piles to the floor.

Emily stepped around the books and went right for the scrawny little cats. She scooped them up, turning to Bobby, who had stayed in the doorway.

"They look like they're starving to death...."

He had more pressing thoughts on his mind than scrawny kittens.

"Emily, we really have to get out of here."

That's when she saw the sketch pad that her mother had given Riddle. It was in the corner under a plastic milk crate. Emily handed Bobby Ellis the two bony kittens, not listening as he said:

"I'm allergic to cats."

She picked up the sketch pad and thumbed through the pages. It was Riddle's work. But it was stuff she'd never seen before. Instead of drawing the electrical circuitry of a toaster oven, these line drawings were all of food.

*　*　*

The kittens, wide-eyed with fear, now sat in the milk crate, which was positioned between Bobby and Emily in the front seat of the SUV. Bobby kept the windows down, doing his best to minimize the fact that his eyes were feeling itchy and it was getting harder and harder to breathe.

Emily was on the phone talking to her mother. She had the sketch pad she'd taken from the room in her lap. Her eyes darted from the road to the crying kittens. She was explaining how Bobby had taken a photo of the house and how he had the license plate of a truck and how they'd gone to the place together and how they'd found something she called a riddle book, which wasn't what it looked like to him, but he wasn't about to correct anything she said.

Because he wasn't calling the shots, that was for sure.

He was the driver; he was along for the ride, and that would have to be enough for now. Up ahead, the light turned red and he put on the brake, easing to a stop. He glanced over at Emily's profile. The wind whipped her long hair back and forth in front of her face as she spoke to her mother.

She was so brave and so bold and so determined.

And he was mesmerized.

20

Emily's parents met Bobby's parents at the Black Angus Steak House where the two families met to discuss the events of the day. After dinner, the fathers went together to the police station.

Emily wanted to go with them, but everyone felt that she'd had enough for one day. Plus the two kittens were at home.

Debbie had taken them in to the vet, and Emily was persuaded that she should be with the cats, since they'd been given antibiotics and were supposed to be watched.

Bobby told Emily he'd call her before he went to bed and give her an update from his side of things. They seemed to be in this together now.

When Bobby got home, he took a long, hot shower and silently thanked Jessica Pope, who had asked him to go with her to get a double mocha after school and had changed his life.

If Jessica hadn't forced him into the lie about investigative work, he'd be right now watching the Cartoon Network, which was something he kept secret from even his closest friends. He still liked little kids' shows. And he still had day-dreams that he was the most popular and interesting guy in high school.

And now those dreams seemed to be coming true.

* * *

Detective Darius Sanderson knew the Ellis family. So when Derrick Ellis and Tim Bell arrived, a front-desk officer took them straight back to Detective Sanderson's office.

The detective had on bright sweatpants and a multi-colored parka. An unlit cigar was in the corner of his mouth, which he chewed at night instead of smoked. Once he got started, he couldn't stop, so even though during the day he wouldn't have had the nasty thing in the office, now it was wedged in between his back left molars, sticking out the side of his mouth like a wet stick.

There weren't many African Americans on the force in town, and Sanderson was conscious of the fact that he was often scrutinized in a different way than his white counter-part, Dave Wilson. And now, with a late-night call that he'd been told was important, Sanderson wished that he wasn't wearing running shoes when the two men were ushered into his office.

Sanderson got to his feet and shook their hands. He

wanted to get this over with fast. With no need for small talk, he launched right in with:

"So what do you have for me?"

After he'd heard the story, told mostly by Tim Bell, the detective settled deep into his seat.

Two minors. Neither in school. One showing signs of physical neglect. Single-parent father calling the shots. Kids seemed afraid of him. License plates that didn't match a vehicle. Abandoned house out on Needle Lane, which was the area where stolen property had spiked in the last three months. Vandalism to Tim Bell's car.

Certainly there was a need to find these people and question them. And to help, there was a trail. A vehicle, a license plate, and a photo.

It was a nice package. After he said good night, Sanderson could have waited until the morning to go to work, but instead he took off his shoes, got himself a cup of coffee, and went online to start the file.

By the time Tim Bell and Derrick Ellis shook hands on the sidewalk and promised to stay in touch, the picture Bobby Ellis had taken had been uploaded into the state law enforcement system and an APB had been issued for the vehicle and the license plates.

* * *

They'd been in the Liberty Motel for ten days when Mrs. Dairy, the old lady who changed the towels and emptied the wastebaskets, insisted that she had to do the carpets. She claimed it was some kind of state law.

Sam, half-asleep, wondered if after all the things his father had done, he'd be arrested for not allowing a woman, who looked like she was over a hundred years old, to vacuum their dirty motel room.

But instead of arguing, Clarence told the boys to get up, and they all filed out into the truck and let the ancient lady push around a red Hoover upright vacuum originally purchased in 1972.

Other people would have looked at Mrs. Dairy's life and seen sorrow and disappointment. But she refused to view it that way.

While it was true that her husband had left her early in their marriage with a disabled child and a stack of unpaid bills, she'd managed to get by. Her little Eddie had suffocated when he was eight years old, after he'd climbed into an empty refrigerator that someone had left in a back alley. They had all kinds of warnings about doing that now. But Eddie had a heart problem that couldn't be fixed, so maybe it was all a blessing.

She liked to think so.

That's why she went to St. Jude's. They dealt with the positive and with the life hereafter, and Mrs. Dairy was looking forward to that. Plus the church was on the better side of town, and they served cream and milk with their coffee after service, not dry nondairy creamer. Her name was Mrs. Dairy after all. She wasn't going to shake a can of white powder into a hot beverage.

She was now eighty-four and a half years old, which seemed like the time most people would have long ago retired. Still she appreciated that she had a job at the Liberty. But her vision was no longer that great, and the vacuum seemed to slam into the sides of things more with each passing day.

And on this morning, while Clarence and the two boys tried to fall back asleep in the truck, Mrs. Dairy drove the vacuum straight into the corner floor lamp. It tipped over and crashed onto the bedside table. There were pieces of cheap white milk glass now speckling the carpet, and Mrs. Dairy got down on her knees to try to find the bigger shards.

That's when she saw the green velvet box taped to the underside of the bed.

What the hell was that?

Thick duct tape was holding a small container to the wooden slat, and that just wasn't right. Maybe there was some kind of explosive in that little box. And maybe terrorists were out there who were going to blow up the Liberty Motel because of its name.

But she doubted it.

Mrs. Dairy was a God-fearing woman, but she was also a realist. So she got back up to her feet, which took considerable effort, and she went to the fake-wood-paneled door, locked it, and slid on the corroded privacy chain. She then returned to the worn carpet and pulled the thick tape off the green box and took it down. When she opened it, she saw Gertrude Wetterling's jewelry.

There was no mistaking it.

Gertrude also went to St. Jude's on Ratsch Street, and her father had been the town's only real jeweler. Gertrude had the family's diamond brooch and two rings and a pearl necklace and the little platinum Christmas tree that Mrs. Dairy secretly coveted because it had little glittering ornaments that were precious stones.

Gertrude Wetterling wore it every Sunday morning in December, like clockwork.

So hadn't the town been buzzing with the talk of the robbery at Mrs. Wetterling's only three days ago? And now, she, Edith Luanne Dairy, had captured the criminals.

Okay, so she hadn't captured them, but she'd found them. And maybe there would be a reward.

It was never too late in life to have your luck turn around.

* * *

Mrs. Dairy returned the green box to its hiding place under the bed, but she kept the Christmas tree pin. Not for herself but for evidence. She had the feeling people wouldn't believe her. She was old. Her hearing was marginal. Her vision was worse. She had macular degeneration but was keeping it from everyone.

She could put two and two together and still get four, but she needed to get the rest of the world to spring into action, and that was going to mean producing some proof of her accusations.

And that's why she kept the Christmas tree pin. Plus she loved it. So for right now it was hers, tucked into her right peach-colored smock pocket, hitting the top of her lumpy thighs as she walked out the motel room door.

* * *

Clarence took one look at the old broad wheeling the vacuum out of the motel room and he knew. Something had energized her step, and it sure as hell wasn't cleaning his rat hole. Now she wouldn't even look at him. Before she was one big coffee-stained, toothy grin.

You just never could tell when people were going to ruin things. He had his eye on a carton of cell phones he'd seen at the audio/video store that was unopened near the unattended and unlocked back door. And just like that, Grandma Gum Disease had taken them from him.

Once Mrs. Dairy had cleared the doorway, Riddle moved to get out of the truck and Clarence snapped at him:

"Shut the door. Now!"

The tone of his voice left no room for argument. Clarence turned over the engine, and the truck fired up. Sam, who had said less than a dozen words to his father in as many days, leaned forward:

"What're you doing?"

"What's it look like I'm doing?"

Clarence threw the truck into reverse and backed up into the parking lot. Sam looked at Mrs. Dairy. She was moving faster now. As fast as her eighty-four-year-old frame would carry her, which was a crooked, wobbly trot.

As the truck swung out of the parking lot and onto the highway, Mrs. Dairy abandoned her cleaning cart and took off for the front office in what was, for her, a full-on sprint.

Sam watched, staring out the side window, with no visible emotion. And then Riddle, gasping for air and realizing that they were not just going but gone, took hold of Sam's arm. Tears filled his eyes as he murmured:

"My inhaler..."

*　*　*

Emily ate lunch with Bobby and Nora and Rory the next day, and when Bobby asked if she wanted him to drive her home after school, she easily agreed. So Bobby went and lifted weights while she did soccer conditioning.

When he was done, Bobby came to the edge of the oval track, where he stood waiting for her to finish. Emily was surprised that she found herself having to look away from his pumped-up body in his sweat-soaked T-shirt.

Was he always that ripped? His upper arms were kind of amazing. It was so unnerving.

But everything now was unnerving. Because all of her senses seemed heightened and exaggerated. That's what Sam and Riddle's leaving had done. They had taken her world and given every corner, every shape, a sharp edge.

And so now a very small thing could have a very big impact.

Did the color of the sky at night just after the sunset always look like the inside of a dirty seashell? And why did the sun disappearing behind the mountains now feel like such a loss? It would be back the next day. But now she couldn't even trust that because she was raw and exposed.

Instead of going straight home, Bobby asked if Emily wanted to stop by Kel Hoffs and get a milk shake. She didn't, but he had been so good about things and he was helping her now. So she had to say yes.

She knew that his favorite milk shake wasn't banana and date, but when she said that was the one she liked, he claimed he felt the same way. Most people thought the banana-date combination was gross.

While they were in Kel Hoffs having the milk shake, Moye Godchaux came in. She was friendly with Emily and was best friends with Jessica Pope. Emily and Bobby Ellis each had a straw in the single milk shake and they were leaning in when they spoke, not because they were some hot couple but because they were talking about the house on Needle Lane and they'd both agreed that it was off-limits to discuss with anyone else.

But of course to Moye Godchaux it didn't look that way.

To Moye Godchaux it looked like Emily Bell and Bobby Ellis were now together.

* * *

Mrs. Dairy knew when someone was fleeing the Liberty.

People left the motel all the time in a panic after they'd broken something in their room or tried to jack the room's

187

crummy TV set but then discovered that an ear-piercing alarm went off when you unplugged the thing.

She burst into the front office completely out of breath but still able to shout for Rowdy, who was supposed to be behind the counter doing the accounting but instead was sitting on the floor on a dog bed in a meditative pose humming.

"Call nine-one-one! The robbers are getting away!"

Rowdy had never seen Mrs. Dairy so full of life. It was inspiring. Rowdy had always wanted to report an actual emergency, and he was now thrilled to have the chance to press those magic three digits on the phone.

It didn't take long for a patrol car to pull up and for Mrs. Dairy to show the officer the taped green velvet box under the bed in room 7.

Things were suddenly crackling at the Liberty.

More police arrived. One officer started taking finger-prints; another began putting the many items that had been left in the room into clear plastic bags as possible sources of evidence. Mrs. Dairy watched him use what looked to her like salad tongs for the process.

Three out-of-state phone books were being removed when an officer noticed drawings on the back of one. He then opened up the first phone book and stared at the precise mechanical renderings.

If this wasn't evidence of something, he didn't know what was. Maybe these people were domestic terrorists. There was something that looked like a cruise missile, and it had been drawn many, many times.

Two of the ten rooms at the Liberty never got maid service that day. Mrs. Dairy answered dozens of questions on site, and then they asked her to come downtown for a more documented interview.

She rode the blue bus everywhere since the state had unfairly taken away her license after she twice failed the eye test. But now they loaded her up into a police cruiser, in the front and not the back, and drove her straight down to the station. She was disappointed that they didn't turn on the swirling lights, but she didn't say anything.

When she got downtown, she had two cups of coffee and a bowl of chicken soup with the officer who was now in charge of the whole thing. Toward the end of the lengthy process, they put her in front of a computer screen and showed her a picture of a man standing next to a black truck. They had to blow it up to ten times its normal size, but once they got the image to where she could see it, she knew.

It was him.

The officer wanted her to take her time. He wanted her to be sure. Mrs. Dairy's fist hit the desk and she shook her head.

"Hell, I'm blind as a bat and I'd bet my life on it."

Now that she'd identified a suspect, a sworn statement was typed up and she had to sign it in front of two witnesses. She was pleased with her own stamina, but she was starting to come down from the biggest rush of adrenaline that she'd experienced in decades.

She suddenly just wanted to lay her head on the metal desk in front of her and shut her eyes forever.

Mrs. Dairy assumed that she'd take a bus from there over to Hillside, but they wouldn't hear of it. That was when one of the officers even went so far as to call her a hero. She just laughed and felt herself blushing. She hadn't had that feeling in a lifetime.

Late that afternoon, when she got home and sat in the one really comfortable chair in the tiny house that she'd rented for years and years from the Rouse family, she pretended to herself that finding the little jeweled Christmas tree in her smock pocket was a complete surprise.

She actually said out loud as she held it in her slightly trembling hand:

"Dear Lord, I forgot all about this adorable little Christmas tree pin...."

* * *

Detective Sanderson got a call from Cedar City, Utah, two days after he'd put up the alert. His suspect had been identified fleeing a cheap motel on the outskirts of town. Stolen property had been recovered. Several phone books, all with intricate drawings, were among the possessions that had been left behind.

It was a satisfying start.

The suspect and the boys had traveled eight hundred miles. They were still at large, but the detective now believed that it was just a matter of time before the net of law enforcement would close in around them.

Sanderson spent the rest of the afternoon reading through the report filed in Cedar City. One item caught his attention: a Proventil inhaler in a plastic bag was found stuffed under the cushion of a chair in the Liberty Motel room. It had been dispensed from Sacred Heart hospital to Debbie Bell.

Sanderson leaned back in his desk chair and felt a kind of dread seep through his body. He'd had asthma when he was young, and he'd been one of the fortunate ones to have outgrown the condition.

But that was only because, in his opinion, he had a devoted mother who spent every moment of his childhood fussing over his malady.

He was now even more worried about the two boys.

21

Clarence was out of his mind.

That was a simple fact, but now it was a different kind of wide-eyed madness as they sped down the open highway.

He'd pulled off the road after they'd traveled thirty miles and switched license plates, but that wasn't going to change things. The bad guys were now actively looking for him.

He tried to calm himself. He'd hit a streak of rotten luck. That happened. What do you do when you're really down? You pull back. You change things up. Suddenly it felt like his head was going to explode.

It was the boys.

This was their fault. All of it. Riddle, sitting in the back, was again breathing fast gulps of air. It would drive anyone mad. The wheezing and the coughing. The gurgling throat spasms. Listening to it made Clarence's skin crawl. The kid had to be doing it on purpose. He had to be just trying to see if he'd get a reaction. Well, he would. Oh yeah.

And Sam. He was the one who had set off this chain reaction of pain. He was the one who had met a girl. The oldest story ever told. Boy meets girl. And then everything goes bad.

When a highway patrolman passed going the other direction, Clarence made a decision. Before the police car could swoop around and come back after them, he turned onto a road that led up into mountains.

*　　*　　*

Riddle, panting like a nervous dog with his eyes closed, suddenly sat up when the truck left the asphalt road and hit the big-stone gravel.

Sam was staring out the window. Riddle looked over at Sam and his brother's eyes said what they always said: it would be okay. Because he would make it okay.

But inside Sam knew this time it was different.

When Clarence got out of the car and removed a pair of wire cutters from the back of the truck and sliced the lock off the U.S. Forest Service chain that was slung across the logging road, Sam knew that this time he wasn't going along for the ride.

As the truck climbed higher up into the remote mountains of the national park, Sam knew that there was another world out there, and he and Riddle had to get back to it.

Or end it all by trying.

*　　*　　*

Bobby Ellis's new SUV pulled up in front of the Bell house. He wanted more than anything to just be invited inside. But Emily grabbed her bag and opened the car door before he could even think of anything to say other than that he'd be on the case, which made him sound like some kind of idiot in an old television show.

But Emily didn't take it that way because she said:

"You're going to do more investigating?"

Bobby nodded and then came out with:

"Yeah, well, I was thinking I'd go to my mom's office and check with her contacts at the police department to see if they'd found anything. You know, off-hours kinda stuff."

Emily nodded.

"Sounds good."

Bobby nodded back.

"I'll call later and give you an update."

Emily nodded again and then headed to her house. Bobby realized he should have pulled away instead of watching her walk across the lawn and onto the porch. He should have left before she took out her key and disappeared inside.

She gave him a small wave from behind the front window and he silently hoped he looked considerate, not obsessed.

Bobby Ellis pulled away from the curb and turned in the opposite direction from his house. He was headed downtown. If there was news about *the Enemy*, as he'd come to think of his rival, he needed to have a jump on it.

* * *

Emily took her backpack and went straight upstairs to her room. She shut the door and sat on the bed and allowed herself to feel numb.

She'd gone to school and studied books to learn about literature and history, math and science. She'd been taught a foreign language and how to play an instrument, although never very well. She'd learned the rules and the strategies of at least a dozen sports. She had taken a scuba-diving lesson once, and she knew how to use a potter's wheel. She could cook all kinds of foods, and she practiced first aid.

But they hadn't taught her this.

There was no piece of paper that had the ten steps for her to memorize that would make it go away. None of the stories she'd heard about other people's losses gave her insight.

Emily rolled over onto her side and felt her eyes blur with liquid.

There was no manual to consult. This was just life.

* * *

When Bobby got to his parents' building, his mother was with a new client in the small conference room at the end of the hall. Nice. Bobby went into her office and shut the door. His mother's e-mail account was open. The best way, he'd learned, to get answers when it was important was to simply impersonate her.

So Bobby Ellis pressed Compose and wrote a short note to Detective Sanderson.

Checking in to see if any new developments on Needle
Lane case.
— Barb

Bobby then sat back and waited. Several moments later, an e-mail appeared in the inbox:

Following lead in Cedar City, Utah. Have made positive
identification and recovered identifiable stolen property.
Interested parties still at large.

Bobby stared at the computer screen.

This was not good news. He was hoping no one ever heard another word from these people again. Bobby pressed Delete and got to his feet. The last person he'd share this with was Emily Bell. He had to convince her that *the Enemy* would never return. But in a kind way.

He had to be her shoulder to cry on.

22

The gravel road was impassable for half the year.

Originally built for logging, it was one of the mazes of forest-service-only slashes that were maintained now purely for seasonal fire use. Dirty patches of snow still dotted the wet ground.

Clarence had no idea where he was or where he was going, but he kept his foot on the gas, chugging in low gear higher up to nowhere.

The rust-colored rock of the jagged mountains had given way to scrub pine, which had turned into taller, towering trees. The road now clung to the side of an imposing peak. Uphill was more rock and trees; down below was a sheer drop-off.

After they'd been at it for almost three hours, Clarence rounded a bend to see that the chunky gravel had completely washed away and a heavy stream of runoff flowed straight across the road, dumping down the mountainside in an icy waterfall.

Clarence threw the truck into park and got out. The boys

wordlessly exchanged looks. They were still in the backseat and, as they both had to pee, they opened the doors.

It was cold outside. Much colder than in the truck. Sam tried to shake it off but then turned around to get his coat. And then he remembered. What coat? Almost all of their stuff had been left in the motel room.

Riddle swung his feet down and as they landed on the lumpy rocks he took a breath. The cold air was actually easier for him to inhale. He put his hands on his cheeks and held his head as he sucked in the chill.

There had been so many times when it had been awful. So many times when he'd felt like he was in a box and someone had closed the lid and wouldn't let him out.

But this day, even by those standards, was bad.

Riddle took his hands away from his face and realized that Sam had come around to his side. He was holding out an old sweater that he'd found in the way back of the truck. He motioned for Riddle to put it on, and he did.

While Clarence continued to stare at the stream as if a defiant glare were going to cause the water to change directions, the boys moved together to the edge of the road to take a leak.

Sam looked down. Way below, through the dense pine trees and sharp rock, he could hear the wild rushing water of what sounded like a real river. But he couldn't see it. He and Riddle finished up and turned back to the truck.

Sam could feel his stomach rumble. He'd been nauseous since they'd left the motel hours ago, but now that was wearing off and his body was asking to be fed.

Clarence suddenly reeled around, his face twisted in anger.

"So what do you boys think we should do?"

Sam and Riddle were both silent. Clarence was louder now.

"I asked you a question."

Sam didn't look at him but finally said:

"There's no room to turn around, so I guess we have to back up down the hill...."

Clarence's tone changed to a small whisper.

"So that's what you'd do? That's how you'd handle this...?"

Sam only nodded. Clarence then exploded.

"I'm not backing down. I don't back down. Anywhere. Anytime. Any way!"

Clarence turned around and climbed into the front seat and slammed the door. He then threw the truck into drive and in a fury stepped on the gas.

The truck lurched forward straight into the stream. It was deeper than it looked, but Clarence was right. The old truck was going to make it across.

But then the front right tire suddenly dropped into what was an unseen hole. The left side of the truck pulled up out of the water while the back tires kept spinning, spitting rocks and water in all directions.

And then the front axle snapped.

The sound echoed through the forest like a gunshot.

* * *

They'd had different trucks in the last dozen years, but this one, this beast, had been with them since outside Tucson. And now it was immobile, stuck in the middle of a stream in the middle of a steep incline in the middle of nowhere.

Clarence stayed behind the steering wheel and didn't get out. Sam motioned to Riddle, and they walked to a fallen tree on the uphill side of the road and took a seat to wait for the next episode of Life with Father.

It was so quiet.

Sam heard only the sound of the wind in the tops of the pine trees, which made the most gentle swishing.

And then gradually he could hear the other sounds. Birds and chipmunks. The stream rushing by. The louder, distant river far below.

He was turning it all into music in his head. Everything became an instrument. Add in the strings. It was a symphony. He shut his eyes and imagined how he would play the piece. A stirring melody over a pulsing beat that was angry and constant. His fingers were gliding now over his old guitar. Riddle coughed, and Sam included the sound as a set of cymbals.

He was in the forest above the high desert, but he was transported. Gone. Safe. But for how long? He didn't know. That's what happened when he played guitar, and now that's what happened as he sat on the side of the mountain with his little brother.

And then the music abruptly stopped as the truck door opened. Sam's eyes snapped wide and his body tensed in anticipation. He looked over and saw Clarence getting out of the stranded vehicle. He was carrying his shotgun. Riddle's eyes darted to Sam. What now? Sam gave him the look to say *We're good* when of course they weren't.

Then the lanky teenage boy simply got to his feet, and as the music in his head returned to full volume, he walked straight toward his father.

*   *   *

Clarence had only one thought and it kept hitting him from all directions. The road. The truck. The dead tree he could see in the distance. The voice in his head was talking now:

All things must end. Yes. All things must end.

He wouldn't get anywhere if he had to keep the two boys. Not happening.

He'd tried his best. No, he'd tried harder than his best. And they'd let him down. Like so many before them.

Once they'd crossed that line, there was no turning back. He should have figured that out earlier. But this was an opportunity. Yes. It was clear to him now.

He'd put the boys out of their misery. The youngest one was a lemon. That was obvious. He couldn't even breathe right. And the oldest one was his faithful protector. The only question was which one to take down first?

Once he got it over with, then he'd disappear. He'd head up into the mountains. He had survival skills. Hell, he'd spent all those years in Alaska. He'd hunt and fish and ride out the storm. When he'd walk out of the wilderness in a few months, he'd start over again. He'd head north.

All things must end.

Yes.

All things must end.

*   *   *

Clarence took the shotgun and checked to make sure it was loaded. He opened the door and then stepped out into the icy water to see Sam get up from the log where he and Riddle had been waiting for forty minutes.

Clarence took two leaps forward out of the cold stream and then lifted his gun. He aimed at Sam, but the boy kept right on walking straight at him.

This surprised Clarence.

He thought the kid would turn and run. He wanted to shoot them both in the back. That had been the plan. But now that wasn't going to be possible. He checked his finger on the trigger, and Sam, still moving toward him, said:

"It's over."

Clarence didn't answer. He kept the shotgun pointed right at Sam, and then behind Sam he heard Riddle yell. Riddle never, ever yelled. It took too much lung power. But he was yelling:

"NOOOOOoooooooo!"

Clarence shifted the barrel from Sam to Riddle and shouted:

"Shut up!"

Sam jumped at him just as Clarence pulled the trigger and the gun fired. The shot went wide, missing Riddle, who was now on his feet, not running away but running for Sam and Clarence, who had both fallen to the ground.

The shotgun hit the gravel just after they did, and another shell exploded. This time the backlash from the rifle hit Clarence in the chest and propelled him, with a thump, right over the drop-off.

But when he fell, he reached out, grabbed hold of Sam's arm, and took the teenage boy with him.

Riddle, still screaming, ran to the edge and watched as Clarence and Sam, now separated, tumbled down, down, down like two rag dolls, over rocks, into trees, finally disappearing from view.

Riddle opened his mouth and screamed:

"Sam!"

Suddenly the wind seemed to abruptly die down.

The pine treetops stopped swaying.

And then Riddle threw himself over the cliff after them.

23

Emily had given the photo of Sam from the PennySaver to the police. But in the chaos surrounding Sam's leaving, she had never thought that the haircut place might also have taken a picture of Riddle.

But then Nora, of all people, said something when they were at school. She asked if Emily still had the PennySaver ad with the name of the hair salon, because she was thinking of having Rory get his hair cut at that same place for prom. Didn't Emily think that was a good idea?

"The before-and-after shots of Sam were pretty amazing. And Rory has been thinking of just buzzing his head, and I'd die if he did that. I mean, the shape of his head is just plain weird, don't you think?"

Nora was massively insensitive at times.

Emily shut her locker and walked straight out the front doors of Churchill High. She had never left school in the middle of the day without a written excuse, and she was surprised that she didn't feel guilty.

Six blocks away, she caught a blue city bus across town and, sitting in the back, she thought of Sam and Riddle. Maybe they'd ridden on this bus when they'd come to see her family. Maybe one day they would ride on it again. But she was good at math, and she knew the difference between the probable and the possible.

When Emily showed up at Superior-Cuts, Rayford was sitting by the door wondering why short-short hair couldn't sweep the country so he could afford to take a trip to Hawaii. If only some actress or model or singer would burst onto the world stage with hair three inches long in a cut that required heavy maintenance and was highly open to imitation.

This was his wish. This is what gave him hope.

Rayford smiled at Emily as she stood on the sidewalk in front of the shop. She didn't smile back. She was very pretty, but she looked incredibly serious for someone her age. And she looked sad. It was the perfect combination for a makeover. He pushed the door open wider and asked what he could do to help.

*   *   *

It didn't take long to find the picture of Riddle, because the file had been transferred on the same day with Sam's photo. And Sam's photo had been accessed often. It was now used in all of the store's publicity. Sam was on the new Superior-Cuts business cards and on the half-price Monday coupons.

Emily stared at the computer screen while Rayford electronically sent her the image. Riddle looked odder than she'd come to think of him. His eyes were squinted, and he looked smaller and like more of an outcast. Rayford saw the confusion on her face and said:

"Isn't that who you're looking for?"

Emily nodded, still staring.

Across the room, Crystal finished applying chunky, blond highlights to a woman who was in denial about her current age. Crystal pulled off her smelly purple gloves, dropped them into the deep sink, and came over to join the discussion.

"So they're both in trouble? I mean, I can see the little one crossing the line, but not the older guy . . . I mean, he was—"

Emily interrupted:

"They didn't do anything wrong. They're victims."

Neither Rayford nor Crystal knew what that was supposed to mean. But Crystal nodded to be supportive. And then, not knowing what else to say, she added:

"I'd be happy to do your hair—you know—if you wanted to try a new style or something."

Emily looked at Crystal. This young woman had cut Sam's and Riddle's hair. For Emily, that was enough of a connection.

"I don't have enough money. I just came about the pictures and—"

Crystal reached over and grabbed a pink smock.

"On me. If, you know, I can take a before-and-after shot to use for publicity."

*　　*　　*

Emily asked if she could donate her hair to one of those charities that made wigs for kids with cancer, and they said it could be done. So they put Emily's hair into one long brown braid and then, after a single snip with oversize shears, Rayford took it away.

Emily had heard that when a woman's heart was broken, she cut off her hair. Her heart did, in fact, feel as if it had been punctured. She closed her eyes for the whole haircut. She'd always, even as a toddler, had a sheet of brown hair that looked in pictures like a velvet curtain.

When Crystal was done and Emily finally looked up into the large oval mirror, she was surprised. She thought short hair would make her seem younger and that maybe she would now be someone who would disappear completely in a crowd.

But she was wrong. It was so stylish. She looked older and more sophisticated.

No one would miss her now.

*　　*　　*

Crystal printed out the picture Rayford took of Emily and pinned it alongside the shot of Sam.

Emily found some comfort in the fact that they were together, even if only on the almond-colored wall of the Superior-Cuts located in the corner space of a mini-mall next to a dog groomer's (that, because of the bad economy, had been out of business for over a year). Wasn't it just a fact that there were now a lot of dogs in town that looked shaggy?

Emily left the hair salon and went back to the bus stop's foul-weather enclosure, where she took a seat and waited.

A silver pickup truck with three young guys, all sitting together in the front seat, slowed as it approached the bus stop and the red traffic light.

The guy closest to the passenger-side window leaned out and shouted:

"Wanna ride?"

Emily looked away. All three guys were now laughing, and the driver was making some kind of hooting noises.

"Come on, I know you wanna sit on my lap!"

More laughing from the truck.

Emily didn't move. Her eyes remained glued to the sidewalk. Up ahead, the traffic light turned green. The truck stayed still. The driver leaned across his two friends and hollered:

"You'll be in my dreams tonight, pretty baby!"

The other two guys laughed again, and then Emily met their gaze. Her voice was so lacking in emotion as to be scary.

"It would only be a nightmare."

The driver exchanged looks with the guys sitting next to

him and then stepped aggressively on the gas and the truck sped off. They wanted no part of her.

Emily looked down the road. What was that about?

Were women sitting by themselves always some sort of target? And did men think that women found that kind of attention flattering? Or were they just amusing themselves at her expense?

Emily exhaled. How had she ended up across town in the middle of the day waiting for a bus when she should have been in math class? And why did she feel like getting on a bus and staying on it across the country?

Because what she wanted now, more than anything, was to escape her life.

Is that how knowing Sam and Riddle had changed her?

* * *

Clarence had been right about one thing: the state highway patrol was now thick in the area. Because of the various reports filed, and because there were minors involved, Clarence had been upgraded from a suspect of stolen possessions to a man in flight with much bigger problems.

Detective Sanderson had been on the phone with Utah, and he had supplied more details about the two boys. He had half a mind to head out there himself.

And then he got a phone call from Tim Bell that there was a picture of the second boy, the younger one. That would help. It was from a hair salon, and the shot was only a few months old.

When the picture arrived, Sanderson posted the photo, along with the other one of Sam, on the hot site for missing children. It circulated to every law-enforcement agency in the country.

And then, while he probably should have returned to investigating a tip on a local businessman who was rumored to be running a big marijuana business on some leased logging land, Sanderson decided to dig around for more info on the boys.

He knew their ages. And now he had both of their photos. They had to have come from somewhere. The Bell family had told him that the kids had been on the road for years. So he'd start looking back when they were toddlers.

It was the opposite of most of these kinds of cases.

Instead of photos of little children who had disappeared — photos that computers and artists tried to reimagine as missing teenagers — he had two images from today that he'd like to connect to baby pictures.

Ten years ago, who had lost two little boys?

* * *

Emily sat staring out the bus window at the blur of small businesses that lined the street.

Two blocks up, the bus stopped, and a girl, carrying a Baine College backpack, got on with a guy right behind her. They took a seat in the row in front of Emily and before she knew it, they were kissing.

It was suddenly very, very uncomfortable on the bus. Emily leaned her head against the glass and shut her eyes.

What was choosing someone all about, anyway? Did it come down to understanding how the way the person felt about you made you feel about yourself?

That seemed messed up, but maybe it was true.

Were people really just mirrors for each other?

Did everyone want, really, just to be told that they were great? And did validation have more meaning if others saw the person who was telling you how great you were as good-looking or smart or somehow unique?

Did everyone simply just struggle to feel special and to be acknowledged for that?

Or was there something else?

Was there some ingredient to the connection that was unseen and not able to be measured? Was there something other than mutual validation that made a bond?

Emily remembered that her grandmother Risha had told her that it was important to remember, always, what made you first love someone.

Long before Emily knew that Sam could play the guitar like some kind of protégé, and before she knew how devoted he was to his brother, she knew he had empathy. He had come to see if she was okay after she had sung one of the worst solos ever heard at the First Unitarian Church.

So he had compassion. And she responded to that. But what Emily really knew for certain was that there was something in him that challenged her. He was so different. Sam might have been so intriguing to her because there were so many doors to unlock.

And maybe unlocking them made her feel good about herself.

But when it came down to it, hadn't she failed?

Hadn't she been kept out of the biggest part of his life?

24

Riddle hit rocks and trees and tumbled down, down, down. When he stopped, when his right arm finally caught hold of a branch that was connected to a dead tree, he was close to the bottom of a deep ravine.

He slowly got to his feet and squinted up into the hard light. He'd fallen a long way. But he was, miraculously, in one piece. His left foot hurt, and he had a cut over his right eye.

Blood, like warm gravy, was oozing out of the gash, but otherwise, as his mind cleared, he realized that he'd thrown himself off a cliff and he'd survived.

It was only now, staring up and looking at where he'd come from, that he suddenly got afraid. He felt a kind of panic sweep over him.

That was very, very, very far. And that was very, very, very dangerous.

I'm not doing that again.

Ever.

Ever.

Ever.

He called out, shouting now:

"Sam!"

But he heard nothing back.

* * *

Clarence could hear Riddle's distant voice echo up from far below.

How had Riddle ended up down there? And how had he ended up here on this rocky ledge?

He'd fallen.

That was the only part he remembered. And he had to have broken his right leg when he hit the rock. It hurt like hell. He looked down and saw that part of the bone had splintered and was sticking out of the skin. He could see blood but also bone and cartilage that was yellow and not what he thought it would look like.

His collarbone on the same side as the busted leg must have snapped, because if he put his hand there, he felt a lump. And when he moved, a shooting pain, like being shocked, jolted straight through his system.

He shut his eyes and tried to concentrate.

The road was up above him. And the bottom of the basin, the river, was way down below. He was stuck between the two.

Well, he'd be damned if he was going to freeze or starve

to death on a rocky ledge partway down the side of a mountain.

He hadn't gotten this far in life by sitting back and taking the easy way out. He could hear Riddle's voice, hoarse now, still hollering for Sam. He'd never heard him shout so loud.

Clarence had to get away from them.

He suddenly threw up.

The world started spinning. Now he had two things to get away from. The boys and this stinking mess.

He looked up again. He wasn't even halfway down the incline. That's when he made his decision. He'd pull himself up the jagged side of this damn mountain back to the road. There was vodka in the truck. And saltine crackers in the back. He'd give anything for one of those crackers.

It hurt to move his throbbing, bloody leg, but if that's what it took, then that's what it took. *Slowly, slowly, reach and pull. And like a bug, move up until you are there. Like a bug, travel on all fours and keep moving.*

Because there are saltine crackers up on top.

* * *

Riddle continued, for what seemed like hours, shouting out Sam, Sam, Sam. And he heard nothing, nothing, nothing.

So he began working his way across the rocks and through the trees.

He knew that if he looked everywhere, very carefully, he would find him. So he made a map in his head of the bottom of the gorge. Like he was making a drawing. The three biggest rocks. The tallest trees. The river down below. And then he started to search each part of the map that was in his head.

And when the light was low in the sky and night was almost upon him, he finally saw a shape. A lump. A body.

* * *

Sam was on his side.

Was he dead?

No, his chest was moving. He was asleep. And he wouldn't wake up. But he made small noises. Little sputtering sounds. But his eyes stayed shut and he wouldn't answer, even when Riddle got frustrated and yelled at him to *wake up now!*

Then Riddle went down close to the water, which was a wild river, and he cleared away all the rocks in an area where the earth was soft and there were brown pine needles all over on the ground.

But there were also still small patches of snow. Maybe that was okay. Maybe the snow would feel good, because Sam's face was red and hot.

Riddle snapped off branches with new green needles, because they weren't crunchy but were bendy, and he made a pillow. And then he went and got Sam, which was maybe wrong.

Sam was so heavy, and Riddle wasn't strong enough to lift him. He had to drag him by grabbing the top parts of his shirt and pulling.

At first he could tell he was hurting him because Sam's face tightened, but he still didn't wake up.

But Riddle pulled him anyway. He could sleep down by the wild river, and there was water there. It took some time, but he got him to the spot he made.

And then he laid him down to rest.

*   *   *

He opened his eyes, and it was dark.

He was dead.

Obviously.

So this was what happened when you died. You just saw black. And you felt fuzzy. And sick to your stomach.

But then his eyes slowly adjusted, and he could see something inside the black. It took a while for him to realize he was looking at stars. An entire sky full of them.

And then he heard something. A hooting. A bird. An owl?

Maybe he wasn't dead.

He closed his eyes and tried to sort out the many, many sensations in his body. The first was cold. He was freezing cold.

The next realization was that his shoulder was throbbing. And so was his chest. The side of his chest. His ribs on the left side of his chest.

And then he heard another sound. Very close. Movement. An animal. A large animal.

So he hadn't been dead before, but now, he was about to die. Okay. Bring it on. Because maybe when you die, it's not so cold, and the pain in your left side doesn't hurt so much.

He shut his eyes and moaned. He couldn't help that. It just came out. So go on, animal. Do it. And then the movement, the animal that was so near, said:

"Sam...?"

The animal spoke.

Sam opened his eyes and they adjusted again to the dark and then he saw the sky field and then he saw the silhouette of his brother.

"Riddle...?"

And then Riddle put his arms around him and started to cry. Deep, full sobs. And it really hurt. The squeezing on his shoulder was a new torture to add to his other sensations.

But he just let Riddle hold him for what seemed like forever and ever, though he knew it wasn't forever and ever, and then finally Riddle pulled back and managed to say, through his tears:

"Are you okay...are you okay, Sam? Are you? Sam? Are *you okay? Sam?*"

He now realized that his mouth was very dry. Like cotton. Like dirt. Like sand. Like sand with ground glass mixed in with it. Like bloody sand. It was hard to even move his tongue. But he managed to say:

"Is there water...?"

Riddle got up. Sam could see that. Riddle could walk.

Well, that was good. But he walked funny. Sort of limping. Was he dragging his foot? It was too dark. He couldn't see. Riddle came back, and he was now holding out a shoe. A shoe filled with water.

Riddle held it to Sam's mouth and he lifted up, a small bit, and it was a mistake. A huge mistake, because now the pain was shooting down his shoulder and into his ribs and across his hips. His head now was going to explode.

But Riddle understood and he moved the shoe and the water touched his lips and it was icy cold and sweet and it ran down the sides of his mouth, but he was able, despite the pain, to swallow.

He now knew he was alive.

He drank the whole shoe full of water and if he moved, even slightly, it felt as if his shoulder were on fire.

Someone had a blowtorch aimed at his shoulder and was burning a hole straight through the top of his arm and into his neck.

He cried out in pain, and Riddle began to touch him again as he frantically said:

"Are you okay, Sam? Are you?"

And Sam shut his eyes and now realized that his head was resting on branches of pine needles that had been piled up. Like a pillow. Riddle must have done that. Sam said:

"I'm cold..."

And then everything was dark again.

* * *

Sam was shaking from the freezing night air, so Riddle picked every fern that he could find on the riverbank. He had armfuls and armfuls of them.

Then Riddle took off the old, oversize sweater that Sam had given him from the back of the truck and he wrapped it around Sam's legs. He then carefully covered Sam with layer after layer of ferns, all positioned in the same direction, like the insides of a circuit board, until only Sam's head was now visible.

And then Riddle lifted up the ferns and got right up against his brother and he fell asleep, hoping his body heat would help keep them both warm.

* * *

Riddle woke up at first light. Sam's chest was moving up and down. He was breathing. So he was still alive. Riddle was hungry. Really hungry. But it was warm next to Sam under the ferns, and he waited until the sun was higher up in the sky, sending spots of bright yellow light onto the riverbank and onto Sam. And then he finally got to his feet.

Riddle filled his shoe with icy water from the churning river and he drank, hoping that the liquid would stop his stomach cramps. But it didn't. He took a seat on a rotten log that lay on the mat of forest debris.

Sam always got them out of trouble. But now Sam was under the ferns and he was still having trouble waking up. Riddle stared at his left hand. He felt something small. Shiny black beetles were burrowing into a hole close to his left thumb, which rested on the decomposing reddish bark.

They look like candy.

Candy with legs.

Riddle reached over and plucked a beetle off the log. It struggled in his fingers. He then pulled off the insect's six angled legs. Now it wasn't struggling.

And now it really looks like candy.

Riddle popped it into his mouth and chewed.

It doesn't taste like candy.

It tastes like a spicy nut.

A nut that's been stuck in the backseat of the truck and that I find after a long time and I eat anyway but don't tell Sam.

Riddle reached over and picked up four more beetles and ripped off their legs and ate them. With each beetle, he got more comfortable with the taste, until he was digging into the log, pulling out beetles by the handful.

And the crunch is a good thing.

*　*　*

Using a sharp stick to dig deeper into the rotten log, Riddle found hundreds of beetles.

He ate until his tongue started to feel thick. The beetles were tart and like licking a lemon wedge that was covered in ground pepper. Knowing that Sam would need something to eat, he then collected many more beetle bodies, removing the insects' legs and putting them in the empty shoe.

But Riddle worried that the nutty snack beetles wouldn't be enough, so he continued searching along the river's edge and was rewarded around the next bend with an inlet.

Here the water was stagnant and sat in shallow, cold pools. Around the edges of the brackish water, it was like a marsh. As Riddle got closer, he saw that the area was filled with cattails.

Riddle stared. They looked like corn dogs.

He liked corn dogs.

Sometimes Sam bought them corn dogs at the 7-Eleven.

Riddle knew that these weren't corn dogs, but that didn't stop him from reaching into the rushes and breaking off a stalk.

Riddle held the fuzzy, brown spike in his hands. He shut his eyes and let the soft brown cylinder rest against his cheek. It was comforting. And it smelled good. When he opened his eyes, Riddle was looking down and could see the fresh green new shoots of future cattail spikes poking up out of the water.

They looked like the vegetable that Debbie Bell made. What was it called? Ash. Pear. Gas. But it had nothing to do with ashes or pears or gas.

Riddle reached down and broke off a new shoot, peeling back the outside green layers to reveal a soft white interior. Didn't Debbie Bell say that sometimes they could be white? He dug his thirty thumbnail into the fleshy, creamy pulp, and it gave way.

He then instinctively took a bite. It was like raw zucchini and fresh cucumbers.

He took another bite.

It tasted good.

Really good.

Especially after eating a lot of black beetles.

*   *   *

Moving was intense.

If Sam could just stay in one place and keep his shoulder steady, everything would be fine. But of course he had to breathe, and that hurt his side. His ribs. They must be broken. And his shoulder was massively messed up. But he was alive.

And then there was Riddle.

How exactly had Riddle gotten down the mountainside? And how had he stayed in one piece? The last thing Sam remembered, he was up on the road. They were all up on the road.

So where was Clarence?

Hadn't he tried to kill them? Or did he imagine that? He remembered his father aiming the shotgun. But then it all went blank. Did he kill his father? Maybe that's what this was about. The end of Clarence. Is that what happened?

He felt like it might be the end of something.

For him anyway.

But except for the fact that Riddle had a cut on his forehead, his brother looked fine. He looked better than that. He looked good. Sam had spent his whole life taking care of his little brother, and somehow Riddle was now the strong one.

And to think he always worried about the kid just crossing the street.

25

He got back to find Sam awake, staring up into the swaying pine branches.

Riddle was carrying a stack of the cattail shoots with a shoe full of beetles balanced on top.

"Sam...!"

Sam managed a small:

"Hey...could you get me some water?"

Riddle carefully put down the cattails and then quickly scooped up some of the cold river into his other sneaker and brought it back. Riddle felt a huge sense of relief, which he kept to himself. But inside he was saying, in a swirl of repetitive circles:

Sam is still Sam. Sam is still Sam. Sam is still Sam.

After Sam had swallowed the water, Riddle presented the other shoe, removing a handful of what looked like black currants. He placed them in Sam's hand. Sam didn't even ask what they were. He put them in his mouth and chewed. Riddle could not stop smiling.

"Nuts…"

Sam ate most of what was in the shoe and then, after more water, he started in, slowly, on the crunchy cattail shoots.

* * *

After Sam ate, he painfully, incredibly painfully, rolled to his side and took a leak, which had to mean his kidneys were still working. But the reality was that he had broken bones, and maybe something inside was bleeding. And he needed a doctor.

Small black flies, exploding into the air in spring, now appeared in a swarm, like a filter of fine netting, waving above his head. Sam watched the chaotic frenzy. What were the insects doing? And why? The frantic motion suddenly was translated in his head into sound.

His physical pain lessened when he could fix his mind on something else. He'd learned years ago how to make this happen. And now, more than ever, this is what got him through the agony of a broken shoulder, six broken ribs, a fractured collarbone, a concussion, and multiple bone bruises.

Sam had no idea how long Riddle was gone.

But when he again appeared at his side, he was using the old striped sweater as a large sling. Dozens and dozens of fuzzy cattails were inside. Sam watched as Riddle obsessively arranged the cattails on rows on the ground.

And then after he'd completed his work, Riddle carefully moved his brother off the damp pine-covered earth to what felt to Sam's broken body like the sweetest cushion imaginable.

*   *   *

Clarence slowly pulled himself upward over the rocks.

His broken leg, a compound fracture, now stiff and swollen, was discolored from pooled blood vessels and almost twice its normal size.

Clarence's collarbone was still electric, but if he held his arm folded when he rested, close to his chest, he could keep the searing jolts to a minimum.

Any normal person would have quit. The pain. The insanity of scaling the jagged rock face. It would have been too much. But the very thing that made Clarence irrational was the same thing that kept him going.

And the following afternoon, under a partly cloudy sky, a full twenty-four hours after they'd gone over the edge, he dragged himself up onto the gravel road.

His truck was at a distance, stuck in the rushing water. With his last ounce of energy, Clarence stumbled into the icy, running water and drank for what felt like ten minutes. He then staggered to the passenger door, opened it, and fell onto the front seat as he lost consciousness.

*   *   *

Since Clarence had always left the boys to fend for themselves, being all alone deep in the forest didn't panic Riddle. He and Sam were survivalists even when they were in the heart of a city.

So as Sam drifted back asleep, Riddle snapped off brush and used it to make an enclosure. He stacked the branches into a wall, which was nearly four feet high.

Satisfied that they'd now be warmer at night, Riddle sat down next to Sam. He was exhausted. Riddle shut his eyes, and his fingers twitched.

I need to make lines. I need to make the shapes.

But I don't have my drawing book.

I need to make lines.

And that was when Riddle suddenly realized that he still had a pen shoved deep in his back pocket. He took it out. Holding the ballpoint made him feel better. He stared at the print on the side.

State Farm Insurance: Agent Dewey Danes Says Be Prepared!

Riddle unscrewed the pen and looked at the different parts.

It had two plastic outer pieces and a thin metal ring in the center. There was a metal clip at the top and a small spring inside that pressed on the plastic tube of blue ink.

Riddle pulled on the spring, and it elongated into a thin piece of curved metal. Riddle pushed the pieces of the pen from his cupped hand back into his pants pocket. And then he curled up right next to his brother and fell asleep.

When he woke up, several hours later, Sam's eyes were

open. He was staring up at the big clouds, hoping they didn't hold rain.

Riddle looked at his brother as he said:

"I'm hungry."

Sam ever so slightly nodded. Riddle was talking to himself now as much as to his big brother.

"I saw little fish in the water."

Riddle didn't like to eat fish. But he knew Sam did. He continued:

"I'd eat a fish sandwich. I'd even eat one with that bad sauce."

Riddle dug into his pocket and pulled out the pen parts and began fiddling with the uncoiled spring. Sam watched. The metal looked sharp.

"Be careful with that. You could cut yourself."

Sam closed his eyes.

Riddle kept pulling on the former spring, which was now a piece of kinky metal. Sam opened his eyes. Riddle was still doing it. Sam was not in shape to fight about anything. He shut his eyes. Riddle sucked in his breath and said:

"Maybe we could catch a fish."

Sam's eyes stayed closed.

"Maybe."

Riddle had tears in his eyes now.

"I don't know how to catch a fish."

Sam opened his eyes.

When Riddle got started on something, even on a good day, it could be tough. The unsprung little metal spring had a curl on the end. Riddle was trying to straighten it. It caught the light. It was pointy. Sharp.

"Put the pen parts away. And take this..."

Sam was still wearing Emily's grandfather's old gold watch. It had survived the fall.

Riddle had always been fascinated by it. He had asked many times if he could take off the back and look inside, but Sam had never allowed it.

Riddle's eyes now widened.

"Can I take it apart? I'll be careful."

Sam didn't even answer. Moving his arm was too painful. The last thing he remembered for the day was feeling Riddle undo the strap.

* * *

Riddle used a piece of the pen to pry open the back of the watch. The working mechanism was a thing of beauty. Just looking at the shiny moving parts calmed him. Now he wanted to disassemble the whole thing. Using the clip from the ballpoint pen, he was able to get the crystal off the front. He carefully placed the glass dome on the pine needles at his side and continued his work.

Overhead, the sun was still strong. Riddle needed a drink. He got up to his feet and, using his shoe, scooped up some of the river. When he came back, water was still dripping from his chin. A drop fell on the glass crystal front of the watch.

And then, while Riddle continued to analyze the intricate

gold timepiece, the sun hit the drop of water on the curved glass. The intense light turned a tiny spot into a powerful hot point.

One of the pine needles, dry tinder at just the right angle, began to burn. Riddle smelled it before he saw it.

But it didn't take long for him to realize he'd stumbled, accidentally, upon greatness: fire.

*   *   *

Sam opened his eyes and as they adjusted to the darkness he saw Riddle's face, bathed in the orange light of flames. He was in hell.

"No...!"

Riddle was positively euphoric.

"I made a fire. With the glass from the watch. Now we'll be warm. And we can cook food! But we don't have food. But I can find us food. I promise. Because now we have fire."

*   *   *

The next day they ate more of the white, crunchy cattail stalks and drank more of the icy water.

But when Riddle, looking for distraction and comfort, took the parts of the pen out of his pocket, Sam again saw the uncoiled spring. And the piece of wire, he now realized, held the makings of a hook.

Riddle understood how things worked. He'd spent his life

drawing mechanical parts. So he listened to his brother. He broke off a switch from a birch tree. He then peeled off the bark into long strips. He attached the metal clip of the pen to the bark, braiding the green bark together until it was strong.

Along the icy riverbanks, the soil was dark and rich. Riddle did what he was told and dug in the ground, finding plump, purplish pink earthworms. He carefully worked the metal spring through the body of a struggling earthworm and then fastened it to the pen clip.

It took him most of the day, but sitting on a rock next to the water, Riddle finally caught a two-pound rainbow trout. It flopped on the shore, furious to have swallowed a dead worm with a devastating secret.

Riddle picked up a rock and slammed it down on the fish's head, ending its life.

He stared at the glistening trout. It was beautiful. Riddle felt an ache run through his entire body, until he realized that, for the first time in three days, he and his brother would go to sleep with a full meal.

Riddle went to check on Sam, who was sleeping. His arm, twisted in a funny way because of his broken shoulder, lay at a strange angle.

Sam had let the fire go out.

Riddle couldn't get mad.

He'd been gone for hours, and Sam was barely mobile. So Riddle put the fish down and climbed the hillside.

He'd discovered that the sticks he threw on the fire that had sticky ends burned best. So now Riddle carefully examined the gnarly pine trees and found what he was looking for: a large ball of amber tree sap.

Riddle used a rock to chip away a fist-size glob, and then he returned to the river. He picked an area in full sun, close to where he'd built the brush enclosure. He then held the glass front of Sam's watch at an angle in the light, aimed at a corner of the sap.

Riddle had focus. To a fault. He'd learned long ago to find his own reality. He was wired that way. And in doing that, he was patient. He had waited for ten years for a mother. He was still waiting. So he could wait for a hot spot of refracted light.

It took fourteen minutes.

The sap bubbled, and then smoke finally rose in a single wisp.

Riddle fed it carefully, like he was tending a baby animal, coaxing it along. He added tiny bits of dry, dead wood, then larger sticks.

And an hour later, he had a roaring fire and was roasting his fresh-caught rainbow trout.

26

Everyone loved Emily's haircut.

She had done it not as an act of defiance but as an act of solidarity. It had turned into an act of redefinition.

The old Emily was gone.

And this new Emily felt, with every passing day, her disappointment growing. No matter where Sam was, no matter what had happened, she believed he could figure out a way to call, even if only to say that he was never coming back, that his life had complexity that she could never understand.

But he didn't.

Not calling was a form of communication in its own right. She began to believe that his silence was his way of definitely telling her that they weren't returning. Because Sam and Riddle's father was some kind of criminal, and maybe Sam was some kind of criminal, too.

Emily was coming to believe that everyone made choices. Sam was making his. If he called and asked for help, she would have been there. Her whole family would have been there. She'd seen her mother's face at night, worrying about Riddle and Sam, but these boys weren't little children.

One of them was a young man.

As the shock of their disappearance gave way to the guilt that she hadn't known their real circumstances, the pain of that was now turning into resentment and then loneliness. Which was why she said yes when Bobby Ellis asked her if she wanted to go with his family to the country club for Sunday dinner.

She'd been to the club once before, but that was just to swim at Anneke Reeves's birthday party. She'd never been in the dining room or on the terrace that overlooked the golf course, where they served drinks and little plates of bite-size finger food before mealtime.

But it wasn't like she'd ever wanted to go.

Emily had never even given it a thought. Her parents didn't run their own businesses or have companies with their names in the titles.

So when Bobby Ellis said that the last Sunday of every month was the club's all-you-can-eat seafood buffet, and that his parents always went and that he could bring a guest, she said yes.

But she didn't want it to be like they were going out, or hooking up, or were some kind of special friends, because they weren't.

She told herself that over and over again.

Going to the Viewpoint Country Club didn't mean

anything. It just meant that she had to wear a dress, and it had to have sleeves, not spaghetti straps, and she had to wear shoes that weren't open-toed.

She'd never heard of rules like that when it came to a place to eat.

But Bobby Ellis had explained that he had to wear a shirt with a collar as well as the jacket from a suit. And all men had to always wear socks with their shoes in the dining room.

Emily thought that the men-wearing-socks rule was funny.

If she wore her running shoes without socks for a few hours, they smelled as bad as her brother's stinky high-tops. But maybe at the country club, they didn't realize that.

And she wasn't going to wear her running shoes, so no one should worry.

* * *

Bobby Ellis didn't even like seafood.

But people went crazy for the towers of plump pink shrimp and the mountain of cracked crab at the country club Sunday buffet. It seemed to Bobby Ellis to be unsanitary.

All those stubby fingers reaching in and grabbing at things. There were large trays of smoked salmon and gooey shucked oysters. There were buckets of gray clams and greenish blue mussels flown in from another continent.

There was herring, which looked to Bobby like sliced-up filleted garden snakes lying in a creamy white pool of smelly sauce. And even though they flooded all the tables with garlic bread, to him the whole place still reeked like a bait shop.

But just as he did with almost everything in his life, Bobby Ellis hid his true feelings and imitated the general mood of the crowd. So when they walked through the double doors with the beveled glass windows that had VCC etched on the front, Bobby turned to Emily and said in an intimate whisper:

"They used to have lobster tails, but they've cut back because of the economy."

Emily didn't remember ever eating a lobster tail, unless you counted the deep-fried langostino bites that she'd once had at Long John Silver's. But those tasted just like breaded shrimp and didn't seem like anything fancy.

Bobby's mother, Barb, sighed.

"I loved those lobster tails...."

She seemed to really mean it, because a kind of deep sadness filled her face, which had a smooth finish, owing to her heavy application of liquid foundation. Bobby found himself feeling bad for her, on account of both her makeup choice and the lobster.

Inside, the Ellis family (plus Guest) was directed to a table next to the windows. Bobby explained that, during the day, this was a great table because you could see the seventh green.

Emily stared outside and saw only pitch black.

A waiter came to take their drink order, and Bobby's parents both had martinis straight up with extra, extra olives. Bobby had a Diet Coke. And Emily ordered lemonade.

The drinks came with plastic stirring sticks that each said

VCC in gold letters on a shield the size of a postage stamp that topped the tip. Bobby had never noticed the stirring sticks before, and it was only when Emily pointed them out that he wondered how he could have missed them once a week for his entire life.

Bobby hoped that ordering a Diet Coke didn't make him seem like a girl, but he was used to the taste and liked it better than regular Coke. After the waiter brought their drinks, Bobby's parents started asking Emily questions. Bobby was cringing inside, even though on the outside he kept his usual, friendly expression on his face.

He knew that his father and mother couldn't help it. They were a lawyer and a detective. Interrogation was their game. In their world, it substituted for all dialogue and small talk.

Since he was small, Bobby Ellis had learned to answer a question with whatever people most wanted to hear. It had a way of stopping them. But Emily didn't know this trick, and her answers only opened up all kinds of new inquiries.

Barb Ellis finished her second martini with extra, extra olives, and the group got up to get their buffet plates.

Bobby didn't go because he'd ordered a chopped Salisbury steak with extra mushroom sauce from the regular menu.

He was the only one in the large dining room eating beef.

*   *   *

Emily was surprised at how much food everyone was taking.

Most people had at least a dozen jumbo shrimp and then

equally big portions of all the other seafood crowding their overflowing plates.

There was a long line at the cracked crab mound, so Emily bypassed it altogether.

Unlike at a regular restaurant, these people all seemed to know one another, so they chatted while they dolloped on their cocktail sauce or waited for their turn to pour creamy pink dressing from a silver pitcher over their crab piles.

And while the eager club members were all polite, they struck Emily as too excited about everything. Her eyes moved around the dining room tables. There were little paper skirts covering the bottoms of all the glasses. She hadn't noticed them before. Were they to catch the drips? They were an ecological nightmare.

And then there were the pieces of fabric stretched across the lemon slices and tied with glossy yellow ribbons. Seed catchers? There was a lot of effort going into all this stuff.

But she wouldn't be the one to point that out.

* * *

A bad shrimp can hit anyone anytime.

That's what her mother told her. It didn't mean that they'd done anything wrong at the Viewpoint Country Club.

Emily was fine during dinner. And she felt okay for the first two hours when she got home.

But right at bedtime, her stomach began to stage a revolt. She felt instantly sweaty, and only moments later had her head in the toilet bowl, where it remained for forty minutes. She'd never been sick that bad that fast, at least not that she could remember.

And somehow, in the back of her mind, she felt that she'd betrayed Sam by going out with Bobby Ellis that night, and now she was paying for it.

27

Clarence had been in the cab of the truck for five days.

He'd emptied two brown prescription bottles of stolen codeine cough syrup. He'd drunk all the vodka. He'd eaten the saltine crackers and some rotten string cheese that Riddle had hidden in the glove box. He'd chewed up a whole bottle of aspirin dry, like it was candy, and he'd licked the edges of four empty soda cans until he'd sliced open his tongue.

But he now had to face the facts:

He had a broken truck. And a badly broken leg.

The road down the mountain led to help.

But he couldn't walk down that road.

And his leg now had a massive infection around the exposed bone.

Even Clarence, who knew nothing about medicine, felt that the gangrene moving its pus-black fingers up his body to grip his throat would kill him if he didn't get help.

And then he remembered that he had some woman's

stolen cell phone in the far back. The service would have long been cut off, but hadn't he heard that the phone sent off some kind of signal? If he pressed 911, wouldn't that signal notify someone that there was a person in an emergency?

And then wouldn't the authorities, the people he hated with all his heart and soul and very being, have to come check on that?

Wasn't that some kind of law?

And so, in complete agony, he inched his way over the sticky seat and into the far back. After clawing through boxes of stolen jewelry, credit-card statements he'd lifted from mailboxes for identity theft, old baseball cards, and someone's collection of semiprecious stones, he finally found the phone.

Clarence held it in his twitching palm. Victory.

But when he dialed 911, nothing happened. The battery had long since died.

And then something broke inside the already broken part of his soul, and he began to weep.

It was all so unfair.

All of it.

So…

Unfair.

*　　*　　*

Jim Lofgren was an extreme cyclist.

He routinely rode over one hundred miles in a single day. He'd first gotten the bug after college, when he decided to commute on a bicycle and bought a ten-speed to get around Berkeley. The ten-speed gave way to a better bike, which turned into a racer, and from there it was a lifetime of pedaling.

The more Jim rode, the more he had to be challenged. He'd ridden six hours in heat above 115 degrees. He'd pedaled through rain and even snow across desert floors and up tall peaks.

Part of the reason that he'd stopped living in a city in California and moved to Utah was to give himself access to more demanding rides.

And on this day, Jim loaded his six-thousand-dollar, carbon-body mountain bike on top of his hybrid and headed out to Manti-La Sal National Forest.

It was late spring, and most of the roads heading up into the mountain peaks were still closed off. But Jim was an expert bike rider; and experts know that "closed to the public" doesn't mean closed to them.

Jim turned off the highway onto the service road. Mount Peale loomed in the background. Jim knew the spot where the road widened and where he could tuck his car unnoticed for the day.

By the time he adjusted his helmet and clicked his feet into the pedals, soft, puffy clouds dotted the sky. A gentle breeze made the tops of the trees sway.

It was a perfect day to scale a mountain.

* * *

Riddle and Sam had been by the river for almost a week.

And for nearly every waking moment, Riddle was focused on their survival.

He caught fish, gutted their bellies with the ballpoint pen, and roasted them over the fire. A fire that he had to keep going, with Sam's help, day and night.

During that time, they'd eaten four frogs. Dozens and dozens of cattail stalks. Toasted grasshoppers. They didn't know the names, but they had eaten lady fern fiddleheads, the flower clusters of fairy bells, sweet cicely, wild ginger, and licorice ferns.

Riddle had dug up the tuberous roots of plants in the soft parts of the riverbank and put them in the hot embers of the fire, just as he'd seen Debbie Bell put baked potatoes alongside her barbecue coals.

Riddle brought back everything he could find to Sam, who wouldn't allow them to eat the big bunches of wild oyster mushrooms, which looked like layers of soft babies' ears. Sam rejected the black and yellow morels and the camouflaged king bolete fungus Riddle found growing in a dead cottonwood.

Sam said it was better to be safe than sorry, not knowing that Riddle ate half of the king bolete anyway.

And once Sam realized that the crunchy black nuts were actually beetles, he put an end to that as well.

The days were long for Sam, who was always flat on his back.

The nights were long for Riddle, who stared at the stars

and worried that rain would come, or something worse, before someone would find them.

* * *

Sam had stopped worrying about Clarence appearing out of nowhere with a gun in hand.

And he'd started worrying about how they would ever get out of the forest.

He had hoped that the smoke from their fire would be some kind of signal, but he watched in despair as the swirls of white disappeared as soon as they moved up into the moist, cold mountain air.

They were deep down in a narrow gorge, and unless they burned the place to the ground, it didn't appear that anything visual would ever give them away. And that was assuming that someone was even looking for them, which was a big "if."

Sam's ribs had stopped hurting so much, but his shoulder was a major problem. So he spent most of the week asleep, and even in his unconscious state he was amazed at his little brother.

* * *

Jim Lofgren had seen the chain lying on the ground instead of pulled taut between the cement pillars when he started up the incline into the national forest.

But he didn't think twice about what it meant. And he

had no way of knowing that it was cut, not simply lowered by a ranger.

Jim had been pumping uphill on the gravel road for nearly four and a half hours when he rounded a bend and saw the black truck in the middle of the stream.

The vehicle was at an odd angle, and it was obvious that it was stuck. Jim slowed. The rushing water seemed to have made adjustments to accommodate the wheels, and there was something about the dust on the truck that said to Jim that this all wasn't recent.

Jim slowed to a stop and got off his bike. That's when he saw the shotgun on the side of the road. Jim felt his heart rate, which was slowing down now that he wasn't pumping like a maniac, again increase. Was this a crime scene?

Jim called out:

"Hello…!"

No answer. Jim laid his bike down on the uphill side of the embankment and, stepping cautiously around the gun, continued slowly toward the truck.

"Hello? Anyone there…?"

No answer.

Jim now stood at the edge of the stream. He'd have to wade into the water to get a look inside the vehicle. His shoes had been heated and custom-molded to his feet. They cost a lot of money and, as he stared at the racing water, Jim seriously wondered what he was getting into. Now would be the time to turn back.

The icy stream swirled around his legs as he waded

toward the front door on the driver's side. The windows were rolled up, and the way the harsh light hit the glass made it impossible to see inside.

Jim put his thumb onto the handle and pulled up, half hoping the door would be locked.

But it wasn't.

It opened, and the air trapped inside was released. It was the worst smell Jim had ever encountered. A combination of rotting flesh, urine, spit, and alcohol sent Jim's hand reflexively to cover his nose and mouth. He stepped back into the rushing water, nearly falling over as he saw Clarence's twisted body in the backseat.

And then he heard a raspy voice say:

"What the hell took you so long?"

* * *

Riddle had been up, searching the rocky part of the riverbank for food, and his feet hurt.

He had little cuts and scratches all over his body, and some of these were now puffy red, a starry field of minor infections that stood out on his sunburned skin. Some of the scrapes itched. Riddle rubbed his eyes and looked down at his shoes. They were a problem that he could at least do something about.

His sneakers were caked with dirt and debris. Riddle wore socks, even though they were always wet, because without them the blisters and abrasions couldn't be tolerated.

Now, with the sun overhead in the middle of the afternoon, Riddle allowed himself to stop the endless searching. He had to take off his shoes. He had to free his aching toes.

The first shoe came off easily, but his second shoe required that he work open the tight, waterlogged knot.

But when Riddle got frustrated, his fingers didn't have the dexterity they needed to manipulate the laces. Instead of taking a moment to collect himself, he pulled hard, and the canvas and rubber piece of footwear suddenly came off his heel and flipped up into the air, beyond his grasp, landing in the river.

The shoe bobbed in the cold water and began moving downstream, and Riddle took off on the shoreline after it.

*   *   *

Throwing himself off a cliff had been an impulsive act, but since then he had been methodical. Riddle took careful, deliberate steps as he gathered firewood and tried to find things to eat.

But now, eyes on his traveling shoe, Riddle was reckless.

He did things he would never have done had he not been locked, irrationally, on the shoe. He scrambled over rocks and ripped his way through thickets of brush, all the while gasping for breath, following the beat-up sneaker. He took two big falls, one nearly landing him in the river and one twisting his ankle so severely that he hobbled as he continued to give chase.

And then, after almost a mile of running and scrambling, just when he thought it was all over, when the shoe was too far ahead and disappearing from view, the renegade piece of footwear maneuvered into an undercut, and the chase was over.

*　*　*

Strong currents can erode a riverbank, leaving an overhang of topsoil. Rocks can then get lodged in such a way as to form a kind of trap, and it was here that the shoe stopped running. Riddle had tears in his eyes when he finally reached the undercut. But he did not feel victorious for long. His ankle was now throbbing, and he had used more energy than he actually had.

While he was gasping for breath, his head hung low, something unnaturally red caught his eye. In the snarl of rushes that had grown up on the other side of the undercut, a spot of cherry was peeking out.

He was too curious to let it go. And after a full twenty minutes of arguing with himself, Riddle put the soaking runaway shoe back on his left foot and went farther downstream to investigate.

*　*　*

It was a tandem kayak.

Flipped over, wedged between a rock and the shore, it had

to have been there for a long time, because slimy green algae covered most of the red surface.

It took Riddle almost an hour to untangle the lead rope and dig out the hull. But he was able, finally, to get the boat free. By the time he made it back upriver to Sam, the sun had long set and darkness had closed in.

Despite the pain, Sam pulled himself up when he heard his brother. He'd been eaten alive inside with worry. Riddle had never been away for this long.

It was another surprise. Not only was his little brother safe, he had his biggest catch ever.

Riddle's face, despite his exhaustion, had an expression of wild excitement.

"I found—"

He was sputtering. He could barely breathe.

"I found—a—"

Riddle was wheezing now. It was all too much for him. He opened his mouth and managed to get out:

"A boat."

Sam at first thought he was seeing things when he realized Riddle was pulling the kayak.

Sam could only use his good arm, which was on his weaker left side, to help. But finally, with great effort, he and Riddle were able to drag the boat out of the water and up onto the shore.

And they were rewarded for that effort.

In the hull of the molded red plastic kayak, in the front area tucked in a waterproof plastic case, was a first-aid kit.

Inside were Band-Aids, a small pair of scissors, aspirin,

sunscreen, lip balm, a bar of antibacterial soap, salt pills, a small roll of duct tape, and a pamphlet on emergency aid.

But the greatest treasure was wrapped in tinfoil and tucked underneath the first-aid kit. The jackpot was the discovery of two Snickers bars. The slogan "Hungry? Grab a Snickers" brought tears to their eyes.

The two boys stared at the bounty as if they'd just robbed a convenience store, which had always, in their lives, been a possibility.

This was better than any holiday, any birthday, and any celebration. It was a gift. It was a reward. It was a triumph.

And it was theirs.

* * *

Jim Lofgren carried a cell phone when he rode. He also carried gorp mix, energy gel, peanut butter pretzel nuggets, hard candies, and beef jerky. While Clarence ravaged the sack of food, Jim dialed 911. His call didn't go through. He was too high up to get any reception. So he'd have to head back down the mountain on his bike in order to get help.

It was a huge relief.

The man in the stinking truck freaked him out. It wasn't just that he was on death's doorstep; he was straight out of a horror movie. He was the Crypt Keeper. That was the only way to describe him. Jim knew that if the guy wasn't starving to death, with a rotting leg that looked like it was about to fall off, he would be dangerous. Very dangerous.

The guy had the wrong attitude. Instead of being grateful, he was enraged. He kept swearing and spitting and making impossible demands.

Jim filled one of the vodka bottles he found on the truck floor with water from the stream, dropping in an iodine tablet to kill bacteria or viruses. When the Crypt Keeper took a sip of the water, he spewed it out, as if firing a weapon, straight into Jim's startled face.

"Are you trying to poison me! Did you take a leak in this first? What the hell do you think you're doing?"

Jim tried to explain water sterilization, but it was useless. And so he climbed back on his bike, his own stomach growling now with hunger, and took off down the mountain.

Jim said that he'd be back with help, but as he heard the man sputter more obscenities, he made a decision: he'd let professionals deal with this guy. He never wanted to see him again.

28

In spite of the bad shrimp, Emily felt closer to Bobby Ellis after the night at the country club. He hadn't made a greedy run at the seafood buffet. He hadn't freaked out at his parents when they'd put her on trial at dinner, and most kids would have. And at the end of the night, he'd thanked her as if she'd given him her left kidney.

But at the same time, she felt even more uncomfortable about the situation.

He was easing his way into her life.

If she went outside by the metal picnic tables to study during free period, he found her. If she stayed late after school to talk to a teacher, he was waiting for her at her locker. If she went over to Spumoni's to grab a slice of pizza with friends during lunch, he'd somehow show up minutes later.

It was like he had a computer with her coordinates programmed 24-7. She wasn't sure, but twice, late at night, she'd gone downstairs to get something to drink and she thought that she'd seen his SUV cruise by on the dark street.

And her house wasn't on his way home.

She was thinking what to say, how to get him to back off, but then they were together when she got the Big News.

And that changed everything.

*　*　*

Detective Sanderson hung up the phone and swallowed a mouthful of his cold coffee. He'd taken notes from the call and now his eyes fell on the yellow pad.

A man claiming to be named John Smith had been found in Manti-La Sal National Forest in Utah.

He was in the truck matching the picture Bobby Ellis had taken, which was in the report that the detective had circulated.

The truck also matched the one identified by the officers the week before in Cedar City. The plates had been changed and belonged to a vehicle in Nevada, but positive identification from contents had subsequently been made.

This John Smith, found in Manti-La Sal National Forest, had a counterfeit driver's license in his wallet. Also at the site was a shotgun. Two other illegal firearms were found in his truck with other identified stolen property.

John Smith was currently in the custody of the Utah County sheriff's department and a patient in the Landon

Regional Hospital, where he was recovering from the amputation of his right leg.

Once his condition improved, he would be moved to Andryc Prison to await his arraignment on multiple felony charges.

The suspect had not said anything about children until the second day, when he came out of surgery. After he'd been positively identified by an elderly woman named Mrs. Dairy, and then interrogated by Cedar City officers, he asked for a lawyer. And then he made a statement:

He had done nothing wrong.

There had been an accident.

And his two sons were dead.

* * *

Bobby Ellis had driven Emily home from school after practice. She didn't want him to come in, but when they pulled up to the brick driveway, Bobby's father's car was parked at the curb.

That was alarming.

To both of them.

They quickly went inside and found all four of their parents in the living room. There were empty coffee cups on the table, so they'd been there a while. Debbie Bell's eyes were puffy. Emily stared at her mother. Had she been crying?

Everyone immediately got up, but Tim Bell was the first to say anything.

"We got news from the police department that Sam and

Riddle's father was found in the mountains of a national park in Utah. He's right now in the hospital —"

Emily interrupted:

"And Sam? What about Sam and Riddle?"

Now her mother was talking.

"They weren't with him."

Emily exhaled. This was good news. They'd gotten away from the horrible man.

But none of the adults looked like it was good news. They were all so anxious. And then her father said:

"Both of the boys were with him in the truck when he left Cedar City. He appeared to have abducted them. All of their things were left inside a motel room."

Bobby Ellis was staring at Tim Bell. He was stuck on the word *abduct*. Can you abduct your own kids? Especially when one of them was a teenager? He didn't think that was the right word.

Emily's head swiveled from her father to her mother and then back again.

"Well, what did he *say*? Where did he say they were? What did he *say* happened to them?"

Silence.

Barb Ellis wasn't looking at her son or at Emily. She was looking at the hardwood floor. Her husband was staring at a book on the coffee table. Tim Bell stepped toward his daughter. He opened his mouth but nothing came out.

Debbie Bell, the person in the room who dealt daily with emergencies, now spoke directly to Emily. Her voice was strong, reassuring. Her daughter knew the voice. It was the voice that took care of you when things were very, very bad.

"There is no reason to believe anything the man said. He's a proven liar and a thief, and he's right now still experiencing the effects of heavy medication...."

Debbie Bell took a moment and then continued:

"But he said that there was an accident. He told the police that the boys were standing on the edge of the road up in the mountains. There was a big drop-off. He said that Riddle slipped, and that Sam tried to keep him from falling, and that he went over the cliff with his brother....

"Their father said that he went down after them and broke his own leg. The state is sending out search teams."

Debbie Bell was still in control as she continued:

"It's been a week now since this all happened. But they also know that two shots were fired from a shotgun. It's possible they may not have survived."

*   *   *

Debbie hadn't thought much of Bobby Ellis until that afternoon. He seemed likable enough, but there was something competitive about him that made her uneasy.

And the same thing could be said for his parents.

They were accomplished and impressive, just not the kind of people who would ever be her good friends. She would have been hard-pressed to articulate why, but that's how she felt.

But after they told Emily the news, and after she sank into the sofa and began to cry, the person who seemed to comfort her best was Bobby Ellis. His parents left right away. They felt out of place and uneasy. They assumed Bobby would leave with them, but he didn't.

He stayed, quietly, by Emily on the couch, and just his existence, the reality of his being, was stabilizing.

Debbie decided that the very part of Bobby Ellis's character that was off-putting to her now became reassuring. His disconnected emotions were now a plus. And the simple fact was that the situation had changed. Her daughter needed someone.

And so Debbie Bell was grateful.

*   *   *

Emily wanted to go to Utah, but of course they wouldn't let her. She didn't believe that Sam and Riddle were dead.

No.

It was not possible. She would see Sam and Riddle again. She would find them. They would be back.

The police were wrong. She was right.

It could not be.

She would be with Sam again. She would. Because what was the future if she could not be with him again? She had been telling herself that he was gone and that it was his choice and that it was over.

But she had never believed that.

Not really.

It was just something she had told herself because she knew Sam would be back at some point, maybe not for years, but one day.

Everything was now fuzzy. Everything looked different.

She hadn't seen the stains on the armchair in the living room until then. Were they always there?

Her mother looked like she was getting older. Her eyes. Was she tired or was she aging?

And her father. His hair had gray in it now. When had that happened? Even Felix the dog looked worn-out.

Is that the way it goes?

She drank a glass of water, and it felt different when she swallowed. Not like water. Like pudding. She was drinking pudding, but it was clear. That's why it was so hard to swallow.

And Bobby Ellis was with her. And he was quiet. He was the only one who wasn't talking or touching her. Everyone else kept talking. Or trying to hug her. What were they saying?

They seemed to now be whispering. In other rooms she could hear the muffled voices. They made her little brother go to the neighbor's and he didn't want to go to the neighbor's.

Her father asked if she wanted to call Nora or Katie or Anne or Lucy? Shouldn't she call one of her close friends? Maybe Anneke or Haley or Remi? Wouldn't that help?

Everyone wanted her to eat.

But she wasn't hungry. Why did they want to feed her? They needed her to have a plan.

Bobby Ellis didn't want to eat. He didn't have any kind of plan.

And then her mother wanted her to take a pill. It would put her to sleep. That's what they wanted. They wanted her to go to her room and rest.

She didn't want to rest.

She wanted to go find him.

Outside it got windy. She watched and the trees were moving in all different directions. She didn't remember that happening before. Did they always move like that? Shouldn't the wind blow in one direction? Shouldn't everything move one way?

Even the grass on the lawn was wiggling weird. If you looked carefully, you would see that the little blades of grass trembled. They all felt it blowing cold even though it was now late spring and almost summer and the chill was long gone.

Because now you could put on a sweater and still not feel any heat.

A chill was out there now.

And it was everywhere.

* * *

Bobby had no idea what to do.

He'd never been with someone when they got devastating news. Even when his nana died, they didn't tell him until after the funeral. They said that he was too little to understand, but he was ten years old and he understood very well what it meant to die. Plus he liked his nana. She gave him candy and cupcakes and she knew secrets and shared them. He still felt bad that they hadn't let him be a part of it.

So he had no experience with any of this.

But this bad news was the kind of good news he'd been hoping for. And now that it was here, it was hollow and empty and he felt horrible that he'd ever wished such a thing.

That's why he was so quiet.

He felt guilty inside.

He'd been pretending to help. He'd been pretending that he wanted to find the two boys. Now he was so ashamed.

He'd thought of Sam as *the Enemy*. And that was wrong and maybe somehow this was now partly his fault. You just never knew.

None of this was going the way he'd planned.

And then she said she wanted to go for a walk, and he said he'd go if she wanted him to go, but he was sure she'd say no because she was saying no to everything.

But she said yes and then she put on a heavy coat like it was winter, but it wasn't cold outside. And her parents were so happy that he was there to go walk with her, and it was the first time he felt like Emily's mother might not hate him.

They went out onto the empty sidewalk and the light was low in the sky and night was coming on fast and he didn't know what to say. He couldn't think of anything to say. So he didn't say anything.

And then, at the end of the block, she reached over and

she took his hand and she held on and gripped it hard and suddenly he started to cry.

It was what he wanted for so long, for her to reach out to him and to need him physically. And he couldn't help it.

Tears just showed up in his eyes and spilled out down his cheeks, and he tried to hold on to his breathing and get it under control, but he couldn't.

And he felt so stupid and like such a big baby.

But she didn't see it that way. She wrapped her arms around him when she saw his tears and she held him and she was crying now, too.

But they were crying for different reasons.

29

The boat was just a bad idea.

The whale, as they called Riddle's kayak, was now out of the water and used as one side of the den where they slept. Riddle wanted to ride it down the river to find help. He couldn't stop talking about it.

Sam discussed this idea with himself as he lay on his back, staring up at the trees, which were always moving while he moved as little as possible.

First question: should two people get into a boat and head into rapids when they don't have life jackets? Obvious answer: hell no.

Second question: should two people get into a boat and head into rapids when they don't have life jackets and when one of the two people is terrified of water and when they both can't really swim? He had tried to learn in Mexico. Would it come back to him? Obvious answer: hell no.

Third question: should two people get into a boat and

head into rapids when they don't have life jackets and when one of the two people is terrified of water and when they both can't really swim and when they don't have oars to row the boat? They just had sticks. Long branches, really, that Riddle thought would work. Oh, and one other thing, one of the people probably had broken ribs and a broken shoulder.

Not worth even answering.

And so he told Riddle: no.

They would stay where they were. Someone would come. It was just a matter of time. Maybe it would be another week. They were surviving.

And then they made a mistake.

* * *

If you're asleep for ninety-four days, you wake up hungry. Before you go down, you pack on the weight around the belly, about forty pounds was the way it usually went, and then you find a hollow log or a small cave and you call it a night.

But that night ends up being about three months. And by the time spring rolls around, you'd eat dirt if it had some ants or worms for seasoning. So it takes a few months to settle down when it comes to food.

Now there are roads and power lines out there, and they lead to all the places you can't go.

The people places.

But despite all of the things they've built, and all the land they've taken over, we're still standing in thirty-eight states.

All ten Canadian provinces. And even a lot of parts of Mexico.

Being a bear is a commitment. Not just to loving fresh fish and wild berries.

Every year there are people who take shots. Every year we're run over by cars and trucks and even trains. We're poisoned. Trapped. Attacked in all kinds of ways, really.

And every year, one of us strikes back. And that's bad for all of us, because there is the issue of reputation. In order to get respect, it's better to be dangerous but not deadly.

But some things can't be helped.

They call it mauling. What we do.

Most of the time, when this happens, it's because we are surprised. We're caught off guard. We're scared, really. And if you weigh three hundred pounds and have forty-two razor-like teeth, claws with sharp points, and a temper, stuff happens.

Sometimes, when things really go wrong, there can be some eating after the mauling. A leg or an arm. If the situation presents itself. Because, if no one is fighting back, the buffet table is basically open.

But again, not a first choice.

We love sweets. That's often the downfall. We'd walk ten miles for honey.

And we'd find it, because we can smell it.

That's how we find each other. And that's how we find the good stuff.

And that's how the two boys were found.

*   *   *

After they had eaten, Riddle would take the fish bones or the leftover bits of the greens, if there were any, and throw them into the river. He did this because little black flies and armies of ants would appear out of nowhere, hungry for any remains.

But after they'd eaten the chocolate bars that they'd found wrapped in tinfoil in the front of the kayak, Riddle kept the candy wrappings. They were a connection to the outside world. And they still smelled sweet.

But to a black bear, fresh from winter hibernation, the chocolaty aroma of the paper wrappings was something that, when the wind was blowing correctly, could be smelled for a quarter of a mile.

It was dawn. The sun had not yet cleared the rim of the mountain due east. Riddle got up twice in the middle of the night to throw wood on the smoldering embers, so he knew that the fire would still be going.

He took the old candy wrapper out of his pocket and inhaled. It comforted him. In the morning, everything was so quiet. There was only the rushing water and the sunrise chill. Even most of the birds were still asleep.

Riddle lay on his back for twenty minutes, thinking about how cold his feet got in the middle of the night, and then he heard what he assumed were the cracks and pops of the burning wood on the fire.

But these sounded different.

265

Sam, at his side, was still asleep. Riddle did not want to disturb him. He held his breath and listened.

More snaps. More cracks. Not the fire, he decided. Something else. Something taking steps?

And then he heard breathing. Not his breathing, because he wasn't breathing now.

Riddle pushed off the pine needles and the ferns and the branches that they used to cover their bodies and he slowly pulled himself to a sitting position.

He could now see over the kayak, which was turned on its side as the barrier between them and the world.

And there, right there, only ten feet away, staring straight at him, was a mature male black bear.

Riddle was startled. And the bear was startled. Riddle sucked in his breath in a high-pitched gulp, and Sam's eyes opened at the sound.

The bear then reared up onto his back legs, standing now over six feet tall. He held his head high, and his nostrils flared as he took in Riddle's and Sam's scent.

Sam could now see the bear. And the bear could now see Sam.

Would he maul them? Would he sink his teeth into the tops of their skulls, puncturing their brains and causing instant death?

Riddle didn't move.

He stayed looking right at the bear, but not a muscle flinched. They remained that way, the bear on his hind legs, towering over them, and the two boys, staring back in horror.

Any normal kid would have collapsed in fear.

But not Riddle.

He was afraid, but he was also in awe. And he was so close that he could smell the bear's warm, sour breath.

The bear opened his mouth wider and began to blow air at the same time that he clacked his teeth together. It was a show of something. His teeth, shiny with his thick saliva, glistened.

After several moments of this explosive blowing and jaw rattling, the bear lowered his body to the ground and slammed the dirt hard with his front right paw. It left a perfect imprint.

And then, having delivered his warning, he turned and ran into the underbrush.

*　　*　　*

The bear is what changed Sam's mind.

He decided that he'd rather die in the freezing water than from a bear ripping him to pieces. He was now ready to try the kayak, because it would be impossible for him to sleep knowing that the bear was out there.

Sam didn't realize the candy wrappers were in Riddle's pocket. And Riddle didn't know that they were what the bear wanted. They both didn't know that the bear had no interest in them. The panting and paw thump had been a bluff.

But they assumed the worst.

And so they made a decision. They would get in the red boat.

They would try to make it down the roaring river.

* * *

Riddle used the duct tape found in the first-aid kit and wrapped two sticks across Sam's back. The emergency pamphlet in the kayak said that a broken bone should be stabilized. It was going to be a rough ride. When he was done, Sam looked like a scarecrow.

The boys stuffed handfuls of green acorns into their pockets to chew when they got hungry. Riddle poured water on the fire that he and Sam had struggled relentlessly to keep going. They put sunscreen from the first-aid kit on their already sunburned faces. They coated their lips with waxy lip balm, and Sam took four aspirin to help dull the pain of his shoulder. And then very carefully, using Riddle's help, Sam got into the kayak.

Riddle had branches from an aspen tree to use as oars, but they were more like ineffectual brakes that he held in the water. Climbing into the back, Riddle pushed the kayak away from shore, and they began their journey down the river.

* * *

I have seen people in boats, and they do not look afraid.
But maybe they can swim.
We cannot swim.
Can bears swim?
Sam cannot help with the boat.

Sam is afraid.
I am afraid.
It is a ride.
It is a wild ride.
It is a wild ride in our red boat for someone to find us.

*   *   *

The Utah County Sheriff Search and Rescue dogs verified that both of the boys had been on the road where the truck was found. And the two dogs followed the scent from the log on the uphill part of the road to the sheer drop-off on the edge.

A person couldn't see many clues as to what happened. But to the scent hounds, it was clear: the boys had disappeared over the cliff.

Using global positioning to mark and map, the three search teams looked for a way to descend, with the dogs, down the steep terrain toward the river.

It took a full day for the lead search-and-rescue team to get halfway down the incline. Working with ropes and climbing gear, with the dogs lowered in harnesses, the team checked the sharp rocks, searching the layers of ledges and indentations. It wasn't until the afternoon of the second day that both hounds again picked up a scent.

Once the dogs located where Sam had first landed, the team radioed back for more support. It wasn't long before they tracked Riddle's scent as well. They now knew that the boys had been at the bottom of the ravine.

They were putting the puzzle together.

* * *

Timing is everything.

And Sam and Riddle left their place at the river just hours before the search-and-rescue team arrived.

If Riddle's shoe hadn't come off, if the kayak hadn't been discovered in the rushes, and if the bear hadn't smelled the candy wrappers, they would have been sitting by their fire waiting to be found.

Instead they were hurtling down an icy river.

* * *

The rescue teams had no way of knowing about a kayak.

What they discovered was evidence that the boys had been, for some time, camped at the river's edge. They found the trampled area where they had slept and the still-warm fire pit.

They also, at a distance, found bear tracks and bear scat.

Had a bear scared the boys into the water?

The dogs found no scent of the boys past a two-mile radius from their encampment.

If the boys had gone into the river, they would have drowned. Had one fallen in and the other gone to rescue him? A water team, with wet suits and scuba gear, was brought in to search the river in the area where the boys had camped.

They found nothing.

Junie and Faith, the two UCSSAR dogs, sat at the river's edge where the kayak had been launched and whimpered, driving everyone crazy. The dogs could smell what the people could not. And they were trying to say:

They were in a boat. That's what happened.

But no one would listen.

30

On the night that they'd received the bad news, Bobby Ellis and Emily fell asleep on the couch in the living room.

Emily was coiled in a ball in the corner like a cold puppy. Bobby's over-six-foot body was stretched out long, like someone who was accustomed to a king-size bed and didn't know when he wasn't in one.

Debbie covered them both with quilts and then called Bobby's parents and said that she'd like to just let them rest. Barb Ellis said she understood, but she really didn't. The Bells were nice enough, but the whole family seemed sort of artsy to her.

That was the only way that she could think to describe it. There was too much stuff in their house. Too many paintings on the walls, too many little ethnic knickknacks that, to her eye, should have been sold at a garage sale.

And there were so many books everywhere. They needed to get more bookshelves or, better yet, start using the public library.

Barb had wall-to-wall, ultra-plush taupe carpeting at her

house, and it wasn't just that she liked the look; she knew that things were clean. Which was part of the reason they didn't have any pets.

Bobby was allergic, but even if he weren't, she wouldn't want animals in her house. She liked them in zoos and in trees and from a distance, like when she could see the squirrels on her neighbor's lawn fighting.

But the Bells had that overly friendly, fat dog. And then the two paranoid-looking cats. And they had plants inside their house, which was another thing Barb didn't like. It was dirt in pots on the inside. And bugs lived in dirt, and when you watered plants that were inside a house, you ran the risk of the water getting on the floor or the carpet. That was just a fact.

Barb liked cut flowers. But she didn't like mixed arrangements. She liked everything to be the same color. Like all white, which appealed to her sense of order and hygiene.

And she liked flowers with super-long stems, because that just said right away that they didn't come from your own yard.

It said that these flowers were purchased and someone cares enough to do that, because they care about things like having fresh flowers in her house.

And that was important.

*　*　*

After that night, Bobby was Emily's shadow. They went everywhere together.

They did their homework, usually in the Bells' living

room, and a lot of time with ESPN *SportsCenter* on the TV, because that's how Bobby did it at home.

After a week of this, Bobby asked her to go with him to the junior/senior prom and she just shrugged.

That night, before he left, he kissed her on the lawn chair in the backyard. He got his hand under her shirt and he was in heaven. She barely noticed.

* * *

The way to make the pain go away was to put your mind somewhere else. You let your mind leave and float above you, where it could watch you.

So now there were two of you.

Always.

And then the two Emilys did what was expected, which is what you have to do because you need everyone to leave you alone.

You don't think about the future, because it doesn't matter anymore, and you never, ever think about the past, because it is gone. And thinking about what is gone is the pain.

You try to smile, but it feels really fake, but you are a fake now so that isn't a problem. What is a problem is how trivial everything is. The things that get people anxious or upset are not worth anyone's time.

But they can't see that.

So while the world around you obsesses over all the wrong things, you know the secret. You know that there are things that matter, and then there is everything else.

And what matters to you, besides your mother and your father and your little brother and your dog and your two new cats and your nana and your pop-pop and your best friend, is him and his brother.

But now Sam and Riddle are gone. Really gone.

Get used to it.

Or at least pretend to everyone that you are.

*　*　*

Clarence's right leg was amputated above the knee.

And on the first day after the operation, he experienced what half of the people who have lost a limb feel for the rest of their lives: phantom pain. He had an excruciating ache coming from where his foot, which was no longer there, would have been.

It felt like someone was hammering nails into his toes.

The feeling started with the uncontrollable urge, in the middle of the night, to scratch his foot.

And it got a lot worse from there.

By morning, the nurses were doubling up his pain meds and calling the attending physician for help. Clarence, bleary-eyed but filled with rage, demanded that they cut off his foot. When they tried to explain that they already had, he did more than lash out with his mouth. He swung his fists, upending the table by his bed and sending his IV stand crashing to the floor.

By the afternoon, after he'd bitten a nurse in the forearm, he had been put in a restraining device. By evening, the chief of staff had signed orders to have him moved to another facility.

An ambulance came the following morning and transported Clarence, known on his paperwork as Clarence Border/Also Known As John Smith, to the Brimway Medical Clinic, which was run by the state.

That afternoon, Howie P. McKinnon, wearing a dark green suit, paid his first visit to see Clarence. When Howie came into the room, Clarence took one look at him and said:

"Whatever you're selling, I ain't buying. So piss off."

Howie stood immobilized several feet from the bed, wrestling with how to shake hands with someone in a straitjacket.

Howie was only four years out of law school, and only two years from having passed the bar exam, which he'd taken three times. And thus far into the game, his public-defender work had consisted of mostly Driving-Under-the-Influence cases, which he had roundly lost. His only defense for these cases being that the state's Breathalyzer was defective.

Howie could usually get one or two jurors somewhat interested in the antiestablishment-conspiracy defense, but the people he represented looked like habitual drunks, so his perfect record of never winning a case had stayed intact.

Howie cleared his throat and took a half step deeper into the room.

"Mr. B-border, my name is Howie P. McKinnon, and I'm g-g-g-oing to be representing you."

Clarence squinted at him.

"My name is John Smith."

Howie looked down at the paperwork and managed to mumble:

"Yes, Mr. S-smith . . ."

Clarence suddenly roared:

"I want to sue. They cut off my damn leg."

Howie nodded as Clarence continued shouting. Spit was flying from his mouth.

"And if it wasn't bad enough, they butchered the job, because I can still feel my foot!"

Howie was now edging back toward the doorway. Clarence had a thought and while still glaring lowered his voice.

"I need a cigarette."

Howie stuttered:

"S-smoking's n-not allowed in h-here."

Clarence shot Howie a look of complete disdain.

"You think I don't know that? What do you take me for, a moron?"

Howie didn't say anything. Clarence continued:

"The next time you come see me, you bring a carton of cigarettes or don't come at all. And ask for a wheelchair. You can push me outside."

Howie found himself nodding again. There was something about Clarence Border/John Smith that demanded you listen. Clarence held his gaze.

"And another thing, whatever they said I did — well, I didn't do it. Write that down, pickle-pants. I didn't do it."

And Howie obediently took out a pen.

*   *   *

The report filed by the sheriff's department listed drowning as the probable cause of death. A river alert was posted in two counties, and a story appeared on the television news in most of Utah explaining that two boys were presumed to have lost their lives after surviving alone in the woods for almost two weeks.

Their bodies were still waiting to be recovered.

Detective Sanderson took the sheriff's call from Cedar City and then wrote an e-mail but didn't send it. He decided to go see the Bell family on his way home and tell them himself. He liked Tim Bell, and he knew that this was hard on them. But his experience told him that having some kind of closure would mean the beginning of healing.

The detective looked down into his file. It had been over a month now since the kids had disappeared. It was actually surprising that it was all wrapped up in that time. Often cases like this went completely unanswered. But he'd still feel better when the boys' bodies were found.

The detective didn't go into the Bell house. He explained it all to Tim Bell on the front porch. The official search was now over. Divers had done a thorough exploration of the river as well as the entire surrounding area where the boys had camped, and they had found nothing.

But the conclusion was undeniable. The boys had gone into the water. The temperature of the river, which was in the forties, would have led to hypothermia after exposure of less than an hour.

You don't survive that.

31

It was like nothing Sam and Riddle could have imagined.

With only the branches to drag, they had no real control in the water. The vessel was at the mercy of the river; its currents and obstacles turned the red plastic kayak into a play toy.

They were constantly spinning, so that one minute Riddle was in the front, trying to hold the big branches, and then moments later the kayak would be kicked forward and Sam would find himself heading down the rapids in the bow of the boat.

It didn't take long for both of the branches to be sucked into the swirling current and then they were completely at nature's mercy. For Sam, with his throbbing shoulder, it was double hell.

Every move caused new stabs of pain, until after an hour of what could have been a ride on a bucking bronco with a chain saw in his ribs, something seemed to give way inside his body.

It was a kind of physical shock brought on by the cold water, the constant motion, and the sounds of Riddle yelping. Once the river turned into a series of rapids, his little brother was like a chained-up dog being beaten. He couldn't escape, and he couldn't keep quiet.

Now he was on a roller coaster that was also a freezing waterwheel, and his answer was to growl and whimper and cry. So while Sam gritted his teeth, wincing with pain, certain that any moment he'd black out and fall overboard, hoping that he'd drown as quickly and painlessly as possible, Riddle was gasping for air, putting up an audible fight.

And then, after three and a half hours of riding the river like a cork in a washing machine, the terrain changed, the waterway narrowed, and abruptly the current slowed.

It was a miracle. They'd never tipped over.

They'd traveled twelve miles. And they were at a much lower elevation. There were now smooth rock formations on either side of the waterway. Tall, rust-colored walls of stone lined the river, which had turned lazy and slow. The sun was out and it reflected off the flat surfaces and began to dry their soaked clothing.

Riddle stopped screaming. And Sam stopped thinking about dying.

And they both were moved by the intensity of the world around them. Overhead an eagle soared, checking them out as it circled.

Riddle finally said his first sentence that didn't include the word *help*:

"I peed my pants."

*　*　*

An hour later, the stone canyon had again given way to a new terrain, and the river had again changed character. The current was picking up, and the rush of the water echoed, making a new kind of roar. The horror show was returning.

Riddle shouted to Sam:

"I'm done."

Sam knew what he meant. He felt done, too. But he answered:

"We'll find someone...."

It made sense when he said it. But hearing the words wasn't very comforting. Riddle said again simply:

"I'm done."

Sam turned his head slightly to get a better look at his brother, and then the flow changed and the kayak swung around for the thousandth time and Riddle was now in front and Sam was in back, except that they were on an angle, not moving straight down the river.

But the roar was now getting louder. Sam wondered if the sound was in his head. But then Riddle said:

"I hear cars."

Sam tried to listen. Is that what it was? A highway? Could they have come that far? It was too much to even hope for.

Riddle was now completely still, intently listening.

Sam, despite the pain in his shoulder and his neck and his back and his legs, twisted at the waist to get a better take on the situation. It certainly seemed as if they were in a very remote area.

But the highway sound was even louder now. Riddle was getting agitated.

"Sam—I hear the cars! I hear them!"

Riddle twisted his body in all directions, and the kayak swayed with him. Sam shouted:

"Riddle, stop that. Stop moving!"

Riddle tried to be still, but he was wide-eyed now. The highway was getting closer. Maybe they would go under an overpass. Maybe they could wave their arms. Wouldn't people see them? Wouldn't people understand that they were in trouble?

Some of the sunscreen that they'd put on hours earlier was now melting off Riddle's forehead and into his right eye. He wiped his eye and made it all worse. He suddenly felt intense stinging.

Riddle leaned over into the water and cupped his hand and splashed his face. The kayak wobbled. Sam didn't understand.

"Riddle, I said stop that!"

"My eye hurts. Maybe from the sunscreen."

Sam snapped at him:

"Forget your damn eye!"

He shouldn't have said it that way. He didn't mean to say it that way.

They were caught up in the moment, in the kayak, both exhausted. Both hungry. Both not really able to pay attention to what was happening on the river, and both not able to do anything about it, even if they had been paying attention. Their drama now involved shouting at each other not to rock the boat.

And only seven seconds later, the rush of the phantom highway revealed itself to be a waterfall, and the two boys and the kayak went straight over.

*　*　*

It was a thirty-one-foot drop, which was like going off the roof of a three-story building. They were on an angle when they slid right over the lip of the river, the bottom of the kayak scraping suddenly on a large rock like a car not clearing a curb.

They both screamed. Like crazed animals, was Sam's thought as the sounds came out of their mouths.

But the river pulled, the rock held, and the kayak flipped. And then the two boys were suddenly airborne as they traveled with the red kayak and the icy water. They hit the river below right with the main flow. The now-empty kayak knifed into the white water and then shot up as if fired from a cannon.

Both boys sank like stones, pounded from above by the black hammer of the wall of falling water. The weight on their bodies was enormous, when suddenly the twists and turns of the sucking snake that was the current shifted direction. A new thrust of motion pushed them upward, and moments later they were both spit back to the surface.

The crimson kayak suffered a worse fate, slamming down on a sharp rock and splitting in two as if cleaved by a giant ax. The two pieces swirled in circles, and the front section promptly took on water and sank. The back piece rode downstream in a spinning fury and disappeared.

The two boys, pushed to the surface as the aerated water churned against their bodies, found that it didn't matter that they couldn't swim. There was no swimming in this situation. There was only the icy hand of fate.

And here it pulled them apart to follow their own destinies.

The last thing Sam remembered Riddle saying was "My eye hurts." And the last thing he remembered saying to Riddle was to "forget your damn eye."

He heard himself saying it now again as the black water filled his nose and pushed the air out of his lungs.

Forget your damn eye.

For, where he was now, only the blind could really see.

* * *

People die every day in rivers.

They die wearing life vests, after years and years of water experience. They die surrounded by boats and onlookers and first aid at their fingertips. They die when they have done everything right in the big book of water safety.

And people live who had done everything wrong.

Sam and Riddle went in opposite directions, thrown to different sides of the river.

Riddle was on the right. His body, semiconscious, bobbed along on the surface. Air pockets inflated his shirt at the shoulders and kept his torso from sinking. Smaller and more compact, he moved at twice the speed of his lanky brother.

Sam was on the left, rolling like a piece of trash. The sticks and the tape that Riddle had put on to stabilize his shoulder were carried off his body like paper products.

The roiling water took the two boys swiftly away from the waterfall and swiftly away from each other. As they tumbled, pulled by the current like rag dolls, their body temperatures rapidly began to fall. Their circulation responded by slowing and, within a matter of only seconds, simple movement was becoming no longer possible.

Everything inside was closing down.

Because it wasn't that you didn't want to swim. It wasn't that you didn't try to paddle. Your body no longer took any direction. It had been thrown in ice water, and all that was communicated to nerve endings was pull in, pull back, exhibit full retreat.

And then Sam's head hit something. Hard. An old tree along the shore had fallen during a flash flood when the water rose and the banks were swollen. The roots had given way and the tree had gone down. A sinker.

The tree now lay partly on the shore and partly in the river. Sam's hand opened, out of instinct, not with any sense of purpose, and it closed on one of the slimy branches. And suddenly, out of nowhere, Sam had a way to make it onto the shore.

Minutes later, he lay on the rocks and mud of the riverbank, feeling a kind of relief that he'd never known. It had stopped, the agony of the motion, the spinning icy world that was pulling him down into the blackness of forever.

And he made a vow to himself that if he survived, he'd never get in a boat again. For the rest of his life.

Just the idea made him feel better. And then his mind, his ability to form conscious thought, turned off.

Done.

He shut his eyes and gave in to the now blinding light and the emptiness of all that was behind him.

I'm done. He now heard Riddle's voice echo.

He answered back:

"I'm done, too."

*   *   *

Riddle, puffed up with air that had lodged into the shoulders of his shirt, was moving feetfirst, riding downstream on his back like a stubby, bobbing pencil. He continued that way, his body frozen from both trauma and fear and an inability to get a decent breath.

And then he hit an eddy that abruptly spun him in circles. His pants twisted around his body, tangling with his legs, cutting off the blood in his ever-stiffening limbs.

The only movement Riddle could make was to use the thumb on his left hand to pop open the top of his old jeans. They were immediately stripped off his legs with his shoes. But the pants and shoes pulling away did something else. It spun Riddle on an extreme angle, heading for the riverbank and, miraculously, seconds later he found himself grabbing at the sandy shoreline, pulling himself up out of the icy water.

Two minutes later, one hundred and twenty more seconds, and Riddle would have been dead. His pulse had slowed. His body temperature had been falling fast, and he was slipping below the surface. He was two minutes from being done. But he was taken out before he was cooked. Or, in this case, before he was frozen.

In just his underwear and his shirt and socks, he moved up onto the rocks and put his head between his knees, throwing up what felt like buckets of brown river water.

The world was spinning.

After what seemed like an eternity, he lifted his head and stared at the river.

Where is Sam?

My Sam.

Sam.

Where is my brother?

He watched every curl of the water for Sam to emerge, popping up out of the frothy sauce that flowed in front of him.

But Sam did not appear.

Riddle waited and waited, shivering as his teeth clattered and his legs shook. It was clear. Sam was gone. Riddle thought about throwing himself back in and joining his brother in the black cold that was the liquid executioner, but he couldn't.

It wasn't that dying made him afraid, but the instinct for survival was strong.

And Riddle had it.

32

Emily remembered Sam saying that he'd taught himself to swim in Mexico.

So even when they explained to her that no one would survive in cold water like what was in the Manti-La Sal National Forest, she would not believe them. He'd left in April and in a week it would be June, and the latest news from the sheriff's department in Utah was meant to be some kind of closure.

At least that's what they were all telling her.

But she didn't want closure. She didn't believe in closure. She didn't accept closure.

The authorities had recovered personal possessions from the truck and from the Liberty Motel room, and Emily wanted something that had belonged to Sam and to Riddle, but she wasn't a relative, so it was not seen as a reasonable request.

Detective Sanderson had contacted the sheriff's office in

Cedar City, which was a back-channel way to see if they could do anything.

Clarence had been moved from a state hospital to a clinic and then to a physical rehab facility, where he was to learn to use his artificial leg before going to prison to await his trial. He had been asked, through his attorney, Howie P. McKinnon, if Emily could have one of Riddle's phone books and Sam's red shirt.

Clarence had answered no.

Or more accurately, "Hell no."

And then Clarence told the authorities that he wanted his kids' possessions thrown away. Instead they were all sealed for use as possible evidence in the upcoming trial against him.

While he was in physical rehab, most of the details of Clarence Border and his two sons, Sam and Rudolph Border, were documented. The boys' abduction from Montana a decade earlier was now public record. Sanderson had matched the kids after painstakingly reviewing hundreds of missing person's files in ten states. And Clarence Border was now being investigated for crimes all over the United States. As Detective Sanderson saw it, it was highly doubtful, when all was said and done, that Clarence Border would ever in his lifetime see the world outside of prison.

Detective Sanderson sent an e-mail to Tim Bell with the information that the two boys' mother, Shelly Thayer Border, had died many years ago after being struck by a car.

Tim Bell read the e-mail over the phone to his wife, and

Debbie Bell went outside and sat in the garden that night until long after it was dark. She put her head down on the picnic table and, certain that no one could see her, allowed herself to cry, not just for the two boys but for the first woman who had lost them.

*　*　*

People at Churchill High School had all heard some account of what had happened.

Emily Bell had been seeing a guy whose father was a total criminal and had taken him hostage, and the kid had died in Utah trying to escape.

That was the headline, but all kinds of things had been added to and subtracted from the story.

Bobby Ellis figured into the narrative because he had information that had led to the arrest of the fugitive father.

That's why Emily and Bobby were so close now.

And that's why Emily Bell didn't hang out now with her friends and kept to herself.

The girls on the soccer team had seen the guy, so they considered themselves more knowledgeable about the whole thing, even if that meant making up details.

Cate Rocce had seen him at church months ago, and she said she knew right away that something was deeply wrong in his life and she had wanted to help. She now claimed that she'd spoken to him that day and that he was a totally cool guy. She said if she hadn't been going out with Emerson Chapman, she would have hooked up with him for sure.

Teachers at Churchill had been sent an e-mail explaining that the community had been part of a tragedy.

By the community, they meant Emily Bell and Bobby Ellis, but the school counselor, Mrs. Beister, found herself inundated by kids who wanted to come in during school to talk, if for no other reason than to get more details and maybe an excuse to miss gym class.

And then, after a week, Taylor Perry crashed her car late at night while coming home from a party where kids were drinking vodka mixed with Gatorade. Taylor got her license taken away and was sent to live with her father in Arizona, and the spotlight shifted.

From Taylor's car crash, everyone moved on to the final social event of the year: the junior/senior prom.

* * *

Emily had no intention of going to a dance. Any kind of dance. But especially prom.

It took everything she had in her to get out of bed in the morning and put on clothes and go to school. The idea of dressing up and pretending to be some version of Cinderella was beyond horrible.

But Bobby Ellis asked her over and over again to go with him, and he said that it was something they should do and he had all kinds of reasons why. None of them made any sense. Emily said no for a straight week.

And then he fell, and that changed things.

*   *   *

He was wearing her down; he could feel it. He did his best work in silence. Bobby had Nora and Rory doing their part, and he'd even brought it up to Emily's parents, who said they'd talk to her when the timing was right.

Bobby dropped off Emily at her house, telling her that he had to do some work for his mom. He thought she looked relieved when he said that he couldn't come in. He hoped that he was imagining that.

*   *   *

Emily shut the front door, realizing that she'd made it through another day. She literally counted the minutes now until she could come home, go up to her room, shut the door, and shut down.

She always took the two cats with her. Even if they were skittish, there was comfort for her in connections. The cats, like Riddle, didn't like to be confined, and they threw themselves at her door once it was closed.

But Emily barely heard their cries.

*   *   *

The Mountain Basin Inn was where the prom was going to be held. It was a place that pretended to be a resort, but it was really just a hotel with a spa. Bobby Ellis's dad always went there before a court appearance. He got a full facial treatment and had his eyebrows groomed. He said it gave him an extra edge.

And that's why Bobby Ellis went to see Olga. It was part of his furtive prom preparation.

The waiting room in the spa played music that sounded like a kid hitting wind chimes with a twisted fork. There were scented candles burning on all the flat surfaces, even though it was the middle of the afternoon and the place was flooded with natural light.

The flickering candles all smelled like fake Christmas trees. One of them might have been tolerable, but a dozen Christmas tree candles made Bobby's eyes water. His allergies were stirring.

Bobby had pictured a tall, slender but busty girl from somewhere in rural Eastern Europe. In his mind she was around twenty years old with thick blond hair pulled back in a messy ponytail.

But the Olga who now greeted him was in her late sixties. She stood less than five feet tall, and "busty" did not adequately describe the massive tubes that surrounded her sausagelike body in the area between her armpits and her belly button.

Olga looked to Bobby like she could have once professionally wrestled in the mud. Bobby tried not to gasp, covering the instinct with a hoarse cough, as he got to his feet and followed her into the bowels of the hotel spa.

More bad news for Bobby. Olga was a talker. And her accent was thick, making it hard to understand half of what she said. However, there was one thing that was perfectly clear. She was calling him Booby.

"So, Booby. We start with analysis and consultations."

Bobby was now positioned in what looked like a reclining dental chair. Olga turned on a light that was as bright as the sun and then swung a magnifying glass over Bobby's face. He shut his eyes and felt his jaw tighten like a vise.

"Booby, you are young. And young peoples have good skins. But we must take care of our skins, Booby...."

Bobby was mute. Great. She was a talker who loved the plural form.

"First Olga will massage Booby. Then Olga will clean Booby. Then Olga will clean Booby again, but this time with brushes. Then Olga will perform the extractions. Then disinfect Booby. Then mask Booby. Then moisturize Booby."

He was stuck on the word *extractions*. What exactly was that about? His eyes flickered open, and he now saw small metal picks in a glass jar on the counter.

Olga swung the magnifier out of the way and moved to a position behind his head. Bobby pressed his eyes closed even tighter, and then Olga's muscular fingers began to rub some kind of grit into his face. Hard. It was possible she was bruising him.

Bobby tried not to squirm, but Olga was now kneading his cheeks as if they were bread dough. Should it really hurt this much? Bobby made a small, involuntary yelp, and Olga laughed at him. He was sure of that. He opened his eyes to glare at her.

But instead of seeing her face, Bobby saw two enormous sandbags, which were part of the tubes of her upper body. And they were pressing right into his head. Suddenly he saw himself only millimeters from possible suffocation.

Now he couldn't breathe.

Someone had turned up the heat and that same person was somewhere unseen, sucking the oxygen right out of the room. Bobby could feel himself start to sweat at the same time that his stomach roiled. He tried to shut his eyes, but everything began to pixilate, like a high-def channel that suddenly freezes when the signal gets messed up.

And then the room started to spin. That's when he forced himself to try to sit up. But when he did, he hit the massive sandbags that were Olga's massive bust, and in a panic he recoiled. And then the room spinning turned into wild swirls as if he were on a carnival ride. He tried to stop it, and the next thing he knew, he was falling.

And on impact, Bobby broke his right arm on the faux-marble floor.

There were two hospitals in town, and it was just Bobby's luck that he was taken by ambulance to Sacred Heart, where the nurse on duty in charge of the ER for the afternoon was Debbie Bell.

33

Very few ranchers in the United States can afford to own the land needed for their cattle to graze. And so the great majority lease terrain from the government.

The last official estimate was that there was livestock on three hundred million acres of public property, and most of that in national parks. A war is being fought between environmental groups who believe that livestock is destroying the natural habitat and the ranchers and farmers who assert that their livelihood depends on the current system.

So while Riddle and Sam were in the middle of a national forest, so was a herd of Black Angus cattle.

*   *   *

Sam opened his eyes.

The warm afternoon sun had dried parts of his clothing so that, as he painfully pulled himself up onto his elbow, it felt as if the front of his pants were made of card-board.

His pockets were filled with sand and silt. Under his fin-gernails were crescents of dried orange mud from when he'd crawled up onto the shore.

His shoulder ached, and his skin and even scalp felt like he'd been shot with a fire hose. It was as if his body had been scrubbed clean and then dipped in orange clay.

Sam blinked in the harsh light and confusion took hold. Who was he? Where was he? And how did he get here, on this slimy shoreline?

He shut his eyes and tried to concentrate.

Impossible.

No answers came to him. He was nobody from nowhere, and nothing was all he knew. And then he heard a noise crashing through the bushes. And it sounded enormous.

Sam opened his eyes again and was able to pick out some-thing black. A bear? This was a very large bear. Hadn't he seen a bear somewhere? Was that a long time ago or was it recently? And where was he when he saw that bear?

Sam didn't have time to even try to get to his feet before the moving black mass burst through the greenery to reveal a cow. A one-thousand-pound Black Angus.

The cow looked at Sam and didn't seem to find the teen-ager to be anything special. She walked right past him to the water, leaned down, and began to drink her fill.

Sam, even more confused, pulled himself to his knees and slowly, painfully, dragged himself up the riverbank.

He didn't go far.

Just over the knoll, through the stand of swaying aspen trees, was a rolling meadow thick with tall grass and wildflowers.

And on it was a large herd of grazing cattle.

* * *

A pool cowboy who was under the employment of three ranchers was driving the cattle that Sam could now see.

He was known to people as Buzz Nast.

Buzz was not made for the modern world. He was a technophobe who had never been on a computer. He refused to use a cell phone. And he wouldn't even take a two-way radio with him when he drove a herd into the Manti-La Sal National Forest for a ninety-day stretch. He was a cranky man who wanted a challenge but was suited to being alone.

The only human contact Buzz had happened once a week, when Julio Cortez drove a pickup truck into the forest on a side road from the highway and then walked two miles to a meeting point where he dropped off supplies.

Keeping track of three hundred head of cattle is a hell of a lot of work. And Buzz spent every waking hour doing some aspect of his job. Most of that time he was on horseback.

When Buzz took off after an Angus that went down to the river, the last thing he expected to find was a disoriented seventeen-year-old boy with a fractured shoulder.

But he did.

* * *

Riddle decided to follow the river because, by his reasoning, he had to follow something. Not having pants was a problem, but not having shoes was a lot worse.

It didn't take long for his socks to become caked with dirt and debris. He considered taking them off but decided against it. They had to be doing something to protect his already torn-up feet.

Riddle stopped a few times to eat river plants and fistfuls of grass. He saw a pair of otters, and they seemed to slightly lift his spirits. But as the minutes turned into hours, he was heartsick over Sam, exhausted, and fast becoming delirious.

I will put my head down. I will shut my eyes. And I will sleep.

And maybe I will never wake up.

And then I will be in a place where it is okay that I can't find Sam. That is all I want. Because I am done.

Didn't I tell Sam in the river?

Didn't I say . . .

I was done?

Riddle moved up the bank away from the water. He was finished following anything. He was finished trying.

And then, in the very moment that he no longer cared about anything, he saw neon orange.

Neon orange was not part of the landscape.

But neon orange was his favorite color. He now had a goal. He would get to the orange spot, and there he would be done.

Minutes later he was close enough to see that the neon orange spot was shaped like a beetle and fastened down into the earth as if it was meant to be part of the scenery.

Riddle stared as if he were looking at an alien spaceship.

It was a breathtaking discovery.

He moved closer and saw that it said Coleman Exponent on the side. Riddle marveled at the printed letters. He put his hand out and touched the words, half expecting them to not be real.

But the Coleman Exponent tent was very much for real.

Riddle cautiously unzipped the opening and peered inside. He saw three green puffy sleeping bags set out on blue convoluted pads. There was also a closed propane cookstove and three mostly full backpacks. Behind the backpacks were clear plastic bags of varying sizes filled with rocks.

Riddle removed his filthy socks and stepped into the tent. He then carefully zipped the opening back shut. The light inside was orange, and it was at least ten degrees warmer than outside. Riddle felt as if he had climbed into the sun. He then lowered himself to the nylon floor and slipped into the first sleeping bag.

Riddle leaned back and his head sank into the inflatable camp pillow. He hadn't felt this physically cozy, this comforted, in as long as he could remember.

And then he thought of Sam.

His eyes filled suddenly with tears, and his final thought before he gave in to his exhaustion was that he was Goldilocks.

And he wondered what the three bears would look like.

*　　*　　*

Buzz Nast could see that the lanky teenager was in bad shape. Besides being injured, he was cold and hungry and in some kind of shock. The boy said he didn't even know his own name. Then, painfully, he started to cry.

It was the first time Sam had cried in a long, long time. And he was frightened by how violent the release of the emotions felt.

Buzz watched, his face expressionless.

And then the old cowboy made a decision to do something he never, ever did. He left his cattle. Because Buzz hoisted Sam up onto his horse and took him back to his campsite.

Once there, Buzz heated Sam a can of chili and beans and then he gave him dry clothes, three Advil tablets, and put him to sleep on a tarp with a thermal blanket.

The kid's shoulder was busted up. That much was obvious. But Buzz wasn't a doctor, and he had no way to call for help. The kid needed rest more than anything. Plus he said that he thought the break might have happened a while ago. But he didn't know how. Or where. Because he just wasn't sure of anything, really.

After Buzz felt the boy was settled, he rode back through the aspen trees to corral the cattle, which were at this point spread out in a mess of bovine freedom. Two of them would never again be found.

*   *   *

Everywhere in Utah, it seemed, scientists were finding things.

Nearly all of the big discoveries in the state had been made on publicly held land. And many of the most important things unearthed had been made on sites in the Manti-La Sal National Forest.

Crawford Luttrell, Dina Sokolow, and Julian Mickelson were paleontologists. And they had received private funding from a television network to investigate a remote area in the Manti-La Sal National Forest.

If what they found proved promising, the network would bring in an actor to join one of the three scientists, and a television special would be made about their work. The split of the money from the special would pay for five more years of scientific research. And it could make one of them, possibly, a household name. It was a dream come true.

And a nightmare.

The three dinosaur hunters had not been getting along. They each wanted a shot at being the on-air personality who would join the actor if funding was granted.

Dina, as a woman, felt that she would be the most unique spokesperson to represent paleontology.

Julian, as the most photogenic, believed that the camera would speak for itself.

And Crawford, being the senior scientist of the group, believed experience trumped all other criteria when it came to research expeditions.

So, after two weeks in the field, and a long day filled with tension while working on rock formations that were seventy-five million years old, the three scientists trekked back to their campsite.

They were barely speaking to one another.

As the sun sank into the horizon, a routine awaited them.

The expensive video camera that they used to do field documentation would be temporarily put aside. The cook-stove would be removed from the tent, and water would be added to packets of mostly freeze-dried and canned food.

After this, each of the scientists would detail to the camera his or her findings of the day, each secretly trying to outdo the other, knowing full well that the television network was going to be reviewing not just the report that they submitted as a team but their individual journals and video diaries.

Lately, Crawford had taken to filming their return to the campsite. He was hoping to catch one of the other two scientists in a moment that would reveal some unflattering slipup. It might be another way to gain advantage. You just never knew.

*   *   *

As they approached their tent, Crawford was shooting when the camera lens swept over a pair of filthy socks just outside the tent door. Crawford held on the socks. Where did they come from?

Had Julian left them?

It certainly wasn't like Julian, who, like nearly all paleontologists, was all about discipline. Crawford didn't say anything, watching as Dina, in her own absentminded professor way, unzipped the tent without even asking about the socks.

And so Crawford had the good fortune of rolling camera when Dina stepped into the tent and then screamed as if someone had slashed her throat.

Her shriek was followed by the sound of someone else, also deeply alarmed, shouting back, and then Dina burst out of the tent and ran.

Julian stood paralyzed. Crawford kept filming. Several moments later, a twelve-year-old sunburned boy, ragged and confused, not wearing any pants, emerged wide-eyed from the tent.

And Crawford Luttrell captured it all on high-definition video.

34

So many things in life are counterintuitive.

No one but Morgan Bumgartner (the manager at the Mountain Basin Inn), Olga, Debbie Bell, and Bobby Ellis's parents knew that Bobby Ellis had broken his arm when he fell off a Pibbs facial chair with a hydraulic base and an adjustable back.

Everyone else heard only that there had been an accident at the Mountain Basin Inn. There were two stories going around. One was that Bobby was checking out the ballroom for the Prom Committee, even though he wasn't even on the Prom Committee.

And the second story was that he was doing undercover work for his mother, who everyone knew was a private investigator. Most people felt that the first story was a cover story for the real story, which was the second story.

But whatever had happened, after meeting Derrick Ellis, the management of the Mountain Basin Inn worried about a lawsuit. And so, to engender goodwill, the hotel lowered the price of the Prom Package for Churchill High School from $49.95 per person to $19.95 per person. They were prepared to lose money on the event.

This meant that the international fruit, cheese, and cracker display with side vegetables; the garden salad with warm roll and butter; the lasagna entrée; the iced tea or lemonade; and the strawberry cheesecake was now a real deal.

It was such a bargain that a dozen kids who wanted to go but couldn't really afford it now bought tickets. And Bobby Ellis, who really only liked to eat meat, bread, and cheese, suddenly became a kind of hero. Which meant that Bobby Ellis was the frontrunner for an honor he'd never even dared dream about:

Prom king.

*   *   *

Debbie Bell had heard the real story of the accident from Olga, and she drove home that day thinking that she'd keep the details to herself.

Bobby Ellis had slipped at the resort. That was enough of a story. He was sort of odd, Debbie decided, but everyone had their secrets. Bobby just might have more than his fair share.

And now he had a cast from his elbow to his wrist, and that was another reason to cut him some slack.

*   *   *

Emily felt bad for Bobby. The cast on his right arm made doing just about everything a huge pain.

And so she put off having the Talk. Because she had to tell him that she needed some space and that things had drifted, without her realizing, into something more than she could handle.

But for now, she went through the line in the cafeteria and picked out his food while he waited at one of the tables talking to an increasingly friendly crowd.

* * *

For Bobby Ellis, in the beginning, the broken arm was totally worth it. Because without the broken arm, he might never have been able to convince Emily to go to the prom. But now she'd said yes, and there was no backing out. Everyone was opening doors and carrying his things. Even teachers who didn't really like him were suddenly all smiles.

But the very best part, as far as Bobby was concerned, was that he got a handicapped-parking placard for thirty days. Of course it was a stretch, because his legs worked fine.

When Emily saw it, she thought it didn't seem right. She wasn't there when Barb Ellis bullied the doctor. And it was impressive. His mom had said that he couldn't carry things for long distances. Dr. Gaiser didn't seem to buy the explanation but signed anyway. You have to ask to receive. Lesson again learned.

So now Bobby could park anywhere, never even putting

money in the meters. Since taking a shower was hard, he was getting his hair washed at the Hair Asylum, which was where most of the successful businessmen in town went to get haircuts. His father had an account there. A woman named Rosie massaged his scalp for ten full minutes during each shampoo. Once the arm healed, he was going to miss Rosie, that was for sure.

It wasn't until the fourth day after the break that he smelled something funky coming from his right arm. Bobby had always sweated more than normal. Or, at least to him, he thought it wasn't normal. Who really knows how much other guys sweat?

But for Bobby, who even perspired in his sleep in the winter when he just had a sheet on top of him and not even any blankets, sweating was like breathing. It just happened all the time, really. And now, only days before the prom, some kind of foul stink was making itself known. It was coming, he realized, from his cast.

The sweat from his arm, aided by gravity, was providing a blotter for his body's natural excretion.

So Bobby got his mother to call Dr. Gaiser, who was already booked for the day. But because of Barb Ellis's insistence, Bobby was squeezed in.

When the doctor came into the examining room, he already seemed impatient.

"So your mother called and said you had a major problem."

Bobby nodded, wondering why the doctor seemed to be so full of himself.

Dr. Gaiser continued:

"What exactly is causing all the grief?"

Bobby looked right at him.

"My cast smells."

The doctor took a step closer and appeared to examine Bobby's arm, but he really didn't.

"All casts, with time, give off a mild odor."

Bobby held his gaze.

"This isn't a mild odor. This is nasty."

Dr. Gaiser closed Bobby's file.

"You're scheduled for a cast change in two weeks."

Bobby looked horrified. The man in the white lab coat was heading for the door.

Bobby Ellis made a point of never raising his voice and of never displaying much emotion. He considered this the secret of his success.

But now he couldn't play by his own rules. Now someone wasn't listening to him. And that someone was getting away. Bobby blurted out:

"The prom is this coming weekend! I can't go to the prom with this stinking turd-of-an-arm!"

But the door to the examination room closed hard, and Dr. Gaiser didn't look back.

* * *

The doctor, driving home at the end of the day, found himself thinking about Bobby Ellis.

It would have been easy to order a cast change. His office did the procedure out of regular rotation all the time.

But he was still angry with the pushy mother. And he still was ashamed that he'd given them a handicapped placard.

And now he was getting even. Because he had to admit that the kid was right.

The cast did really stink.

* * *

Emily didn't care what she wore to the prom.

She couldn't believe that she was even going.

She'd have worn any dress from her closet, but the prom committee had made a rule that gowns had to be ankle length, and she didn't own anything that long.

Bobby said that he could come with her to look but was horrified when she said that she was going to go to St. Michael's thrift shop. Her plan was to buy a dress from the rack in the back. Bobby was certain that stuff was supposed to be Halloween costumes.

Emily had bought her favorite sweater at St. Michael's. But a lot of people didn't understand wearing used clothing. And Bobby was definitely one of those people.

So Emily didn't tell him when she went to the Sunday flea market at the county fairgrounds. Everything there had a story; nothing was packaged or presented. And most of the things were odd or damaged or somehow misfits, which was now how she felt.

Emily wandered the aisles and realized that no one knew her. And no one cared if she was quiet or sad or angry. No one knew that she now felt alone even with people around her. It was comforting.

In the far corner of the second room, Emily found a woman with a rack of old party dresses. Emily picked one that the woman said was more than seventy years old. It was made of black ribbons all sewn together to make the soft strips a kind of ribbon fabric. Someone had spent hours and hours and hours sewing those ribbons into place.

The dress had a scooped neck and was fitted at the waist but then flared with a full skirt, which had layers of silk taffeta underneath. The shape was like a sculpture. Emily didn't even try it on.

She wanted the dress because it was made from so many pieces. Like the heart that Sam had made for her out of the small sticks. And what she liked was that someone had become obsessed. The ribbons might have been, for someone, a release.

They might have been a way of blocking out part of the world that didn't make sense and giving it order.

That's what all those ribbons sewn together said to her.

And because of Sam and Riddle, that was now something that she understood.

*　*　*

A few days later, Emily finally tried on her twenty-dollar flea-market dress made from five hundred and twelve different black ribbons. It was still in an old grocery store bag stuffed in the back of her closet.

As soon as she slipped it over her head, she knew it fit. But it wasn't until she pulled up the side zipper that it became clear how well. It was as if the dress had been made for her.

Emily stared into the full-length bathroom mirror. She looked like an old-fashioned movie star. She was Audrey Hepburn dressed by Givenchy. She let out a long sigh of frustration. She was trying her hardest not to try at all — and now this.

Emily wasn't the kind of girl to leaf endlessly through fashion magazines or look online every day at what celebrities were wearing. But even she could still tell that this dress was awesome and, somehow, incredibly of-the-moment.

And that was strange, because its original moment had to have been a long, long time ago.

Her eyes narrowed. Maybe she shouldn't wear it. Her whole idea about the prom was that it was an ordeal she was going to endure.

Emily walked out of the bathroom and bumped into her mother, who had just come upstairs. Debbie literally stepped back.

"Ohmygosh, Emily ... You look just beautiful in that dress."

Emily shrugged. Her mother continued:

"Is that what you bought at the flea market?"

Emily, feeling strangely guilty, nodded as she said:

"Yeah. And I didn't even try it on. . . ."

Debbie Bell reached out and fingered the layers.

"Someone sewed all of these ribbons together...."

Emily looked down at the black strips.

"They were probably crazy, right?"

Debbie was still mesmerized.

"Well, for sure they were focused."

Emily suddenly saw in her mind a woman in a large room surrounded by spools and spools of black ribbon.

"Maybe it was all the person had."

That thought made Emily feel better. She continued:

"Maybe the woman needed to make a dress, and it was either the ribbons or the fabric on the patio furniture."

Debbie looked at her daughter. While Emily was logical, she was also imaginative. For a flash Debbie Bell saw a dress made from the rubber cords of the rocker on the front porch.

"Whatever the story, it was made for you. Even if it took years for the dress to end up in your closet. It's a perfect match."

The words hung in the air. Debbie Bell regretted saying them. But Emily just looked at her mother and said:

"If it's a perfect match, it won't last. Something will destroy it."

Debbie saw her daughter's eyes fill with tears, and then Emily turned abruptly and headed back down the narrow hallway to her room.

35

The dinosaur hunters had everything.

They had a location system, and they had a satellite phone that worked even in the national forest. They had food, and they had extra clothing, and they were scientists who knew how to spring into action.

With darkness now upon them, they made an emergency call and reported to law enforcement that they'd found a boy. Or that the boy had found them. They weren't sure of his name. Or age. He seemed to be in shock and was lacking in verbal skills.

The decision was made to spend the night and then leave the next day. A good night's sleep would clear things up.

But when Riddle didn't want to communicate, he didn't communicate. So while he answered a few questions, he didn't answer the big question: Who was he and what was he doing out in the middle of nowhere?

It was Crawford Luttrell who decided to film a lot of the next twenty-four hours. He was rolling when they'd discovered Riddle, and he kept recording. He rationalized this by telling himself that there were potential legal issues. Their discovery, after all, was an only partially clothed, lost minor.

And so Julian Mickelson gave Riddle his sleeping bag (since he'd already climbed into it once that day). Dina gave Riddle another pair of pants and new socks. Crawford had a sweater and T-shirt for him to wear.

They arranged the sleeping pads in the opposite direction and then positioned themselves in a row. Julian put on extra clothes and got in the middle of the group under a sheet of plastic. He was the toughest of the three scientists.

Riddle couldn't remember ever sleeping without Sam. Just the thought of his brother rendered him mute. But after he'd had three servings of Backpacker's Pantry chicken Saigon noodles with a sweet Thai chili sauce, he was snoring.

It was the deepest, most sound sleep of his life. He slept without dreams and without even turning over for the first six hours.

Because he was lost, and now he was found.

*　*　*

The paleontologists were met by the Emery County sheriff's department thirty-six hours after Riddle appeared in their lives.

There had been severe thunderstorms in the southern portion of the state that night, and the next day the entire central computer system that connected all of Utah's law enforcement was down.

So when Sheriff Lamar Wennstrom finally went out to investigate the incident, he hadn't yet spoken to Cedar City, and he hadn't connected Riddle to the missing-person report first filed in Oregon.

Lamar wasn't happy when one of the egghead professors insisted on pointing his video camera in his face. This wasn't, after all, some episode of *COPS*. He had some experience with these academic types before, and the best thing to do was to ignore them.

But in this case, he couldn't.

There was a minor involved, and that meant he needed everyone to go back to the station and file reports. Because according to subsection (8) of the Utah state 102-56 legal code:

> *When a minor is found unharmed but with any person other than his parent or guardian, all reasonable means need to be taken to delay the exit of that person or people who found the child until all circumstances of the situation have been determined.*

That was a shame, because he was understaffed in the office.

* * *

Lamar finished his chili-bacon cheeseburger and wiped his mouth with his already-dirty paper napkin. This was shaping up to be a helluva mess.

The recovered kid was odd.

Who knew if he was odd before he crawled into someone else's sleeping bag without his pants, but he was odd now.

He didn't answer questions. He took quick, short breaths that were gasps, and the only thing that could get him to come out of the hall and into the interrogation room was a bowl of hard rock candy.

Dr. Hardart was going to come down to the station and give the boy a physical examination, but there was a car accident out on the old Red Bluff highway, and she'd been called off to that. And Dr. Wallent was out on tribal land doing a two-day women's health clinic.

It was just a big mess.

And all of this was thrown at Lamar at the same time as the news that his brother Clyde had accidentally-on-purpose fired three shots at their first cousin Pinky after an all-night game of poker at Boomer Heap's place. Fortunately, none of the shots had landed.

But investigating his own family drama would have to wait.

For now, he'd called in a member of the Utah health-services trauma team. They happened to have a big muckety-muck out in the field. Maybe he could get something out of the boy. Because, so far, they'd gotten little more than that the kid wanted a bowl of cereal with very cold milk.

He said he was sorry for getting into the sleeping bag without asking.

He asked for a ballpoint pen and a phone book.

He said he'd seen a bear stand up on two legs.

He said he'd eaten a salamander with an orange belly and that he'd thrown up right after.

He said that the pants they gave him itched.

He said that he was all alone in the world.

Lamar had a headache. After two days of interrogation, it wasn't a lot of information.

*   *   *

Buzz Nast picked up his fresh supplies once a week.

He'd drive the cattle down into a low meadow that was protected on three sides by steep terrain, knowing that when he got back he'd still have his work cut out for himself rounding them all back up.

Sam had rested for three and a half days, eating nearly all of Buzz's food. He hadn't done much talking, because he was too confused to have much to say.

Did everything stop making sense when his head hit the log? Or did the icy water freeze some vital part of his brain?

He was a blank.

The only thing Sam knew, really knew, was that he'd done something wrong. Deeply, horribly wrong.

It was possible, no, it was probable, that he'd killed someone. That's what he felt. The loss. Complete and total emptiness.

And so it was clear that he had done something very, very bad. Because how else had he ended up here — in the middle of nowhere? Where were the people he cared about in his life? But an even bigger question was *who* were the people he cared about?

He had no answers. Fortunately, Buzz Nast wasn't the kind of person to ask a lot of questions.

Buzz thought Sam was between hay and grass, not yet a real man but not a kid anymore. The boy had obviously been through a hell of a rough time. He sometimes called out in his sleep, and his legs twitched like dogs do when they're dreaming.

So on Tuesday, Buzz left earlier than usual, knowing that his palomino, Maska, who was no longer honey-colored but bleached out light from working outdoors in the sun, would need to go slower carrying them both.

*   *   *

Julio Cortez didn't like surprises.

And Buzz Nast showing up with a busted-up teenage boy qualified as a big surprise. Julio was paid by the ranchers to do drop-offs, and there were always special requests. Cowhands needed help with snakebites, bad cases of poison oak, and even the delivery of love letters, but he'd never had a cowboy try to stick him with a six-foot-two teenager.

It presented all kinds of problems.

Buzz wanted Julio to drive Sam into town and let the authorities sort it all out. Buzz had a job to do and his cattle to tend.

So Buzz loaded up his cans of extra-spicy chili, his

packages of Western Cut teriyaki-style beef jerky, and the bottle of Tullamore Dew whiskey. He put a new bag of coffee in his coat pocket along with a sack of dried apple pieces. And then, after barely more than a nod to Sam, he and the sun-bleached palomino were gone.

Sam was still wearing the worn jean jacket with the fleece lining that Buzz had given him. He still had on the beat-up blue shirt and the thick wool socks. Sam called out to try to give the clothes back, but Buzz didn't even look over his shoulder.

Buzz wanted to wish the kid good luck and all.

But he wasn't the kind of person who could say those things.

*   *   *

So now Sam was Julio's problem. He stood in the hard light sizing up the teenager.

"You feel good enough to walk out of here?"

Sam nodded. And Julio continued:

"'Cause I parked my pickup truck about two miles down."

"I can do it...."

This was all making Julio very uncomfortable. He turned toward the trail and started walking, mumbling:

"Okay then. We'll just go easy...."

After five minutes, Julio knew he wasn't going to have to carry him or anything. Granted, Julio was going slower than regular, but the tall guy behind him was steady enough on his feet to keep moving.

As they walked down the rocky trail, Julio tried to figure out a plan.

He knew that what he should do was take the boy to the sheriff's station. Somebody had to be out looking for him. Buzz, in his ten-word explanation, had said that the kid's memory was off.

But Julio didn't want to be questioned by the sheriff. It wasn't that he didn't want to help. He already liked the young guy. But he had his own problems.

Julio had lived in Utah for twenty-two years, and even though he had a son and a daughter both in junior high school in town, and even though he worked as a volunteer firefighter and had a brother who had joined the army and died over in Baghdad, Julio was illegal in the United States.

The idea of law enforcement interviewing him, asking to see papers confirming where he worked, looking at his driver's license, checking his social security number and his address, these were very bad things.

And Julio knew what could happen. It could be the beginning of the end for him, and twenty-two years of a life might suddenly be gone. So Julio decided to just tell Sam.

"I got a problem, you know, dropping you off at the sheriff's. I can take you into town. But I can't do no more than that."

Sam didn't say anything. Julio mistook his silence for judgment.

"Don't worry. I done nothing wrong. But it's immigration. You understand what I'm saying?"

Sam didn't understand the system, even when he was of the mind-set to understand something. And so now the idea of going to it for help was as frightening to him, in many ways, as it was to Julio.

Buzz had asked Sam about his parents. He couldn't remember a mother. And when he thought of a father, his mind started playing tricks on him. He only saw a shotgun, pointed at his own chest.

So Sam said:

"It's okay, because I don't want to go to the sheriff."

Sam took his time as he chose his words.

"I want to go back..."

But Sam couldn't say to where. Julio took a moment before he said:

"But you should see a doctor — don't you think?"

Sam considered that notion.

"I don't have any money for that...."

Sam closed his eyes. He remembered the inside of a hospital. He could see the waiting room. And an emergency room. He remembered the green color of the walls and a sign that said not to use cell phones.

And then the thought of the cell phone made him anxious. Did he have a cell phone? He remembered one. Sam suddenly said:

"I want to get on a bus...."

Julio continued walking. A bus? Was the tall kid hiding something big? Something dangerous or illegal? Julio glanced back over his shoulder. Maybe he was part of a drug deal gone wrong? Julio tried a different approach.

"What about if I take you into town and you call your parents. Or your friends. What if they help you figure it all out…?"

The brainstorm was back. What parents? What friends?

He didn't know family or friends. Sam wanted on a bus. Now if he could just figure out where to go.

"No. I'm going to take a bus. I've ridden on buses before."

Julio mulled it over. This could be some kind of solution. He could put the boy on a Greyhound bus and get him away from the small town where he lived and the many questions that would follow if he left him there.

So Julio nodded.

"Okay… We can do that."

And then, satisfied that they had a plan, they continued down the fire trail that led out of the wilderness.

*　　*　　*

Walking down the single-track fire trail, Sam's mind, now a blender with broken blades, flashed memories of sounds. Small, damp towns with arguments coming from low-rent apartments. Trailer parks. Cramped rooms next to alleys and businesses. He could hear the past. Music had come out of bars late at night. He heard sirens and freeways. Dogs were barking, and pots and pans were clanging. He heard car horns and low-flying airplanes.

And then, walking behind Julio, he suddenly heard waves crashing and, this time, the sound had an image. Mexico. He remembered being there. Hadn't he gone in an ocean? He believed that he liked the place. Baja. That would be the plan. He would start over there.

But he didn't have any money. And he had nothing on him to sell. Would the man walking in front of him pay for a bus ticket to Mexico?

When they stopped to drink some water, minutes later, Julio brought out a candy bar. He split it in two, handing Sam one part as he said:

"Where do you plan on going...on the bus...?"

Sam waited.

"I was thinking to Mexico."

Julio shot him a look. That was ironic. Was the kid trying to provoke him? Sam looked too earnest, too hesitant, for that. Julio asked:

"Do you have any money?"

Sam shook his head. Julio considered his options and decided upon:

"I'll get you a ticket."

Sam looked at him, overcome with gratitude.

"I'll pay you back. I promise. I'll send you the money. I can do jobs, you know, when I'm feeling better and —"

But Julio interrupted him:

"We'll figure things out. I'll get you to a Greyhound bus depot. There isn't a station in town, but we'll head west on 138 till we find one."

Julio was doing the right thing—for the lanky teenager and for himself. If he could wash his hands of the mess, it was worth it. He'd pay to have trouble go away.

36

Sam stood at the ticket window in Price, Utah.

He had two hundred-dollar bills that Julio Cortez had given him in his pocket, along with a chocolate bar, a bottle of water, and a handful of aspirin. Sam paid eighty-two dollars and sixty cents for a one-way ticket to Las Vegas.

The man behind the counter told him that from Vegas a bus left every ninety minutes headed to Mexico. Nine were scheduled a day to Tijuana. Eight had routes to Mexico City.

The bus didn't leave for two more hours, so with the ticket in the pocket of Buzz's old jean jacket, Sam took a seat in the waiting area next to an elderly lady in a tracksuit. She told him that, because she was afraid to fly, she was traveling by bus to see her cousin in San Diego. It was going to take her two days.

Sam nodded and said he'd never been on an airplane. He didn't add *as far as he could remember* he hadn't. But who knew — maybe he was really a pilot. The old woman took his statement to mean that he was also afraid to fly.

Having a young man as handsome and rugged as Sam tell her that he'd never flown in his life was a huge comfort to Irene Robichaux. The bus station had been remodeled many times over the decades, but the inside still looked close to the way it did sixty years ago when Irene had dreamed of sitting on a bench with a young man like Sam.

And so, when he fell so deeply asleep that his head tilted over and he slid onto her shoulder, she didn't mind. He smelled like pine trees and campfires and the outdoors.

Irene shut her eyes, and for a long moment felt exactly as if she were seventeen again. Only now she was out late with the most handsome boy in town.

*　　*　　*

Riley Holland had a lock on being crowned prom king.

At least he did, until the prom ticket price was discounted after Bobby Ellis was pushed down a flight of stairs at the Mountain Basin Inn by one of two men under surveillance who had serious underworld crime connections.

Rumor also had it that the FBI was now involved, because Bobby had gotten a good look at the main guy. Now everyone knew the suspects were foreigners. That's what Bobby had told Farley Golden, but she was sworn to total secrecy.

Riley Holland was smart and funny, but more than that, he was a good guy. He was considerate — and not because he thought it was going to get him somewhere. It was just his nature.

So of course, when the tide turned and the general consensus went from voting for Riley Holland for prom king to voting for Bobby Ellis, Riley made it appear that he was a little disappointed.

In fact, he was the one behind spreading the word that voting for Bobby was a way to acknowledge what he'd done. To Riley Holland, being prom king was embarrassing. It was like when a pack of girls chanted your name in unison in a big chorus during a football game. Not cool.

But Bobby Ellis didn't know that.

At Churchill High the result of the prom voting was announced during the week prior to the event. Six years before, two girls who were vying for the coronation of queen got into a fistfight in the bathroom, and after that the administration decided they needed to be there to monitor the election results. Since it was a junior and senior prom, both classes were eligible. But most years, seniors won.

When the results of the balloting were announced during the assembly in the gym on Thursday before the Saturday night prom, Bobby Ellis went out to the podium to put on the goofy gold crown and have his picture taken next to Summer Maclellan, who was the prom queen and the hottest girl at school. Bobby raised his good arm into the air and repeatedly pumped his fist.

Victory.

It really got the crowd going.

Sitting high up in the fold-out bleachers, trying to

appear interested, was Emily. But she found the whole thing impossible to even watch. And so she turned her head slightly and looked away.

And that's when she had the surprise of seeing Bobby Ellis's parents in the far corner of the gym. Bobby's father had one of those mini-video cameras that fit in the palm of your hand, and he was recording the event.

And next to him, Bobby Ellis's mother was doing the fist pump.

* * *

Riddle took the pad of yellow legal paper that was on the table and a pen that was on one of the desks and began to draw. He had been craving using lines to escape for what seemed like forever. And now he would not be distracted from drawing an exact replica of the inside of the dinosaur hunters' tent by answering a bunch of loud questions.

I will never forget finding the tent.

We slept in tents before. Sometimes when we didn't sleep in the truck. I will never sleep in the truck again.

Never.

And that is a very, very good thing.

I will never, ever live with that man again. I don't know where he is, but if I tell them, they might try to find him. That's why I tell them nothing about what happened.

Because now that is my choice.

And I will never see Sam again. But I will not tell them, because they did not even know him. So they do not miss him. I will never stop missing Sam.

I tell them what I want to tell them.

Because now that is my choice.

*　　*　　*

Riddle only stared at the table, refusing to talk to the piece of crumpled green felt with eyes that looked like fried eggs. He was at least eight years too old for a hand puppet, and it wouldn't have worked even back in the day when it had been age appropriate.

After two hours, Dr. Pincus, the regional director of child services, reported to the sheriff:

"After intensive evaluation, it is my determination that the minor has been through a traumatic event."

Lamar waited for more, but Dr. Pincus was now signing some kind of form and appeared to be done with his evaluation.

Lamar shot him a look of total disgust and said:

"You gotta be kidding me! It took you two hours to come up with that?"

Dr. Pincus was in his car and back on the road ten minutes later, listening to his favorite call-in talk-radio program.

Arrangements were made for Riddle to continue to sleep in the juvenile holding area of the law enforcement facility. The three scientists were still on the hook and had been asked not to leave until Riddle was able to reveal more information. And since there wasn't much else to do, they kept filming.

* * *

You had to attend school on Friday, or you weren't allowed to go to the prom on Saturday. Emily woke up early and spent twenty minutes debating whether she could stay home sick.

Because thinking about the prom did make her feel ill.

But didn't everything now make her uneasy?

And then, as she plotted a possible fever, another realization hit her. She was given special treatment now. She could miss class, and Bobby Ellis and his parents would call the school. They'd get permission for her to go to the dance the next day. She could see that all happening.

Hadn't someone said once that love was attention? No more. No less. But there was attention. And there was obsession. And there was possession.

Sam had never considered possessions. There wasn't a place in his life for ownership of any kind. It was so unlike everyone else she knew who defined themselves, at least in part, by their things.

From her position in bed, Emily stared across the room at the heart that Sam had given her. It was mounted on the cream-colored wall. The heart was made of so many pieces. But they fit together in such a way that, from a distance, it looked like one piece of gnarled wood.

Emily shut her eyes and allowed herself for just a moment to hear Sam's guitar, and she could suddenly see him that last night walking away into the dark. And he had Riddle at his side.

She knew that if Riddle fell into the water, Sam would have gone to save him. She knew that. He would have done anything for his little brother.

How do you get over someone who changed the way you see the world? She had no idea. But she did know one thing:

You don't just randomly replace him with someone else.

* * *

After seventy-two hours and many, many, many inquiries from many different people, Riddle said that his mother was named Debbie Sweetcake Bell and that she worked in a hospital.

But he didn't know her phone number.

There were no hits on the Internet for Debbie Sweetcake Bell, but when they went online and searched *Debbie Bell* and the word *hospital*, it was discovered that she was employed by Sacred Heart Medical Services.

It was midmorning on Friday when Randall Monte, working the admitting desk in the ER, placed the caller on hold and went to find Debbie.

She was with a patient, but Debbie could tell by Randall's face that the call was important. It wasn't until they were in the corridor heading to a phone that Randall told her that it was someone from the police department in Utah on the line.

Debbie felt her pulse double. And she was an expert in heart rate and adrenaline surges.

Were they calling her to say that they'd located bodies?

She punched the line to take the call and with what she hoped was a steady voice said:

"This is Debbie Bell...."

A voice on the other end of the line responded:

"My name is Henry Wertheimer, and I'm calling from the Emery County sheriff's department...."

Debbie wasn't breathing. The man had stopped talking midsentence. Just say it. Bad news needs to flow quickly. Didn't they give these people any trauma/crisis instruction? Finally the man took a breath—or was it a swallow of a cup of coffee?—and continued:

"...And we have a boy here who was found in the Manti-La Sal National Forest, and he says that he's your son...."

Debbie's hand was trembling now. But she managed to say evenly:

"He's alive...?"

The voice continued:

"Yes, ma'am. He's here, and he's very much alive. And he wants you."

Debbie felt her knees start to buckle. She reached out and steadied herself against the wall. She could hear the shuffling sound of the receiver changing hands and then Riddle's voice, very low, in what was a hoarse, wheezy whisper, said:

"I tried to take care of Sam. I tried...."

And then Debbie could tell that he was crying.

And now she was crying. And she was talking and crying as she said:

"Of course you did. I'm coming there, sweetheart. Right now. I'm coming to get you. Right now, Riddle...."

* * *

She had a son. His name was Jared. But when the man on the phone had said they'd found a boy in the Manti-La Sal National Forest, and he'd said he was her son, she knew that this was also now true.

And she also knew that somewhere, deep in her soul, she had never stopped believing she would see him again.

37

Debbie Bell's first call was to her husband. Together they made a plan, and part of that was an agreement not to tell Emily the news until they had everything sorted out. She was going to the prom with Bobby Ellis the next day. There was no reason to derail that. Finding Riddle was a miracle, but it would of course point out the obvious. Sam was gone.

Being the head nurse of an emergency room in a large hospital means that you understand rules and regulations. And that means you speak the language of bureaucracy.

Debbie's second call was to Detective Sanderson. She knew that the state of Utah would not release Riddle into her custody without documentation. Sanderson couldn't believe that the authorities hadn't identified the boy right away. But it was typical. They were looking for two kids. And one had turned up. He'd been with three adults. Those people were now the focus of the investigation.

The detective reminded Debbie that they had found the

inhaler she got for Riddle at the Liberty Motel. The inhaler was checked out in her name. This meant that she had dispensed medicine to him. That fact was a good thing.

After Debbie arranged to have her shifts covered for the next three days, she paged Dr. Howard, who signed out two more Proventil inhalers for Riddle. And then Debbie remembered something else that could be used as evidence of prior association.

Debbie had filled out preliminary forms with the school district in an attempt to register Riddle and Sam. The forms were incomplete, but they had been recorded as received at the end of April. Debbie could get a letter from the woman in the Board of Education office verifying this.

She and Tim would have to petition the juvenile court for legal guardianship, but she believed, given the circumstances, that they could be granted temporary custody.

And so Debbie made copies of their income taxes (to show their ability to care for Riddle). She took pictures that Riddle had drawn while at their house. She took her latest letter of commendation from the hospital, and then she drove home, where Tim was now waiting.

As quickly as she could manage, she stuffed clothes into an overnight bag. She gathered together a thermos of just-brewed coffee, a turkey sandwich, a bag of oranges, and a slice of banana cake with buttercream frosting that she wrapped in plastic and placed into Tupperware.

The cake was not for her.

Debbie Bell kissed her husband good-bye and told him

that she loved him. She then drove away from the house as anxious as she ever remembered being.

She just hoped that, in the next eight-hour drive, she didn't get a speeding ticket.

* * *

Detective Sanderson, prompted by Debbie Bell's call, spent the rest of the morning on his computer. He was assembling the paperwork needed for her to take Riddle across the state lines.

Without his help, the boy would be placed in foster care until social workers and the state of Utah could make a determination regarding his welfare.

But Detective Sanderson, who considered this to be a miracle, knew where the boy belonged.

* * *

The veteran driver Juan Ramos leaned into the popping microphone of the bus PA system and announced:

"Las Vegas, Spanish for 'the meadows.' Hard to believe, but this place was once naturally a green spot. Enjoy, folks. And watch your step."

Sam had been through this city many times with his father and Riddle, and now as he stood on the scorching-hot blacktop of the bus depot parking lot, it all seemed only vaguely familiar. He knew he'd been here before.

Clarence Border hated Las Vegas.

One of his many ironies was that he disliked criminals and he hated gamblers. He preferred to be around people who he could trust to do the right thing. Good citizens who didn't lock their back doors, and who never thought someone would climb in an open bathroom window, were his kind of people.

But in ten years of crisscrossing the country, Clarence had spent a few dozen nights in the city of neon light. Sam and Riddle had once gotten lost downtown. Riddle had fallen into a fountain. And a few men had propositioned the handsome young kid that was then Sam, but he hadn't understood what they even wanted.

Now inhaling the hot, dry air, Sam seemed to remember the smell of the place. And the sounds. He knew he'd been here before.

He just had no idea when and with whom.

* * *

Inside the Greyhound bus station, next to the counter that sold coffee and sandwiches, was a T-shirt display. Sam stared at the shirts: *Lost Wages*, *Sin City*, *Capitol of Second Chances*. He was looking for clues now, and small things were helping him piece his past together.

The woman selling the T-shirts smiled wide and asked if he wanted anything. Sam shook his head no and went out the main door into the one-hundred-degree heat. He had fifty-one minutes before the first bus pulled out for Mexico.

To Sam's left was the Golden Gate Casino. The sign was

eye-popping orange, even in the daylight. Three tall palm trees stood like tired guards flanking the entrance. A street performer, newly arrived, opened up his guitar case and set it down on the sidewalk in a slice of hot shade in front of the casino.

Sam watched as the man pulled out his guitar and then found a few dollars in his pocket, along with a handful of coins, and tossed it all in the now-empty musical case. He then removed a folding canvas tripod stool from his knapsack and took a seat.

Sam was riveted.

After a few moments, the man was strumming the guitar and singing. This was something Sam suddenly understood. Completely.

Two songs later, Sam cautiously approached. The man lifted his head, grateful for any recognition. Sam dug into his pocket and pulled out a ten-dollar bill. He put it into the open guitar case. The man smiled, exposing a mouth of small, tobacco-stained teeth:

"Thanks, man. Much appreciated."

Sam stayed close, finally saying in a voice filled with apprehension:

"Do you think..."

But he couldn't finish the sentence. The man waited and then shot back:

"Yeah? Go on...?"

It was hot outside, and to Sam it seemed to be getting more difficult to breathe by the moment.

"I think I play the guitar, but I'm not really sure...."

This made the man laugh.

"I know the feeling."

But the man looked at Sam and could see that he was completely serious. So he got to his feet and removed the guitar strap from around his neck and handed the instrument to Sam.

"Go ahead. Play a few chords. You just paid for the right."

Sam's shoulder ached, but he turned his head to the side and put the strap around his back. While his left hand cradled the guitar neck, Sam shut his eyes.

And then he softly, tentatively, let his fingers touch the strings.

Sam had learned years before how to make his voice sound like a trumpet. And now, to his own surprise, he played the guitar and made those sounds, in essence becoming two instruments.

And he did it with such fluidity and confidence that people on the sidewalk, intent on getting out of the heat and into the casino, slowed their step. The kid could play.

When Sam's strumming stopped, a handful of people threw money into the open case. Sam moved to hand the guitar back, but the man didn't want it.

"No way. You play. I'll split the pot."

The music, a language of its own, was bringing things into focus for Sam. He remembered Las Vegas now. He was here with his brother.

Sam's eyes were instantly flooded with tears, and he had to lean against one of the palm trees, fearful that he might lose his balance. The street musician put his hand on his arm.

"Play. You'll feel better. Go on...Get it out, son."

Sam did as he was told, comforted as his fingers slid up and down the neck of the guitar. He played, as he had in the past, to be transported from reality into another place. He didn't just make music. He became the music. And as he played, he remembered what mattered.

His brother. Riddle. Riddle. His little brother.

When he stopped, several hours later, the empty guitar case was filled with money. The sun had disappeared and the bright lights of the neon city chased away the dusk.

"My name's Hal. And you're...?"

Sam turned to look at the man. He opened his mouth and out came the words:

"I'm Sam. Sam Smith."

Hal nodded.

"You are one helluva guitar player, son. So where are you from, Sam Smith?"

Sam was surprised to hear himself say:

"Nowhere. Everywhere. We move a lot."

Hal continued his query:

"You come from a family of musicians — don't you?"

Sam looked down at his fingers and at the guitar. A family. It was all he ever wanted. For him and for Riddle. Did he come from a family of musicians?

Hadn't his life changed direction when he'd heard someone sing?

* * *

Emily walked home from school. She hadn't done that in forever. When she came in the back door of the kitchen, she was surprised to see that her father was there making dinner. He was home early. Tim Bell liked to cook spicy things. This afternoon he was making a big pot of chili, loudly promoting the fact that it would make great leftovers, since he believed that it was always the tastiest on the second day.

Her mom was gone.

That was unexpected.

Something had come up with some relative, and she'd left town to help. Her father was vague. He didn't say which relative. Or where she went.

Under ordinary circumstances, Emily would have asked a dozen follow-up questions until she'd gotten to the bottom of the situation.

But now Emily only said:

"When's she coming back?"

Tim Bell shrugged. But it was such a cheerful shrug.

"We don't know. But we're hoping tomorrow. I know she wanted to see you and Bobby before you went to the prom."

Emily tried not to make a face and silently nodded her head.

Jared, who was sitting by the window carving a figure out of a bar of soap with a bottle opener, stared at her.

"Are you going to marry Bobby?"

Emily blurted out:

"Good God, *no*! What's wrong with you?!"

Her father, alarmed, looked up from the cheese grater. Jared dropped the soap carving and sucked in his lower lip. And Emily managed to say:

"Sorry. I didn't mean it like that."

Emily's cheeks burned red as she walked out of the room. She felt terrible. But what do you do when the person you really need to get away from is yourself?

* * *

Sam played while Hal worked the sidewalk, forcing people to listen to the musical prodigy. The lights of the casinos lit up the never-dark Las Vegas sky, and finally Sam had had enough.

Hal tried to split the money with him, but Sam refused. He'd gotten what he wanted from the hours of playing.

He had lost Riddle, but he'd remembered that there was a family named the Bells. And they had a daughter named Emily. And that was something that eased his heartache.

Playing the guitar, he had been transported. And this time it was back to some kind of understanding of who he was. Clarence had returned to his consciousness. Sam wasn't sure; maybe he had killed his father. But he knew his father had tried to kill him. Many times.

And he also knew that he'd lost his Riddle. That's what

he had been really blocking out of his mind. His little brother. He knew he'd never get over it.

Getting to the Bells was the only thing that mattered to him now. As he crossed the busy street back to the Greyhound station, his damaged shoulder was literally throbbing. He would need to negotiate changing his ticket to Mexico to a fare heading to the Pacific Northwest. But now he had Hal at his side.

And Hal said he knew how to work people behind cash registers.

*   *   *

Debbie Bell didn't arrive at the dusty little town in Utah until six in the morning.

She went to the Motel 6, checked in, called Tim to say that she'd made it, and was sound asleep eight minutes later.

She'd set the alarm to wake her in three hours, when she planned on going to find her boy.

38

He was prom king. Emily was his girlfriend. Sort of. She was at least his date for the prom, which was half the battle. And he had a plan.

First he would sit outside in the sun and get some color on his face. Then he would go to the country club and lift leg weights. Afterward he would eat one of the club's double-bacon cheeseburgers. He then would get a haircut.

After that, he'd pick up a corsage for Emily. And then come home to relax. At exactly five o'clock, he'd start getting dressed.

Bobby pulled himself up out of bed, saying in a loud, booming voice:

"I'm prom king of the world!"

*   *   *

Emily had never been able to sleep in late. And over the years, it was a problem. But things had changed. She now could close her eyes and roll over, only to wake up hours later to find the afternoon light spilling all over her pillow.

But not today.

She stared at the clock. It was seven in the morning. And it was Saturday. This was crazy. It was the old Emily all over again.

But then suddenly she knew that wasn't true. The old Emily was gone. She couldn't get her back. But the new Emily knew a lot more than the old one. The new Emily was going to deal with it. That's what Sam would have done. He had never complained about the pain of his life. He had made that choice.

But today was prom day. It was possible that this was going to be the worst day of her life. And then she realized, no, she'd already lived that. A few times now.

She decided in that moment that she would have a regular Saturday. She was not going to have her nails done and not going to get a spray-on tan like half the girls in her class. She was not going to go to a beauty salon at all. She was not going to buy new shoes or borrow someone's fancy earrings or buy skimpy lacy underwear.

She wasn't going to just eat celery and red Jell-O all day so that she'd have a flat, indented stomach, and she wasn't going to panic and buy a box of whitening strips and try to make her teeth look like the color of a sheet of notebook paper.

She decided to start her day by taking the dog for a long walk. Then maybe she'd make pancakes for her little brother so he'd forget how she snapped at him the day before. She'd send her mom a text telling her she hoped things were going well — wherever her mom was, since she still hadn't gotten that story.

Emily would finish the book she was reading, and if her dad was working on one of his compositions, maybe she'd go down to the basement and listen for a while.

At the end of the day, she'd take a shower and wash her hair. She'd use the blow-dryer, even though it wasn't environmentally cool, and then she'd put on her flea-market dress and somehow get through prom night.

And once the day was over, once it was behind her, she made a promise to herself that she'd never think about it again.

* * *

It was midmorning on prom day, and the weather was sunny and crisp as Bobby took a seat in his backyard on a lawn chair. He put on his sunglasses and closed his eyes. He was relaxed. He let his mind wander.

When he looked down at his watch, an hour and twenty-five minutes had passed. He must have fallen asleep. He should have had coffee or a cookie or something. Bobby got to his feet and went into his house. Now he was off his schedule, and he was pissed. And his face felt really hot.

Bobby lifted his glasses and looked at himself in the hallway mirror. He was red. He looked more closely and discovered that he had an outline from his sunglasses and he looked like a raccoon. Or the opposite of a raccoon. He looked like he was wearing a white eye mask.

This was bad.

He didn't realize that the sun was so strong and that he didn't have, how do they call it, a base?

But he did know one thing: he now looked like a total loser.

*　*　*

Bobby Ellis was driving too fast with the radio on too loud. There were two choices. Wear sunglasses to the prom. Or fix the problem. And then he heard a voice from somewhere say:

"Pull your car over to the right."

Bobby answered out loud:

"What the hell...?"

His eyes darted up to the rearview mirror and he saw a police car. Up the road, a second officer on a motorcycle was writing a ticket to a woman in an enormous cargo van.

It was some kind of speed trap.

Bobby slid his SUV to the curb, and moments later a policeman had his face at the driver's side window.

"I'm going to need your registration and driver's license."

Bobby looked the guy right in the eye.

"I'm Bobby Ellis. I'm Derrick Ellis's son. My mom's Barb Ellis. Do you know my parents?"

Bobby hoped he was striking the right tone. He didn't

want to sound like he was threatening the officer; he just wanted to get the facts on the table. His parents mattered in this town. The guy should know — right?

Wrong.

The officer edged down his sunglasses to get a better look at the tomato-red teenager.

"And you're telling me this about your parents because … ?"

Bobby wasn't sure how to answer that question. So he didn't answer the question. The officer leaned closer.

"Have you been drinking alcohol or smoking an illegal substance?"

Bobby felt his whole body tighten. When he answered, his voice was shrill.

"No!"

The officer didn't like the intensity of the response.

"I'd like you to step out of your vehicle."

*   *   *

Officer Duggan finished writing up the red-haired woman in the cargo van and went to assist Officer Gates, who was now standing on the curb with Bobby Ellis. The red-haired woman in the van, clearly rattled, then put her vehicle in reverse instead of drive, and with her foot hard on the gas, backed up right into Bobby Ellis's SUV.

That's how the accident occurred.

But instead of showing him any mercy, the officers still gave him a speeding ticket and told the woman to give Bobby her insurance information while they pulled over more speeding cars to the curb.

It took a half hour to complete what should have taken five minutes, because the red-haired woman wouldn't stop crying.

Bobby's SUV was drivable, but he was now a wreck. He hadn't eaten since the night before, and the sunburn on his face was feeling worse every second.

But the afternoon was sliding by. Real decisions now needed to be made. He was now doing damage control.

He'd start with his burned face.

* * *

Debbie Bell was sitting in a cramped room in the Utah sheriff's station. She still had not yet seen Riddle, and she'd been in the building for three hours. She'd answered dozens and dozens of questions. She'd filled out all kinds of forms, and she'd signed affidavits attesting to her knowledge of the minor in question.

But now there was a knock on the door, and it opened and she again saw the sheriff, Lamar Wennstrom. But this time, behind him, wearing a sweater that was too large, shoes that didn't fit, and pants issued from child services, was Riddle.

Riddle pushed past the sheriff and, if there was any doubt in Lamar Wennstrom's mind as to who she was, or whether he should release the kid to her, it was now dispelled.

Debbie put her arms around the boy and he literally fell

into her. She wasn't a big woman, but somehow Riddle now looked so small. She had his head pressed to her chest and her hands on his hair and she was saying, over and over again, that:

"It's all right. It's okay. Everything is okay now."

Lamar, who after thirty-one years in uniform was hardened to the world and as tough as they come, couldn't even look. He had a lump in his throat and tears in his eyes, and it was getting hard to breathe.

He'd sign anything now. He didn't even need an okay from child services.

* * *

Driving in a car would have taken fifteen hours. Driving on a Greyhound bus from Las Vegas up to where the Bells lived would take twenty-two hours, because the bus stopped constantly to pick up and drop off people. So Sam would not arrive at his destination until nine at night on Saturday.

A middle-aged woman named Cece was the third person to sit next to him. She had packed enough food for a family of four. On her fifth attempt to get him to try one of her turkey-and-cheese sandwiches, he gave in. Once the dam was broken, she and Sam ate an entire backpack of food, which included a tin with chocolate chip cookies and a bag of caramel-covered popcorn.

Cece never thought to ask him a question. She had a prisoner now, and as long as she kept him chewing, she could recount her divorce, the injustice of her settlement, and then the subsequent misunderstanding that took place after she'd run over her ex-husband's foot in the driveway of the frozen-custard shop.

When Cece finally got off the bus, five hours later, she shook what looked like a packet of birdseed from the front of her smock top. Crumbs ground into the carpet under her heels as she gave Sam her daughter's phone number. The girl was named Cameo and, according to Cece, she was going places in the world of aromatherapy. Sam promised that if he were ever in some place called Calabasas, he'd give Cameo a call.

The Greyhound bus pulled back out onto the highway with only a dozen people on board. Most of them thought the seats were uncomfortable and that it was too bright inside to do anything other than occasionally nod off.

But to someone who had been sleeping outside for weeks on a bed of rocks and pine needles, it was heaven.

39

A woman in a low-cut green top, with skin the color of a blanket of freckles, took Bobby Ellis into the back of the tanning salon.

She'd been concerned about the cast on his arm, so she had taped a garbage bag around the plaster and pronounced it now good-to-go. She didn't look like the sharpest tool in the shed.

Now seated on a small, sticky sofa, Bobby Ellis watched a four-minute instructional video that explained the spray-on tanning process.

There were two people in the video. A man and a woman. They both wore swimsuits. Bobby picked up the remote and pressed the fast-forward button. How complicated could it be?

Minutes later, alone in self-tanning room number 7, Bobby was swept with a wave of panic as he faced his first dilemma. Should he get the spray-on tan in the nude? He hadn't brought a swimsuit. But they were wearing swimsuits in the video. He remembered that much. What was the right thing to do? He decided to keep on his boxers.

Next decision: on the bench in front of him was a paper hairnet. Why was he supposed to wear that? He couldn't remember. So he put it on. He didn't want his hair tan — right? But what about his ears? In or out of the hairnet? He was sweating now.

Ears out.

And then he remembered he'd be wearing a crown.

Ears in.

Forget the crown. His earlobes were dipping down out of the thin band of elastic. The damn hairnet would not hold.

Ears out.

There were little blue foot booties placed on the brown towel on the plastic bench. Again, why? And was the towel they'd given him dark brown because it was really streaked with the stains of past tanners? An ugly thought.

Bobby put on the booties. And then he opened the door to what looked like a porta potty and he stepped inside. A green button the size of an Oreo cookie was on the plastic wall in front of him. Was he supposed to push it? Then what? The light wasn't good in the spray booth. He really should have paid more attention to the instructional video.

Bobby leaned forward and pressed the green button. It sounded like an air compressor went on somewhere, and then the porta potty tanning booth literally started to tremble. And then an explosion of spray was fired from the wall in front of him. Cold, smelly liquid mist shot from three wall jets, starting from his ankles and moving up and down the front of his body.

Bobby squeezed his eyes closed, but he should have done that sooner. His eyes were stinging now. Make it stop!

And then finally, after what felt like the amount of time for an earthquake, the jets hissed off. Bobby exhaled. He couldn't remember the next step. He tried to breathe, and he realized that he was gulping the spray-on mist. Would his lungs now be tanned? What about his throat? It was over. Right? Or was he supposed to now turn around? He wasn't sure. Maybe there were jets on the other wall?

And then suddenly he was being fired on again. But he had not turned. So the front of his body was being coated in the evil mist for a second time.

He couldn't take it.

With his eyes shut, Bobby Ellis reached for the door handle and his hand hit the molded plastic wall instead. The wall was slick, and his hand instinctively recoiled as he lost his balance.

Bobby hit the opposite wall, and all the while the spray was still hissing from the valves. He now had to open his eyes and, through a soup of foggy mist, he grabbed the door handle to regain his balance. The door unexpectedly flew open, and Bobby lurched forward, hitting the sharp edge of the threshold.

It felt like a carving knife as it pierced his skin at the knee.

*   *   *

The good news was that Debbie Bell was not the nurse on duty in the emergency room. The bad news was that Bobby had to have eight stitches just below the kneecap, where the broken threshold had sliced all the way down to his shinbone.

The other bad news was that Lena Buelow, Ilisa King, and Naomi Fairbairn, who all went to Churchill High School, were also getting spray-on prom tans, and they all saw him being loaded into the ambulance.

Since there was metal in the threshold, the emergency room doctor gave Bobby a tetanus shot, which hurt. And then he was issued a course of antibiotics, just to be safe. The physician made it clear that Bobby was not to drink alcohol, because then the medication wouldn't work.

Bobby felt a kind of rage as he listened to the doctor. It was prom night, for God's sake!

It was four o'clock by the time he finally was released, and Bobby still hadn't eaten since the day before. He was now starting to feel weak and dizzy, and his head was pounding like someone had put a jackhammer to his temples. He hadn't called his parents, because after they got over his injury, he knew they'd freak about the front of his damaged SUV. He couldn't deal with that right now.

So Bobby went to Arby's.

He had to get something in his stomach fast. But there was no place to park, so Bobby pulled his beloved, but now damaged, SUV to the red zone right out front. He then put up his handicapped placard on the rearview mirror. Thank God for that.

But Bobby didn't see the handicapped placard fall when he slammed the door shut. It dropped like a wet leaf to the floorboard, disappearing straight under the front seat.

Inside, Bobby ordered two of the beef sandwiches. It was only when he lifted the second sandwich to his mouth that he caught sight of himself in the reflection in one of the fast-food restaurant's security mirrors.

His face looked like he'd been dipped in molasses. Four minutes later, while he was in the bathroom, Bobby Ellis's SUV was on the back of Marlow Hough's tow truck, being pulled down Franklin Boulevard to the city impound lot.

*   *   *

On the second half of the trip, the bus was nearly empty. So Sam went all the way to the back and put up the armrests and stretched out on four seats.

As he drifted off, he allowed himself for the first time to think about ringing the buzzer at the Bells' house.

A woman sitting two rows in front of him had brought a blanket with her. She'd taken it from an airline inadvertently on a cross-country flight once. Or so she claimed.

The woman saw Sam when she first got on the bus and, six hours later, she was still thinking about him when the Greyhound pulled into a sleepy little town where she got off. The sun was low in the sky, and she put the royal blue blanket over Sam before she exited. He looked like he could use some comfort.

Sam stirred but didn't waken.

The roar of the powerful engine, and the slight shimmy of the wide bus as it motored down the highway, had rocked him gently into a better place.

*   *   *

All week Bobby Ellis had told Emily that the only place with good flowers for corsages and boutonnieres was the Green Thumb.

So now she made a point of not going there.

How could one place have a corner on the good flowers? Plus everything was really expensive at the Green Thumb. She'd gone online and checked.

There was a woman named Carla who lived four doors down from the Bells in an old farmhouse from back when the whole area was just bean fields. She used to work in a flower place on Briot Street, and Emily sometimes fed her cats when she went skiing. The flowers in Carla's garden looked more beautiful than anything Emily had ever seen.

Emily asked Carla what to do for a boutonniere for Bobby's tuxedo, and she told her to come over in the afternoon and they'd take care of it together.

So Emily did. And she and Carla looked over the maze of flower beds in Carla's bountiful garden, and Emily picked an orange rosebud with streaks of fiery red running through the petals.

Inside the house, Carla showed Emily how to insert a wire

into the rose for strength and then wrap the bottom with green tape. She then threaded a floral pin with a black pearl plastic tip through the flower and voilà: done.

Emily told Carla she'd feed the cats next time for free, and Carla told her to forget it. She would pay.

Walking back home, Emily thought that the rose was one of the most beautiful things she'd ever seen. She felt certain that Bobby wouldn't appreciate the fact that it came from a neighbor's yard.

But the best thing about it was that she'd made it herself — and that it was such a vibrant hue of orange.

*   *   *

He was orange.

Bobby was staring in the mirror in the bathroom at Arby's, and maybe it was the fluorescent tube lighting, but he looked like a traffic cone. No, a squash. He looked like Nemo. Or a sweet potato. A mango. A prison jumpsuit.

Bobby Ellis splashed water on his face, but it was clear that too much time had passed since he'd been shot with whatever carcinogenic dye was fired from those hissing valves. Because this crap could not be washed off!

And when he began to really rub his cheeks, he had another problem: underneath the stain, he was sunburned. And it now really hurt.

Bobby rested his arm on the edge of the sink and realized that his cast was getting wet. In the horror of the orange face revelation, he'd forgotten that he had a broken arm. He stepped toward the paper-towel dispenser and felt a stabbing pain where the new stitches were now doing their job to keep the skin knitted together under his left kneecap.

It was suddenly just too much.

Bobby reeled around and violently kicked the wall hard and, to his shock, his right foot sank straight into the cheap drywall, which had been weakened by years of toilet-bowl splatter. Bobby now had his foot fully implanted in the wall next to the toilet. Fortunately, it was his good leg. When Bobby pulled it out, pieces of drywall plaster flung around the small bathroom.

And he didn't clean it up.

40

When Emily got home, her father was carrying a single mattress out of the garage and heading to the back door. And he was so happy. Emily followed him into the house, moving things to make the mattress negotiation easier.

"What's going on?"

"I'm putting this in the room off the kitchen."

No one ever knew what to call that room. Emily opened the door.

"We're expecting guests?"

Her father nodded.

"Your mom's on her way back, and she's bringing someone."

That sounded interesting. Emily still didn't know where her mom had even gone.

"Who?"

Her father didn't answer.

The room off the kitchen had at one time been a bedroom. Then it had become a home office for her mother. But that had given way to a treadmill and random storage. Her father was now assessing the room.

"I guess I'll have to take the treadmill apart and get it out of here."

Emily stared at him. Taking apart a treadmill seemed like an awful lot of work for a guest. Even if the person stayed a week. Her father leaned the mattress against the wall and started back out to the garage.

"I've gotta get my tools."

Emily called after him:

"Wait — who's coming again?"

Her father called over his shoulder:

"Family."

Emily watched him go. Duh. So it must be Aunt Jean.

Everyone had a love-hate relationship with Aunt Jean. She was smart and funny, but she was also a talkaholic. You literally couldn't get Aunt Jean to keep her mouth closed. And whenever someone was sick of her, you'd hear the excuse that "well, what are you going to do? She's family."

Hadn't Emily heard her parents talking about Aunt Jean having some kind of health problem? Or was it financial? She really hadn't been paying attention in the last month to anything. And that made her feel bad.

She was going to make a big effort with Aunt Jean.

Emily put Bobby's boutonniere in the refrigerator and headed upstairs to shower, wondering how long Aunt Jean would be in town. She was going to put a Welcome sign in the little room before she left. It was important to make guests feel at home.

*   *   *

Emily realized, as she stepped out of the shower, that she'd had an okay day. The first one in a long, long, long time.

And then she realized that part of what had made it so nice was that she hadn't had the endless stream of texts and phone calls from Bobby Ellis.

It was the first day since April that she could inhale without feeling his hot breath only inches away. She'd let the prom king have his day but make sure he realized that they would never be more than just friends.

Lots of girls liked Bobby Ellis. What did he see in her, anyway? She wasn't ready to be in a relationship. With anyone.

When she explained it all to him she knew she wouldn't have to worry about being convincing.

*   *   *

Debbie and Riddle were making good time. Traffic was light on the interstate, and Debbie estimated they'd get home at ten that night. Riddle hadn't once shut his eyes. He simply stared out the front windshield, his new inhaler clutched in his left hand, afraid that if he fell asleep, he'd wake up in a rock pile somewhere in Utah, only to discover he'd been dreaming.

After three hours, they stopped and had pepperoni pizza and lemonades at a place right off the highway. It wasn't the kind of healthy food Debbie would normally seek out, but they ate with a lot of enthusiasm, finishing a large pizza between them. When they were done, Riddle carefully folded up the paper place setting decorated with a map of Italy. He put it into his pocket for safekeeping along with two packets of sugar.

Back in the car, Debbie gave him the banana cake with the buttercream frosting that she had brought the day before from home. Riddle unfolded the paper place mat and put it on his lap while he ate.

Then Debbie tuned on the radio, and right away Riddle started humming. Debbie was surprised, because Riddle knew the words and the tune. She turned up the volume, and they were suddenly both singing:

> *I'll reach out my hand to you,*
> *I'll have faith in all you do,*
> *Just call my name and I'll be there*
> *I'll be there to comfort you*
> *Build my world of dreams around you*
> *I'm so glad that I found you*
> *I'll be there with a love that's strong*
> *I'll be your strength, I'll keep holding on.*

By the time the song was coming to an end, they were both wailing the lyrics. It took all the lung power he had, but

Riddle was not to be stopped. He'd never sung before in front of anyone except Sam, but his voice was startlingly clear and even.

When the song was over, he used his inhaler twice and found he could breathe with ease. Riddle looked over at Debbie and he exhaled.

Yes, for the first time in a long time, he could breathe.

*   *   *

The Greyhound bus was equipped with a sound system, and it was up to the driver's discretion if he wanted to turn it on. Most people these days had their own music to listen to, but there weren't many people on the bus, and it was illegal for the driver to wear his own audio headset, so now he flipped on the satellite surround system to a channel devoted exclusively to Motown music. That worked for him.

"I'll Be There" came on, and the riders, ranging in age from an eleven-year-old girl traveling with her aunt to an eighty-nine-year-old man sitting up front doing crossword puzzles, all found themselves silently mouthing the words.

In the last seat in the far back, Sam's eyes opened. As far as he was concerned, the song was being sung to him.

> *Let me fill your heart with joy and laughter*
> *Togetherness, well that's all I'm after*
> *Whenever you need me, I'll be there.*

Bobby's mother called Rory and explained that Bobby and Emily wouldn't be there for the photos and would meet up with everyone at the prom. They'd miss the limo ride with all the other couples.

It took a full five minutes just to get his tuxedo pants on. Bending his leg was painful, and at this point Bobby seemed to be made of glass. His stitches were in his left leg, but he kept complaining to his parents about pain in his right foot. He wouldn't know for a week that he'd broken a toe when he kicked in the wall in the bathroom at Arby's.

By the time Bobby was out the door, he was forty-five minutes late to pick up Emily. He didn't have a corsage. And he still had the starchy smell with the patented cucumber-melon scent overlay from the tanning spray.

But the prom king was ready.

* * *

Emily spent the extra time in her room listening to music and putting things away. Lately the place had gotten out of hand. She had stacks of books and papers and clothing everywhere.

Emily had been surprised when she got a call from Bobby's father telling her about the stolen car. Bobby loved that SUV. She hoped that someone would catch the thief.

At 6:45 PM she came downstairs. Even ten-year-old Jared,

who didn't seem to ever notice much about the physical world, said:

"You look like a princess."

Emily didn't want to be mean, but she couldn't help saying:

"I'm wearing black. Princesses never do that."

Jared thought about this and answered:

"Don't princesses go to funerals?"

Emily started to laugh. And then her father appeared. He stopped abruptly when he saw her.

"Wow."

Jared piped up:

"She's going to a royal funeral."

Tim made a face.

"Jared, what on earth are you talking about?"

Emily was now really laughing. Her father realized that he hadn't seen that in a long, long while. Jared held his ground.

"I thought Bobby was the king."

Now it was Tim who corrected Jared.

"They are not going to a funeral."

Jared shrugged. And Emily, smiling, put her arm around her brother, saying:

"If you only knew...."

Tim Bell then took a few photos of his son and daughter, thinking to himself that his shots from now on would be of three kids. Life took unexpected turns, that was for certain.

His wife had always wanted more children and, somehow, her wish had come true.

Jared, suddenly feeling left out, asked his father if they could forget the leftover chili and go eat Chinese food. And as the doorbell rang, Tim agreed.

Debbie and Riddle wouldn't be home until ten at the earliest. He and Jared would do something special together before a lot of change took place.

41

Bobby's parents had to drive them to the Mountain Basin Inn. It was like they were in the sixth grade. But the group limo had left, and now it was just a question of getting them there on time. If you weren't inside the ballroom by seven o'clock, you weren't allowed in at all.

Since Bobby hadn't been able to pick up the corsage his mother had ordered, he insisted that Emily wear the boutonniere she'd made for him. He didn't say that the fact that it was orange made his skin crawl.

Earlier in the evening Bobby's father had called the police station to report the stolen SUV and that was when he'd discovered that the car had been towed. But Bobby was going to stick to his story for tonight. And his parents had agreed to back him up on that.

As far as Bobby was concerned, Emily looked good but not in a sexy way, which was really too bad. Instead, she looked sophisticated, almost foreign, and her dress wasn't strapless or a halter top or sort of see-through, which was disappointing. She looked like something in a glossy magazine. And that was sort of sneaky of her.

He was going to be honest with himself. If he had a choice between him looking hot and her looking hot, he'd have picked himself. It was just the truth. He was the one who was the king. She was just a subject. Or a student. Or whatever everyone else was. And she just had never been into the whole thing to begin with.

But Bobby could see, despite the way she looked, that as soon as she got into the car, Emily was somewhere else. He really needed her to be needy. He stared out the window wondering if there was a way to tell her that.

When they arrived at the Mountain Basin Inn, Bobby took a deep breath and assured himself as they got out of his father's car that the nightmare that had been his day was officially over. Now the good times would roll. And then he heard a voice call out:

"Booby?"

The voice was louder now.

"Booby, how are you doing?"

Emily turned to look, and now Bobby didn't have a choice. He glanced over his shoulder to see Olga, dressed in her spa uniform.

"How is your arm, Booby?"

Bobby mumbled:

"Fine."

But Olga was a licensed cosmetologist. In two countries. Her eyes widened when she saw his face.

"Oh dear mother of Gods, what is wrong with your skins?"

Bobby did not answer. And Emily wondered two things: how come this woman knew him, and why was Bobby being so mean to her? Olga continued:

"You come see me tomorrow. You still have credits for your first session from the accident."

And then Olga reached over and touched Emily's arm, saying in a low voice:

"I never have anyone fall out of the facial chair before. Never."

Once they were inside the hotel and had turned down the corridor toward the ballroom, Bobby told Emily that he'd never seen the woman in his life. Ever. It was a clear case of mistaken identity.

From the look on Emily's face, it was obvious that she realized he was a liar.

*　*　*

Dinner didn't go any better for Bobby.

At their table, a waiter spilled a plate of lasagna on Courtney Kung's back, and her dress was made of white silk. The accident made her cry. Emily tried to help wash off the sauce in the bathroom, but that made the dress see-through. Courtney wrapped a lace shawl around herself, but she was still weeping when she and Emily returned to the table, and Bobby couldn't help but be angry that Courtney and her tears were wrecking the mood.

Rory and Nora were arguing about something in nasty whispers, and finally Rory tried to turn things around by proposing a toast.

Everyone raised their glasses and Rory said:

"To the after-party, and to the Motel Six!"

Emily knew that there was an after-party. There was always an after-party.

But what about the Motel 6?

Emily turned to Bobby. The dinner plates were still being cleared, but a few of the more rowdy kids were back to dancing. Bobby was now intently watching them as if he were a judge in a contest. Emily leaned closer to Bobby and said:

"What's going on at the Motel Six?"

Bobby just decided to come out with it.

"We all rented rooms. I've got one for you and me."

The music was loud, but not loud enough that she couldn't hear what he'd said.

"Why did you do that?"

Trying to be as in control as was possible, given all his problems, Bobby said:

"I called your father when you were in the bathroom and told him we were going from the after-party to a big breakfast at Ryan's. I said we wouldn't be home until the morning. But that was bull. Tonight's the night, Emily."

Emily looked at him.

"What are you talking about?"

She was honestly confused. He couldn't be thinking what

372

she thought he was thinking. He wasn't that out of touch with reality.

Or was he?

Bobby's hand was on her arm, and he squeezed it now. Too tight. Aggressively tight. He knew he shouldn't do that, but he was frustrated with his orange face and his smashed car and his broken arm and his stitched-up knee and even his throbbing big toe. He was angry at everything that should have gone right but had gone wrong and ruined what was supposed to have been his perfect day.

And then the president of the student body, Marylou Azoff, took the microphone from the small podium at the front of the room and called up the prom king and prom queen, and Bobby released his grip.

Bobby didn't even look at Emily as he got to his feet.

He knew that he shouldn't have held her like that. She bruised easily. But she should eat more bananas or something, because maybe she had a health problem.

Bobby raised his one good arm over his head, pumped his fist, and with his back now to Emily shouted to the room:

"Yeah, baby!"

People laughed, and someone threw a lemon wedge in his direction.

Harry Meledandri, the class techie who was standing in the shadows at a place along the far wall, then hit a switch, and a dozen laser lights went on. Colored magenta and blue beams, like in a real disco or a sci-fi movie, now sliced the room.

Most of the room cheered. And then two dry-ice machines, called Peasoupers, suddenly were unveiled. Solid carbon dioxide, heavier than air, was released onto the dance floor, where it made a blanket of soupy fog. The photographer sprang into action, snapping away at the prom king and the prom queen, and Bobby began to strike all kinds of ridiculous poses.

Emily, now obscured from view by the lights and the fog and the general mayhem, took a pen from her small black bag that had been hanging on the back of her chair. She turned over the card with the printed menu that had been part of every place setting, which some of the girls were saving as mementos. She wrote:

Bobby - I had to go home early.
Have a good night. Emily

And then no one seemed to notice as she got to her feet and walked out of the Mountain Basin Inn ballroom.

* * *

The sun had disappeared from the sky, but an afterglow of smoky orange was still on the horizon, and real night was still minutes away. If she'd had on shoes that were more comfortable, Emily would have just walked home. But there was a bus stop right in front of the hotel, and one of the big blue buses was shutting the door when she reached the sidewalk.

She had a choice. She could try to catch it or wait for the

next bus. She looked over her shoulder at the hotel. The idea of waiting was problematic. What if Bobby came looking for her?

And so she slipped out of her shoes and took off in a run, reaching the bus just as it began to pull away from the curb. Emily pounded on the glass, and the driver, surprised to see the seventeen-year-old girl in the black prom dress, hit the brakes.

It was bright inside, and a dozen people watched with intrigue as Emily boarded. She was flushed from running, and her hair, which had been pulled back in a clip, now fell loose around her face. She carried her shoes and her handbag as she fumbled for the fare. She looked not like a runaway bride but maybe like someone who ran away from a funeral. She suddenly wished her little brother could have seen.

As Emily headed to the back of the bus, she thought to herself that everyone had a story.

Tonight she was just one of those people whose story was more interesting.

* * *

They'd gone to Chang's for dinner and had their favorites: sesame shrimp and lemon chicken. Jared's fortune cookie had read: *Expect a big surprise.* Tim's had read: *A journey of a thousand miles begins with a single step.*

Now home, Tim Bell let Jared stay up past his bedtime.

It was Saturday night and he knew that Debbie and

Riddle would be arriving soon, and he reasoned that it was better to explain things now than for Jared to find Riddle as a surprise in the morning.

Emily was another matter.

Normally Emily had a curfew of midnight, which she could extend until one o'clock with permission. But tonight was the prom and the after-party and then the breakfast. Bobby Ellis had explained over the phone that there would be a limo, and no one would be driving, and he'd keep her safe.

So Tim Bell really had no idea when he'd see his daughter.

He wasn't used to keeping track of things like that. Details were Debbie's domain. Now, with three kids, he imagined he'd find himself more in the thick of it. Kids were like farm animals. You had to keep your eye on them. And now he was going to have more to corral. Jared had asked, endlessly, for a brother. And now he was getting one.

Tim Bell doubted that Jared ever imagined an older brother, but with Jared you just didn't know.

That might have been what he meant all along.

*　*　*

Debbie pulled into the brick driveway, musing to herself that so much in life can change so fast. Everything really did need to be taken one day at a time. Riddle didn't get out right away but sat motionless in the passenger's seat staring over at the house.

Debbie had explained during the ride in her calm, matter-of-fact way that he'd be living with them. That this would be his house. But now, as he looked at it, she wondered if that had been the right thing to do. Maybe the best way would have been to ease him into his new situation.

But it wasn't like there was a handbook she could consult for all of this.

Once he'd seen Debbie's car pull off the street, Tim had turned to Jared, who was sitting on the floor looking at a book on frogs. He had a scheme that involved trying to catch a few down in the stagnant pond behind the golf course and bring them home, where he'd start a habitat and sell their tadpoles to other kids as pets.

Tim said:

"Your mom's back."

Jared looked up from the frog book and smiled.

"Good."

Then he went back to the tadpoles. Felix, on the other hand, was going crazy. Debbie was his favorite person in the world, so this was expected. But this was a different kind of going crazy, even for a wildly exuberant dog.

And then the cats suddenly appeared. They looked like regular cats now, no longer skeletons of cats wearing fur suits. But they still always stuck together. And now the two cats jumped up onto the back of the sofa to get a better view of something happening outside.

Tim shot the animals a look. Didn't they say that pets could predict earthquakes? Maybe there was something to that. Tim looked out the window. He could see that Debbie and Riddle were still in the car. Maybe it wasn't going well.

Suddenly Tim decided he'd better give Jared some warning.

"Jared, your mom brought someone back with her...."

Jared looked from the frog book to the dog.

"Felix is losing it."

Tim continued:

"You remember Riddle—"

He had Jared's attention now.

"He couldn't swim. I'm going to learn to be a lifeguard. I already decided that."

Tim kept going.

"Well, it turns out he didn't die in the river like they told us."

Jared shut the frog book.

"No one really told me what happened. What do you mean, he didn't die?"

"He survived. And he was found in Utah."

Jared's eyes were like saucers.

"*Really?* Does Emily know? Does Mom know? Is he okay?"

And then, before Tim could answer, the front door swung open and Debbie and Riddle walked in.

42

Emily leaned her head against the tinted bus window. How many people took a bus home on prom night? How many people had their dates walk out on them? She suddenly felt bad for Bobby. Maybe she should have stayed and told him to his face that she was leaving. But she didn't want to cause a scene. Wasn't it better this way?

And then, up ahead, she could see the marquee for the Motel 6. The red neon sign that said No Vacancy was turned on. Underneath, in glowing yellow letters, she could read: "We'll leave the light on for you."

Emily shut her eyes. She'd done the right thing.

The bus turned at the corner and headed onto Scofield Avenue. They were passing by the old part of downtown. There wasn't much traffic, and the bus went through a half dozen lights before stopping in front of the bus station.

An elderly woman sitting near her stood up to get off. Emily glanced out the windshield and she could see that someone was in the shadows of the bus enclosure waiting to get on.

But with the tinted glass and dusky sky, Emily could barely see the person.

* * *

Checklist. Fire in the fireplace: not good. Cats: excellent. Dog: also excellent. Emily not being home: not good. Cold milk: good. Bed downstairs: not good. Bed in Jared's room: possible. Leftover chili: unknown.

Within the first five minutes, they established that a fire reminded Riddle of being out in the woods, and that reminded him of Sam, and that was really not good. Emily not being home upset him. He wanted to see her.

Riddle held the cats in his arms and tried to pet the dog at the same time, and that was also not good. But the pets were a great thing. They gave the room focus.

The bed in the little room downstairs was concerning to Riddle because everyone else slept upstairs. Good point. He didn't want to sleep alone.

Did they all want to sleep together outside in a tent?

* * *

Sam stood at the front of the bus paying his fare.

Emily, in the back, couldn't clearly see his face, but she could see the shape of his body and she knew.

It was him.

It was Sam.

So she was dreaming.

Or someone put some kind of drug in her lemonade at the prom. Bobby Ellis. Maybe even Rory.

Because she was hallucinating.

Right?

Because what was Sam, who was dead, doing getting on a city bus?

Was there someone else in the world who looked just like him?

Isn't that what people said?

That there was someone in the world who was your twin, visually speaking. The person at the front of the bus stood exactly Sam's height, with the exact same posture. He had his wild hair, but was skinnier. He was angular in a way that Sam wasn't. Plus he moved in a different way. He was stiff. He was hurt.

And Sam didn't have a worn jean jacket, but his pants looked like ones that Sam had worn. And then he turned, and she saw his face.

It.

Was.

Him.

And he now saw her. And he just stared right at her. Unblinking.

Emily opened her mouth, and all that came out was:

"I…"

That was it. Nothing else. Just "I." His eyes were locked

with hers. He came closer and she was on her feet and she was moving toward him and finally she said:

"Sam."

And Sam:

"Emily."

*   *   *

He did not expect to see her on the bus.

He did not expect to see her wearing a beautiful dress, barefoot, holding her little sandals in her trembling hand.

He did not expect to see that.

He was going to find her with her family at her house, and even that made him feel afraid, like he'd fall apart. And now this.

Now, in front of a dozen people under fluorescent lights in the aisle of a city bus, she was there.

And she wrapped her arms around him, and even if he wasn't real, she was never, ever going to let him go.

*   *   *

The city bus route did not go by the Bell house.

Riddle knew that better than anyone, because Riddle had memorized all the routes and had ridden the bus and thought about the bus even when he wasn't riding the bus. He had drawn diagrams of the town and of the bus lines and he had included all of the bus stops.

382

But now, looking out the front window through the gauzy, sheer white curtain, Riddle saw a city bus. And it had put on the brakes right in front of the Bell house.

Riddle turned to the room and said:

"The bus came here."

Everyone turned to look outside, and he was right.

There was a city bus right at the curb. And the door was opening, and two people were getting out.

Jared didn't care much about buses, so he went back to looking at Riddle's hands, which were all scratched up.

Tim Bell bent down to pick up Jared's big picture book about frogs, which was now in danger of getting stepped on.

Debbie, who was exhausted from the driving and the lack of sleep, took a moment to lean against the couch and shut her eyes.

And that's where they were when Riddle screamed.

*　*　*

Sam heard his brother's muffled scream, coming from inside the house, and it was like a razor cutting his throat. He'd heard that scream before.

But then the heavy front door of the Bells' house opened, and Riddle came out onto the brick walkway, and he was running.

He was running straight to him.

And Sam felt his knees give way and it was possible, in just that moment when he realized that he had a little brother and that this little brother was alive, that everything bad that had ever happened to him in his life was erased.

Because he now knew that sheer joy wipes out pure pain.

*   *   *

No one slept that night.

Not Sam or Riddle Border.

Not Emily Bell.

Not Jared, who had never stayed up past twelve-thirty in his whole life.

Not Debbie or Tim Bell.

Not Bobby Ellis.

Not Nora or Rory.

Not Olga from the Mountain Basin Inn, but that was because she had drunk regular coffee instead of decaf served by accident at the hotel concierge desk.

Not even Detective Sanderson, who had received a call from the Bells telling him about Sam, and who then had sat up in bed all night watching films noir and wishing that he had been born in an era where he could wear a fedora to work.

*   *   *

Sam and Riddle held on to each other for what seemed like forever, and then both of them, unable to contain themselves, found their faces wet with tears.

That got Emily weeping, and then the rest of the family joined in, except for Jared, who for some reason couldn't stop laughing. Felix the dog barked for a solid ten minutes.

Once they finally got themselves under control, everyone kept explaining, over and over and over again, what had happened. Then Debbie insisted, despite the late hour, that they go to the emergency room at Sacred Heart hospital and have Sam checked out.

It was there that it was made official that Sam had broken his shoulder. The X-rays revealed that, despite everything that had happened in the intervening weeks since the accident in the national forest, the bones were well on their way to knitting back together. Only an orthopedist would be able to tell if they needed to be surgically reset.

And so they were all squeezed into one car, because no one wanted to be separated, and they were driving back across town to the Bell house at four in the morning when they passed a limousine filled with juniors and seniors from Churchill High School who had left the after-party.

Bobby Ellis was inside the stretch, wondering how so much could have gone so wrong so quickly.

In the backseat of her parents' car, Emily had changed out of her prom dress and was wearing jeans and a hooded sweatshirt from her soccer team. She'd never ridden in a limo that night and didn't even register that Bobby might be inside the one that passed.

An hour later, when the sun rose, the sky was fiery orange, and no one could ever recall seeing it that way.

43

Hiro Yamada of Medford Coin had for ten years kept the valuable penny brought in by Clarence Border.

In the second week of June, a photo of Clarence appeared online with an account of the man who had wrongly taken his two young sons and spent years on the road. Hiro immediately recognized the group.

Hiro contacted law enforcement and was directed to Detective Sanderson, who was coordinating the legal aspects of the case on behalf of the two minors. A judge in Utah juvenile court had awarded temporary guardianship of both Border boys to Debbie and Tim Bell.

Sam and Riddle couldn't remember going into Medford Coin.

But Sam remembered his mother having a penny collection. And he remembered that it was kept in a blue cardboard penny holder. That turned out to be enough identification.

The penny, which Hiro Yamada had certified as authentic, was then put up for auction and sold ten days later for the record price of $48,202 in San Francisco.

Detective Sanderson hung up the phone once he had the news and found himself saying, for the rest of the day:

"Not bad for a penny."

Sam and Riddle wanted to split the money with Mr. Yamada, but he flatly refused. His grandparents had lost their landscaping business during the forced internment of Japanese Americans during World War II. Hiro's father had been born behind the barbed wire at Tule Lake.

Hiro believed in returning property to rightful owners. After the story became public, the reputation of Medford Coin soared to new heights, and Hiro became a national expert on Indian Head pennies, tracking the most famous collections and acting as the sales agent in many high-profile transactions.

Riddle had only heard Hiro's name; he'd never seen it in print. And when he sat down with Debbie and wrote a letter and thanked him, he addressed it to Hero.

No one corrected him.

* * *

Sam sent Julio Cortez a certified check to the post office box address he'd been given. It was twice the amount that Sam had borrowed.

Julio thought it was only fair to give the overpayment to Buzz Nast, who bought a new jean jacket and shirt when he got back from his three months herding cattle. The woman in the general-supply store who found Buzz the right size coat asked him to go with her after work for a coffee. Her name was Marla.

Instead, Marla and Buzz went to a bar called the Golden Horseshoe.

Eighteen days later, they drove all night to Las Vegas and got married. Marla's dream was to raise miniature cattle. Buzz was a willing partner.

*   *   *

At the end of the summer, the dinosaur hunters — Crawford Luttrell, Dina Sokolow, and Julian Mickelson — turned in to the Discovery Channel ninety hours of video from their six-month expedition. The scientists all hoped that the network would see the merit in their work and continue to fund their ambitious paleontology research project.

But it was not to be.

The head of the network, Bernie Smeltzer, looked at a rough cut of a potential pilot for the show and said it looked dusty and boring. He passed on the program, giving everyone involved two weeks' severance pay.

Three days later, an intern named Sarah Allen, who worked in the editing room, cut together the footage of Riddle being found. It caused a sensation when the new vice president of programming, Wei Chen, was walking down the hall and heard people squealing.

Wei took the footage and, from it, the show *The Seekers* was born. The TV program, starring the three scientists, was about discoveries of the sensational kind. Their second story was an exposé of a woman who had lost her pinkie in a boating accident and believed that it was her finger that appeared in a fish sandwich at a fast-food restaurant two weeks later. The scientists led the team doing the DNA testing to verify the claim.

Debbie and Tim let Riddle decide if he wanted to participate in the program. He refused to do any additional filming, but he allowed the scientists to use the existing footage.

He then had Debbie and Tim donate the money he received to the paleontology program at the University of Utah. Riddle hoped to one day study dinosaur bones at a very high level. He'd caught the fever.

*　　*　　*

In Cedar City, Gertrude Wetterling locked herself out of her house one night after a bridge tournament. She had yet to master the new alarm system, which she'd installed after Clarence had stolen her jewelry.

Gertrude tried to break into her own home by climbing a rose trellis up to the second story. The trellis was more ornamental than structural, and Gertrude fell to the ground and broke her wrist.

Her daughter Els, who lived in San Diego, took the injury, on the heels of the robbery, as a sign. And two months later,

Gertrude Wetterling was living in a retirement community with an ocean view in La Jolla, California. The woman in the unit next to her had been a professional opera singer in Italy, and she and Gertrude listened to opera every afternoon for two hours. For Gertrude, it was heaven.

With Gertrude gone, Mrs. Dairy began wearing the gemstone-encrusted Christmas tree pin to church on Sundays.

She told the other parishioners that she'd found one like Gertrude had owned in an antique store in Skylar. Everyone admired the pin, and there were smiles all around.

* * *

Crystal from Superior-Cuts entered the before-and-after pictures of Sam and Emily into the annual North American Hairstyling Awards. She won second place in the nationwide contest, which was an all-expenses-paid trip to Miami to their annual convention.

While at the convention, Crystal met Wade Vilhelmsen, who owned ten salons in the Southwest. Wade hired Crystal to be his new general manager.

* * *

Bobby Ellis hooked up with Marylou Azoff the night of the prom after Emily walked out on him. He knew that Marylou had always liked him.

But Marylou's mother was relocated to Denver when she

got a job promotion, and the Azoffs left town in June. Bobby said they could still be a couple even though they weren't in the same state, but Marylou didn't see it working out.

Once she was gone, Bobby announced that he now wanted to be known as Robb. With two *b*s.

He had a six-month, fourteen-point plan in place for a new identity.

*   *   *

Debbie and Tim Bell had decisions to make.

At first they thought that they'd simply have Sam and Riddle live with them. But their daughter was involved with Sam, and so that wouldn't work.

But then the penny was sold at auction, and the boys had some resources. They decided to take an inexpensive apartment near the college. Sam would be eighteen on his next birthday, and Tim Bell was in the process of arranging for him to get a scholarship into the college music program.

The boys wanted to be together. For now, it was a solution. Riddle walked over to the Bells' house every morning as soon as he woke up, which was always early now. Felix took to sleeping in the boys' apartment, so the two could be seen just after sunrise, walking across people's lawns. Riddle didn't like sidewalks.

The two cats stayed with Emily.

*   *   *

Late at night, several weeks later, in another state, Clarence Border lay awake in his airless jail cell, feeling the agonizing pain of a missing limb. Because a foot that was no longer there was moving.

At the same time, hundreds of miles away, Sam was in an apartment that legally belonged to him and his little brother. He was staring at the plaster ceiling, trying to fall asleep. He still assumed that it was possible that he might open his eyes at dawn and discover that the last six months of his life had been a dream. He might wake to find that his old reality would be in place.

And then in his mind's eye he remembered first seeing Emily. Music was playing. She sang to him, off-key, "I'll be there."

For him and his brother, he now knew, that music was real.

Because all you had to do, really, was be willing to use your imagination.

And listen.

Questions for Discussion

1. Why, do you think, are Sam and Emily drawn to each other? Do they want something from each other, or do they complement each other in some way?

2. How are Sam's and Emily's families different? Are they at all similar? How does the "nature versus nurture" argument apply to each of them? Do you think both Sam and Emily are a mix of "nature" and "nurture"?

3. How do you think Riddle got his name? Why doesn't he talk very much?

4. A big theme in this book is the idea that we are all connected to one another, sometimes in small ways that we don't see at the time. Has anything ever happened to you that seemed inconsequential, only to have it greatly impact your life at a later time?

5. Do you, like Emily, believe in destiny? Or do you think that all events are random and that the things we call "fate" or "destiny" are just coincidences?

6. Another theme in this book is the idea of belonging. Who is the last person in the story to realize where Sam and Riddle belong? What happens to make this person realize where the boys should be?

7. How does each of the main characters relate to the title of the book (and the title of the main song in the book), *I'll Be There*? Do you relate to this song in a particular way? Is there another song you relate to better?

8. What do you think Sam and Emily talked about after they were reunited on the bus at the end?

9. Do you think this book would make a good movie? Whom would you cast to play the main characters?

10. Did you like the book's ending? If you were the author, what would you have written differently? Since every event in the story is connected to the ones before and after it, how would your change affect the outcome of Emily's, Sam's, and Riddle's lives? How would it affect other characters, such as Hiro Yamada, Buzz Nast, and Mrs. Dairy?

An Interview with
Holly Goldberg Sloan

1. *I'll Be There* is a very complex novel with multiple characters, plotlines, and settings. Where did your inspiration for this story—as well as its many different parts—come from?

I was inspired to write this book after hearing about a boy who had been kept out of school by his father, who had a mental illness and had turned to a life of crime.

My father was a college professor. I grew up in college towns, and my playground, in many ways, was the campus of the university where my father was teaching. Many of the opportunities that came my way early in life were from college theater groups (who needed kids for their shows), museums on campus (where we wandered on weekends), and cultural events. I went with my friends to folk-dancing classes, lecture series, concerts— even the bowling alley at the student union at the University of Oregon.

When I tried to imagine what life would be like for someone who didn't have access to even the basic idea of education, I couldn't stop thinking about what that would be like. And because my family moved a lot, I understood what it means to leave things behind.

2. Do you have a favorite character among Emily Bell, Sam Border, and Riddle Border? Or did you find a particular character more difficult or more satisfying to write than another?

I am very attached to Riddle. I understand him and I appreciate what makes him special. Riddle and the bear are the only characters in the story that are allowed to speak in first person. Both Riddle and the bear communicate in a way that is not easily understood. In my opinion, it is a mistake to view silence as the absence of thought. Often it is the opposite. It is an avalanche of feeling waiting to tumble forward.

3. One of the main themes of *I'll Be There* is the idea that we are all connected. You show this by skillfully interweaving the characters' lives through everything from the smallest details to the most important plot points. Did you find it difficult to bring everything together as you were writing the book? Did you have an outline or notes that you followed, or did the story evolve organically as you progressed?

The story evolved organically. I don't write from an outline. I write from character. So I am led by the needs of the people in the moment. I come from the world of screen and television writing, where in most instances, if a person is writing on assignment, an outline or a treatment is required before being given the go-ahead to begin the project. I've made my living in this field for many years, but I still have a great deal of trouble outlining what I will do. I actually once sold a television pilot (for a network) based on a pitch of characters and a situation. I had already written the pilot but didn't show the network. I just took the pilot and turned it into an outline to get their approval to write the show (which I had already done). I know that sounds crazy, but I guess everyone works in their own way.

4. A significant amount of the story takes place when Sam and Riddle are trapped in the wilderness with almost nothing to help them survive. How did you make this part feel as authentic as it does? Did you do any particular research, or do you have experience living in a wilderness setting that may have influenced this part of the story?

When I was in junior high school in Eugene, Oregon, I took a class called Outdoor Education. I remember this class better than any other single course I took in school.

My favorite teacher, Mr. Thompson, taught the class with two other instructors, and we learned about everything from geography, weather, plants, and animals to basic outdoor survival.

But the amazing part was that we put what we learned into practice. We took multiple weekend overnight trips, and the class culminated in an extended camping trip where we hiked into the Cascade Mountains. We carried enough food for five days, and of course our tents and sleeping bags and clothing. We had been divided into groups, each with three boys and three girls. We had to eat all of our meals in these units and set up our tents and take care of our basic needs. Now that I'm writing this, I'm realizing how life-changing that experience really was.

Another thing that heavily influenced me was that when I was a teenager, I had a very close friend named Teri Byrd. Her father was the head of Outward Bound (a nonprofit educational organization) in Oregon, which trained people about the natural world and then sent them off to do a "solo" where they would make their own way in the wilderness for several days. This was, of course, before people carried cell phones or had easy ways to communicate. Teri was the strongest, most dynamic of friends. I guess that makes sense, considering that her father was dropping off people in the woods with a single match and a blanket (or something like that).

In addition to all of this, I come from a family of campers. When I was eight years old, my family lived in Europe for three months in a tent, driving from campsite to campsite. That wasn't outdoor survival living, but we ate reindeer meat (it came from a can) cooked over an open fire, and we washed our clothing in campsite sinks. Every night I went to sleep listening to crickets and owls. To this day I find a level of peace when I'm in the woods, far away from what we think of as civilization.

5. If any character can be called "secondary" in a novel that makes every character seem pivotal to the plot, who would your favorite secondary character be, and why?

Bobby Ellis. I had to be careful with him because I *loved* writing about Bobby Ellis. He could have just taken over the story if I didn't have an editor. I had fun writing Bobby Ellis because I like to place characters in comedic situations. And Bobby is so ripe for that. I think Bobby is much more complicated than people might believe. Yes, he's a compromised character. But he's not a true villain, like Clarence. A big part of Bobby's problem is that he's not authentic; Bobby doesn't actually know what Bobby really likes or admires. Everything for him is external. This makes him the opposite of Sam.

6. *I'll Be There* has a cinematic quality that keeps readers racing from one scene to the next. Do you think your background in film has anything to do with the way you write? How do you explain that there is relatively little dialogue in *I'll Be There*, given that screenplays are typically completely dialogue-driven?

I think it would be hard for me to write without seeing a story told in images. That is what my career has been about. I have written seven films that have been produced, and I directed three of those movies. I have also directed television commercials. My mother is an architect, and when I was little, I wanted to be a painter. So I've always thought in terms of images, which is how I tried to tell the story in *I'll Be There*.

I'll Be There is told primarily via a third-person, passive, multi-perspective narrative. This allowed me to be inside the characters, but with a distance that allowed me to tell readers what was happening without a lot of dialogue. I realize that for some readers this can be frustrating. But ultimately I think this choice is what accelerates the action of my story. It allows me to move quickly from one place to another, both physically and emotionally.

7. How would you compare the experience of writing your first book to working on one of your films?

I experienced great joy in writing *I'll Be There*. That's not to say I haven't experienced happiness while writing films, but that kind of work, by definition, takes many, many people to get over the finish line and onto the screen. Writing a novel is a more solitary experience, and perhaps because of that, it was much more personal for me.

8. What kind of writing routine do you have? Do you write whenever inspiration strikes, or do you have a certain routine you follow?

I get up every morning and I write. After about an hour and a half, I have breakfast, and then I return to writing. I do this seven days a week. But if you subtracted the time that I'm answering e-mails, watching pet videos, bouncing around Facebook, and reading newspapers and blogs, I would say that I write for three hours a day.

9. What do you hope readers will take away from the book?

That the small things matter as much as the big things. That acts of kindness are acts of courage. That everyone has a story. That all of our stories have areas of intersection. That we need one another.

10. Can you give us a brief sneak preview of what a sequel to *I'll Be There* would be about?

Everything is new as the story continues. Emily and Sam and Riddle and the Bells all must adapt to a new life. There is great joy in this, but also real adjustment. Basic issues of education and living arrangements must be sorted out.

The pain of the past doesn't just go away overnight. The shadows remain. So while love and family and belonging have the ability to heal, the fact remains that Clarence is in prison, where a cracked idea burns in his brain every moment of his confinement: someone took his kids. And he has an idea about how to even the score. His favorite line from the song "I'll Be There" is "Just look over your shoulders . . . I'll be there."

But this time when Clarence comes into their lives, Sam and Riddle are not alone.

Stories about **love, loss,** and just **being a girl**

From National Book Award Finalist
SARA ZARR

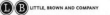 LITTLE, BROWN AND COMPANY   Available wherever books are sold.   www.teen-readme.com

BOB411

FOR VALERIE LEFTMAN, ONE DAY WOULD CHANGE EVERYTHING....

HATE LIST
BY
JENNIFER BROWN

HATE
JENNIFER BROWN
LIST

I didn't mean for anyone to die.

A NOVEL

BITTER
END
JENNIFER
BROWN

And don't miss
BITTER END.

AVAILABLE NOW.

HOLLY GOLDBERG SLOAN was born in Ann Arbor, Michigan, and spent her childhood living in California, the Netherlands, Istanbul, Washington, DC, and Oregon. She has written and directed a number of successful family feature films, including *Angels in the Outfield*, *The Big Green*, and *Made in America*. The mother of two sons, Holly lives with her husband in Santa Monica, California. *I'll Be There* is her debut novel.